Praise

"*Aéros & Héroes* is a witty,
vampire legend into terrifyi̇   ...faint of heart!"

> —Jonathan Maberry,
> NY Times bestselling author of
> *V-Wars* and *NecroTek*

"A thrill ride you won't be able to climb off until the last page. Highly recommended."

> —Gregory Frost, author of *Rhymer*

"An exquisitely detailed world! This epic story blends intrigue, romance, and camaraderie for a steampunk adventure with flavors of Anne Rice and Alexandre Dumas.

> —KC Grifant,
> author of the *Melinda West* series and
> *Shrouded Horror: Tales of the Uncanny*

Praise for Esprit de Corpse

"A rollicking steampunky romp through post-Revolution France. Most delectable!"

> —Tiffany Trent,
> author of *The Unnaturalists*

"A meticulously-built world awaits readers in this delightful steampunk mystery."

> —A.C. Wise,
> author of *Wendy, Darling* and *Hooked*

"A truly delicious story. Deal confidently establishes her world and characters with small historical details and revealing turns of phrase, and leads you through the story's twists to a satisfying end. *Chef's kiss!*"

> —Miriam Seidel,
> author of *The Speed of Clouds*

"A delightful romp suffused in period details [...] Great for readers who love steampunk, are Francophiles, strong women with amazing talents, or just who love a ripping yarn of a tale."

> —Randee Dawn,
> author of *Tune in Tomorrow*

AÉROS & HÉROES

EF DEAL

NEOPARADOXA

PENNSVILLE, NJ

PUBLISHED BY
NeoParadoxa
a division of eSpec Books LLC
Danielle McPhail,
Publisher
PO Box 242,
Pennsville, New Jersey 08070
www.especbooks.com

Copyright © 2024 Ef Deal

ISBN: 978-1-956463-55-2
ISBN (ebook): 978-1-956463-54-5

Copy Editor: Greg Schauer, John L. French
Interior Design: Danielle McPhail, McP Digital Graphics

Cover Art & Design: Mike McPhail, McP Digital Graphics
Interior Art:

DEDICATION

To Johnson and Lubonski, my Barnabas-loving friends,
and to Elizabeth Payne, the writer of vamps.

1.

"JACQUELINE MARIE-CLAIRE DUVAL DE LA FORGE-À-BELLESFÉES!"

The cry reverberated throughout Château Bellesfées' music conservatory concert hall, resonating under the acoustic dome and across the marble floor. Sunlight streamed through six balcony windows and glittered off the facets of a crystal gasolier. Seven clockwork androides ranged around an Érard fortepiano, each seated on an armless Louis XVI chair holding a tuned instrument at the ready. The eighth figure, half-poised with a clarinet, reeked of burning solder and spirit fuel. Having no ears, they did not hear the housekeeper Marthe bellowing their creator's name.

Jacqueline Duval had ears, but she rarely paid attention to anything around her while she worked, and the clarinetist was far from complete. Outside, the harvest in the vineyards to the east had begun in earnest, the fragrance of the Bellesfées varietal grape filling the air with its honey-citrus tang. Finches came to the balcony rails and twittered like rusty wheels to one another. The breezes from the Loire would have tempted any village boy to abandon all chores for an hour of swimming or fishing. Jacqueline was impervious to all. Only the late August heat was enough to make her pause to mop the sweat dripping from her nose and chin onto her soldering. Even that much respite took too long as confused emptiness threatened to fold around her once more.

Marthe's voice broke through at last. "One hundred chairs?"

With a long-suffering sigh, Jacqueline set down her spool of brass, rested the soldering iron on a block of wood beside her, then closed the blow lamp. As she removed her specialized safety spectacles—"gogglers" she called them because they made her look goggle-eyed—Marthe stormed into the concert hall.

"One hundred chairs? Now you expect a hundred guests? Why wasn't I told?"

Ignoring the housekeeper's fit of pique, Jacqueline finished assessing the clockwork clarinetist she'd been working on the past two hours. This final piece was proving tedious with all its refinements. She did not have time for Marthe's little snit.

"Am I to cook for a *hundred* guests? And how do we house them?" Marthe's ruddy, heart-shaped face grew redder as she planted her fists on her hips, her right hand closing on a towel she often used to swat anyone incurring her wrath.

"It's fifty guests, dear Marthe, including the children," Jacqueline assured her, wiping her brow with a heavily insulated glove. "Fifty chairs here." She gestured to the capacious hall. "Another fifty out on the east lawn."

"And if it rains?"

"The chairs will be under pavilions."

Marthe threw her hands in the air. "Why do they have to be on the lawn? Trudging mud and grass up into the château? Falling drunk into the pond? You have not thought this through, ma fille."

Jacqueline stood to confront her stalwart housekeeper. "Marthe," she said, "I'm almost twenty-three years old. I've been running affairs at Bellesfées for seven years. In that time, I've sold hundreds of designs, brought thousands of francs into our household, and dealt with a twin who turns into a wolf, corpses rising from the dead, and all the ghosts of the Paris Catacombs. I really don't want to wrestle with you too. Please?"

Not willing to back down, the housekeeper wrung her towel. "I like to know your plans, since they usually go somewhere you hadn't planned. Like to be prepared for these things. You haven't been yourself lately."

Marthe wasn't wrong. Jacqueline generally lacked the social graces to entertain company, much less fifty notable personages from Paris and the Touraine. Marthe had questioned every decision along the way since the manic moment Jacqueline decided her twin Angélique and her new husband Gryffin Llewellyn *must* be received at Bellesfées with a celebration befitting the restored (*finally!*) prodigal sister. It was as fine an excuse as any to focus on work instead of on her own absent lover.

Conceding Marthe's point, Jacqueline returned to her forte, the clockwork musician. As she picked up the iron rod, she dismissed

Marthe with stern instructions. "Now, the delivery men get well paid *after* they unload those chairs. I don't want Luc or Jean-Paul bothered with the task. They already have enough to do. Fifty up here, fifty downstairs stored in the ballroom, for now. And no one must disturb me again until I finish this clarinetist."

"No one?" said an unexpected and welcome voice — deep, resonant, and thrilling.

Jacqueline's heart leapt. Heedless of her soot-covered work gloves and apron, she flew into Alain de Guise's arms as he entered behind Marthe.

"De Guise! You're home early!"

"Making more work for me," Marthe grumbled on her way out the door.

Giggles burbled up in Jacqueline as de Guise whirled her about.

"I am indeed home. And how fetching you look in that merry bonnet, chérie." Snatching her leather welding cap from her head, de Guise dropped it to the floor and kissed her, combing his fingers through her honey-blonde hair, as sweaty and tangled as it was. "And why must I say it again: *Alain.*"

"Mmm. *Alain,*" she repeated with a saucy grin, never removing her lips from his.

He kissed her again more intimately, eliciting a moan of delight.

"And," he added, "unless you're planning to brand me, please put down the iron."

She complied, laughing, leaving her gloves as well. "I didn't expect you until tomorrow." Wrapping her arms around his neck, she cried, "Oh, you've made my day complete. I've been so lonely."

De Guise surveyed the clockwork musicians and scratched his blond head. "So lonely you've made yourself some new friends? What are you creating here?"

Dancing away, Jacqueline circled each figure to show them off. "Ah, I'm so close to finishing. I call it a panharmonium — sort of a panharmonicon, orchestrion, and componium in one. I'm holding a reception for Angélique and Llewellyn when they return from Wales, and I'm hoping for a grand recital."

She plucked the strings of the violin, violoncello, and bass, tapped the pistons of the trumpet, horn, and euphonium, and twiddled the keys of the flute. "I made a few night runs to Paris in my steam coach to get the clockwork instrument wheels stamped and drilled. Sax gave me the brass—" Here she slid back a panel of the back wall to reveal a rack of organ pipes. "And I was lucky to run into the Kaufman boys to help me put a few things together. And if you look over here—"

De Guise captured her as she flitted past him. She caught her breath, then laughed at herself. "I know, I know. Lost in my plans again. But I want it to be wonderful for her."

He searched her eyes, mischief twinkling in his. "All this for a sister who provoked so much aggravation these many years?" he teased. "Did Prince Abadi ever get his ruby back?"

Her face grew even hotter. "But that was… She… I wanted…"

"You are extraordinary in your grace, my love. You give me hope, for in my line of work, I may need such grace."

She wiped her brow on her sleeve and propped her hands on her hips. "Where *have* you been these past weeks? I have missed you!"

"Then I must atone." He caught her back to kiss her again—warm, deep, soft, sending a wave of heat through her.

Jacqueline sighed in delight and pressed her face to his chest, glad of his height, which made even her feel petite. Beyond the dust of the road on his worsted wool jacket, she breathed in his own spicy scent and the almond fragrance of Savon de Marseille. She nuzzled him but stopped when she barked her nose on the hard metal of the Colt Paterson revolver hidden in his inside pocket, a harsh reminder of his calling as an agent of the Sûreté Nationale tasked with protecting Louis-Philippe, the "King of the French," as he called himself.

She smoothed his lapels. "I prayed you faced no grave peril."

De Guise winked and held a finger to his lips.

"Of course. King's business." Releasing him, Jacqueline twisted her hair into a topknot and put her cap back on. "Well, I hope it was somewhere exotic."

"Hmm. Is Normandy exotic?"

"Mers-les-Bains? You look bronzed. And we all know it's the King's preferred summer retreat, at Château d'Eu." She waved her hand when he tried to protest. "Never mind, your secret is safe with me."

De Guise wrapped his arms around her, and they swayed back and forth to a music only they could hear. She molded her body to his, allowing arousal to fill her.

"Oh, I've missed this," she murmured with a sigh of delight. "When you left, I wandered these halls and the parc absolutely lost. As if a piece of me had been cut away. I forgot everything but you. Days together, nights in each other's arms, it all felt so natural. I didn't realize how much you changed me. Or maybe I changed myself for you?"

De Guise pressed kisses just below her ear. "No, do not change for my sake, unless by change you mean grow (*kiss*), learn (*kiss*), become what you will (*kiss, kiss, kiss*). I love you, and my love will grow with you."

Jacqueline slid her hand below his back playfully. "Come grow with me now," she teased.

"Ho, là, là!" De Guise laughed in surprise. "I take it back. I must have changed something." He pulled her closer. "My oh-so-proper, shy, modest mistress of the forge, what are you suggesting?"

"Something utterly improper," she replied. "And I may be a master of the forge, but I would rather not be called your mistress." She caressed him. "Say, rather, 'lover.'

"Ah, chérie, in front of an audience?"

He caught her hands and kissed them, but the smile on his pretty bow lips belied the tension in his arms and the edge of his voice. She reluctantly stepped back with a moue.

"No, I suppose I'll have to wait to enjoy your favors."

De Guise caressed her cheek, his soft brown eyes pleading forgiveness. "In truth," he said, "I've come to beg a favor from you. I wish to invite a friend to stay here, at Bellesfées. Just a few days."

She knew better than to ask for details. He wouldn't have asked if it weren't desperately needed for national security.

"My bed is yours, Alain. My body is yours," she said softly. "So, of course, my home is likewise yours."

"I promise you," he said with a growl, "he does not get to enjoy the first two." He kissed her deeply again, and he chuckled when she responded.

A shriek from outdoors distracted them, along with metallic banging and the cackling of terrified chickens. Jacqueline and de Guise hastened to the balcony to discover the source of the alarm. A large mechanical man, an animated suit of bronze with a helmet like a diver's casque puffing little clouds of steam, strode determinedly up the macadamized drive to the château. A small boy dangled from the autonomaton's grip, yelling and beating its riveted torso, but the metal man lumbered on unperturbed.

"Oh, dear." Jacqueline quickly untied her work apron. "I told Monsieur Claque I wanted no visitors, but I didn't tell him how to handle them."

As the cries continued, the two hastened through the château halls to the entryway, where Monsieur Claque deposited the boy and bowed. With a poot of steam out the top of his head, he lumbered off again.

Marthe came in from the kitchen wiping her hands on her apron. "Guy? What are you doing here?"

She picked up the red-faced lad and held him close against her fluffy bosom, where he once more fought to free himself with indignation. "My nephew," Marthe explained to Jacqueline as she set him down.

Guy's freckled face reddened as he huffed and brushed himself off, pouting angrily. "This place is crazy," he declared. "Maman didn't tell me you worked with monsters."

"I'm so sorry he frightened you, Guy." Jacqueline stooped and took his hands. "How can I help you?"

In her sweaty work clothes, Jacqueline must not have appeared to be the mistress of the château, for Guy directed his tale to Marthe, in his eyes the greater authority. "It's Anne. She's real sick, Tatie Marthe. Maman couldn't wake her up all morning. Then when she woke up, she couldn't get out of bed."

Marthe's face knit into a worried frown. She looked at Jacqueline, who nodded.

"Go on," she told Marthe. "Take what you need for them."

"But your guests—" Marthe protested, thrusting her snub nose at de Guise.

"We'll manage," de Guise broke in. "I can fend for us for a few days."

The housekeeper eyed him balefully. Jacqueline chuckled. No one interfered with Marthe's kitchen!

"Go, Marthe. Send for me if you need anything more." Jacqueline tousled Guy's head. "And I will tell Monsieur Claque that you are one of our honored visitors. He won't frighten you again."

Guy's pout finally eased to a grin. "I wasn't scared. Didn't you see me punch him?" He trotted off after Marthe.

Jacqueline stood and took de Guise's hand. "Marthe said 'guests.' So your friend is already here with you?"

De Guise cleared his throat. "Ah. Yes. I wanted to ease into an introduction, give you time to finish your work and change for dinner, but I suppose you could meet him now."

"Absolutely not!"

She indicated her attire: a much-abused work chemise, the sleeves rolled up in the August heat exposing her scarred, muscular arms, dirty leather trousers with burn holes and globs of solder spotting here and there, and leather sabots. "I'm soaked in sweat, I smell like a horse, and I look even worse."

His eyes danced as he tweaked her nose. "I think you look adorable." He wiggled the modified spectacles around her neck. "Particularly with your special gogglers." He took her hand to kiss her wrist. "Ah, I've missed the scent of you."

"Pouah!" She shoved him away from her, wrinkling her nose in disgust. "How would your king like you quoting Napoléon? '*Home in three days. Don't bathe.*' Beurk!" Laughing, she stopped him from pulling her into an embrace. "No. You entertain your friend until supper, while I finish the clarinetist. You can introduce him to the water closet and the clockwork porters lest they frighten him the way they did you the first time you visited here."

De Guise winced at the reminder of how he had wrestled with the automated luggage cart that had taken his boots and refused to relinquish them unpolished.

Hours later, Jacqueline got to her feet and stretched, pressing her fists into the small of her back, groaning away the stiffness. The last joint of the clockwork clarinet still smoked, and her own joints burned with the strain of her hours' work.

"Perfect," she declared. She took a final look at the completed panharmonium, then gasped in surprise at the darkened concert hall. Beyond the open balcony doors, the early evening sky had paled, and the sun blazed along the treetops.

"*Zut!*"

Gogglers, gloves, apron, sabots, and tools clattered into the automated porter. It scuttled to the lift beside the staircase, and Jacqueline sent it to the floor below. Racing barefoot out of the music conservatory wing, she took a back stairway to her chambers for a quick wash with rosewater, Napoléon notwithstanding. Muffled voices drifting up from the salon reminded her she needed to dress for company with no one to help her tie a corset or coif her hair. De Guise, naturally, would not mind her casual day dress and unbound locks, but that wouldn't do for a guest at dinner. By the time she had stuffed herself into an appropriate gown, her hair's natural tendency to curl gave her a wild Créole appearance.

"A lady's maid," she grumbled. "One of these days I'll remember to build one."

Jacqueline grabbed a satin ribbon, tied it halfway along the length of her hair, and rolled it up to the back of her head, creating a shower of untamed corkscrew curls. A modest tucker, a shawl to cover her brawny arms, and gloves for her scarred and callused hands finally made her look like la Belle Dame de Bellesfées, as the villagers called her.

De Guise met her at the bottom of the stairs. "Have you sufficiently whetted your appetite?"

"I'm sorry, I was so focused, and then—"

Jacqueline stopped with a hiccough at the sight of the tall, portly, older gentleman behind de Guise, recognizing the pear-shaped face and aquiline nose immediately, the face imprinted on the coinage of France: Louis-Philippe, King of the French. She caught her breath, but before she could speak, de Guise put his finger to her lips.

"Madame Duval, may I present my dear friend Mister Smith of Philadelphia and Boston in the United States of America."

Confused, Jacqueline curtsied in reflex as the King of the French took her hand and kissed it, but her heart pounded, anxiety pressing air from her lungs.

"You have made this a charming home, madame," Smith said, his voice rolling, avuncular. "I am most impressed with the modernity of your system of gas fixtures and excellent plumbing work. Hot-and-cold water, gravity fed, and a bathing room, complete with a tub in every bedchamber. I've never seen the like." He crooked his arm and placed her hand there. "Allow me to escort you to dinner."

Speechless, she nodded. "Mr. Smith" led her to the head of the table in the dining room, seated her, and took a place to her left, deferring to de Guise to take the place of honor to her right. Having no time to prepare roasts, de Guise had laid a spartan meal of cold meats and a variety of fresh vegetables lightly sautéed in butter and herbs. Smith cheerfully allowed de Guise to serve Jacqueline and himself before receiving dishes, although he did take the larger portions once the dishes were set before him.

Her twin Angélique had often spoken of Louis-Philippe's reputation as a bit of a trickster within the palace walls, which explained the twinkle in his eyes as he "held court" at dinner, pretending to be a bourgeois tourist in a country home. Jacqueline recalled the King had been to the United States of America during his years of exile, calling himself "Mr. Smith," but that was over twenty years ago. Louis-Philippe, King of the French for the past thirteen years, often boasted of his "bourgeois" status and frequented literary and social salons, the kind Angélique attended. But Jacqueline remained wary, as the King also hobnobbed with Rothschilds and with that porcine financier Rodolphe Armand, who had been for the past two years pressing a suit against Jacqueline for theft and breach of a contract she'd never made.

"De Guise tells me you built a panharmonicon," Mr. Smith commented. "I do enjoy a good clockwork orchestra. I'm fascinated by your automata here at Bellesfées. Especially that large fellow, Monsieur Clanque. Marvelous! I wonder if I might engage your engineering skills at some point in the future."

De Guise winked surreptitiously, knowing Jacqueline's low opinion of technology in service to political gain.

"Monsieur *Claque* is unique," she replied noncommittally.

"Delightful. As is this wine. De Guise tells me it's your own varietal. You developed it yourself, am I right?"

"De Guise seems to have told you many things, monsieur," she said archly, flashing her lover a questioning look, getting an amused shrug in return. "I cannot boast the same."

Smith and de Guise exchanged more serious expressions. "In good time, madame. In very good time."

Dinner proceeded with no less awkwardness for Jacqueline. Part of her was furious with de Guise for introducing the King of the French with no advance notice and with so little opportunity for propriety. Another part was flattered the King himself was here, at Bellesfées, and she thanked heaven that Marthe wasn't present to be as mortified as Jacqueline was at the plain repast set before their monarch—not that Marthe would recognize him. Marthe knew all the chickens, goats, and cows on the estate, but no one who hadn't spent time in Paris would recognize the King.

But mostly, the untimely visit interfered with Jacqueline's plans. She had so much more to arrange for her sister's return, and while she never resented entertaining guests, this guest would demand more of her energies than she wanted to spare.

De Guise cleared the table to the sideboard and returned with a plate of cheeses. Horrified at the crust of mold on the block of Gruyère, Jacqueline quickly sliced it away. Her cheeks flushed with more than the August heat as Smith and de Guise carried on a light conversation about the excellence of English and Irish cheeses, Viennese pastries, and incomparable French wines. Smith told tales of the cholera epidemic in Philadelphia ("My brothers were both quite ill. I nursed them myself.") and recounted meeting George Washington ("He was their president, did you know?") in Boston, where Smith taught French and German in his "younger years."

But Jacqueline's ears felt stuffed with cotton from shame and with fear she would somehow offend her king by her utter lack of awareness of social cues. Angélique often teased her for being buried in her thoughts, unaware of the insult she inflicted on others while adrift in self-absorbed obsessions and compulsions. Jacqueline grew bored attending to the comforts of others for the sake of passing the time, and she had a propensity for careering off into new plans for engineering designs in the middle of conversations.

Moreover, her political and sociological views were almost diametrically opposed to Louis-Philippe's, and in most other circumstances, she would be pitted against him in angry discourse, but she couldn't afford to lose his favor with Armand's lawsuit at court.

In short, she was trapped in a cocoon of dread.

After supper, when they retired to the more spacious salon, she hurried ahead to make certain the furniture had no coat of dust drifting in from the doors and windows, which were kept open day and night in summer. De Guise set up brandies and made a show of a tray of chocolate confections he had brought her from Switzerland. Her hand trembled as she took one, appalled at presuming to serve herself before the King.

Mr. Smith broke into her thoughts. "I see your consternation, Madame Duval." He raised a brow and smiled his mischievous smile. "I am not here for you to entertain. Please do not think of me as your king. In fact, I would be pleased if you treated me more as a shadow. I would take advantage of your vast library, perhaps practice a little fortepiano—I noticed your little Pleyel over there—or tuck myself away in a corner to write. Hopefully enjoy more of that splendid Bellesfées wine. Go about your day as if I were not here at all. Indulge me in our pantomime, won't you? Can you do that?"

Jacqueline sighed, not quite relieved. "My home is yours, Maj—euh, monsieur." She rose, and the men stood for her. "Please excuse me, but I must retire. It has been a difficult day and there is still much to do before my sister arrives. You will stay for the celebration?"

He kissed her hand. "I should like nothing better."

She hesitated. "There are those among the guests who may recognize you."

His eyes twinkled. "Several old friends, de Guise tells me. That should be fun." He relinquished her to his bodyguard.

At the foot of the staircase, she turned on de Guise. "What were you thinking?" She smacked his chest.

He caught her hand, pulled her into his arms, and kissed her. She allowed herself to melt just a little. When he released her, he caressed her face, then held her and gently swayed.

"I'm sorry." He kept his voice at a whisper, close to her ear. "I had no time to forewarn you."

"De Guise, you know my suit is in court now. How will his stay here affect that?"

"Clemency, I should think. He knighted your father, he received your début, he—"

"He *what?*" Jacqueline gawked in surprise. How could she have not known the King of the French had received her début?

De Guise grinned at her. "You were probably so preoccupied explaining the advantages of your plumbing system to the ladies, you never noticed him." He caressed her hair. "And it's obvious you built no such machine as Armand has declared ruined him."

"But—"

His voice turned grim. "Chérie, with growing talk of rebellion, in Paris and along the routes, the threat of assassination has once again reached my ears."

She gasped and he hushed her.

"Socialists?" she whispered. "I did not think they were organized well enough to mount a revolt, much less an assassination."

"No, the threats come from outside. We decided to make it known the King had already returned to Château d'Eu for the meeting with the Queen of England, then we would "absquatulate"—as the Americans say—somewhere he could safely hide. As it has been noted, when it comes to kings, hunting season never closes."

From the salon came stilted strains of a Bach two-part invention on the Pleyel. Jacqueline wagged her head in a whirl of worries. Marthe gone, the wedding celebration, guests from Paris, Angélique's return, and now the very life of the King of the French.

"What can I do?" she asked.

"Just as he requests. Treat him as Mister Smith of the United States of America, as he once was in his youth. He left behind his ring and his sash. We must leave them behind as well. I've verified the guest list, and I see nothing menacing, even if there are those who do not support the Orléans lineage. His life is in my hands. In our hands, now. My love?"

She kissed him again to seal their pact of silence. Then she pouted. "Does this mean you will refrain from—visiting me?"

For answer, he lifted her into his arms and carried her upstairs. Bach's was not the only two-part invention that evening.

2.

JACQUELINE AWOKE TO A THOUSAND-VOICED DAWN CHORUS FILLING THE air with trills, warbles, whistles, and calls. Sunlight streaming onto the bed quickened De Guise's scent on the pillows, sparking memories of a lingering afterglow. Her thighs tightened, then released as she sprawled across the bed beneath the canopy of gold stars on a blue field above her. Hugging a pillow, she breathed in de Guise and sighed with a soft moan. She traced the indentation on the sheets where he had lain beside her, trying to dream him back into existence there.

The crunch of a wagon rolling up the macadamized drive broke through her reverie, but not as thoroughly as Marthe's voice barking quick instructions to her son, Jean-Paul. Jacqueline yanked trousers over her night chemise, donned slippers, and hurried downstairs. De Guise, fully dressed, was already out the door. Jacqueline didn't doubt he had stood downstairs on sentry, protecting his king, after leaving her bedchamber. Necessary, yes, but she counted it another grievance against Louis-Philippe.

Marthe's niece Anne could barely stand, so de Guise fetched her from the wagon and carried her through to the empty servants' wing, where he set her on a bed in the room closest to the kitchens. Drawing up a chair beside the bed, Jacqueline examined her.

"No fever," Marthe said, her voice frayed with exhaustion. "She perked up a bit with some soup, but she's white as a ghost."

Anne, a tall girl at the edge of womanhood, tried to sit up, mumbling about helping Maman. Jacqueline hushed her and brushed back her hair, damp with sweat, though the girl's pale skin was cool to the touch. There were purplish-red bruises along her neck that worried Jacqueline only because the girl seemed too young to exhibit such intimate tokens.

"What happened? Do you know?"

Marthe shook her head wearily. "Her mother said she had a day like this a few weeks ago. Guy says she fell out of bed with a nightmare. Two nights ago, another nightmare. The next day, well, you heard. I stayed with her, and we both slept deep. I thought I could better keep an eye on her here, though, make sure she's fed and looked after while Cici and Marius tend to the fields. Harvest will be coming in soon. Jean-Paul can watch her."

"But, Maman, Papa needs me, as does the mistress."

Jean-Paul, a tall, strong youth a little more than a year older than Anne, clearly deemed the task of babysitting his cousin beneath his abilities. Jacqueline didn't want to argue with Marthe, but at the same time, she did need Jean-Paul to help Luc set up the pavilions on the lawn for Angélique's reception. She was about to say as much when another voice interrupted.

"I can sit with the child," said Mr. Smith from the doorway.

Still in his dressing gown, cap, and slippers, he came forward and took Jacqueline's seat, lifting the girl's hand. He caressed it with gentle concern. "I've cared for many a sick child in my days, as a brother, as a tutor, and as a parent. I will tend to her as one of my own."

Jacqueline gulped, awaiting the explosion. Marthe's face contorted at the suggestion of a visitor to the household assuming a servant's duties. As her ruddy face puffed and she stammered, trying to shape her indignation into words, Jacqueline quickly took her arm.

"Of course," Jacqueline said. "How perfect. Come, Marthe, you must be exhausted. You're a bit pale yourself. Let me fix you some breakfast. God bless you, Mister Smith. How fortunate we are to have you with us."

Jean-Paul took advantage of his mother's confusion to disappear while Jacqueline ushered Marthe to the preparation room.

"Have a seat at the end of the table, Marthe," she told her. "I'll bring last night's embers up to cooking fires in both the hearth and the stove and get you breakfast."

By the time Jacqueline stood again, Marthe was asleep with her head on the table, lightly snoring; no doubt that, despite claiming she had "slept deep," Marthe had sat sentry all night too.

Jacqueline hurried back to her room to dress for a day of work. By the time she returned to the kitchen, ham and tomato slices sizzled on the hob and de Guise carved stale bread for toasting. The aroma of strong coffee and boiled milk made her mouth water, and she poured a large bowl for herself and one for de Guise.

"What do you think?" he asked her as they drank.

She frowned. "Did you see those marks on her neck and throat? I didn't like the look of those on a girl her age."

"They were more than bruises, I'm afraid, and no, not what you think they are. I found small pricks in the skin, like horsefly bites. Very deep. But horseflies carry no diseases I'm aware of. And their bite usually leaves blisters, not—bruises."

A loud snore ended in an indignant snort as Marthe sat up groggily. "And what do you think you're doing, ma fille?" She got to her feet and pushed Jacqueline away from the stove. "And you, monsieur! This is *my* kitchen."

She clapped on her bonnet, but as she stuffed her hair up under the brim, Jacqueline caught her wrist and stopped her.

"De Guise, look."

Two small pinpricks marked Marthe's throat, and the flesh around them was mottled with red spots.

"Marthe, I don't wish to be indelicate but—euh—has someone been nuzzling you?"

Marthe slapped her hand away. "Ma fille, you go too far!" She snatched up a charger and examined her reflection. "What's this?" She tried wiping the bruises away and winced. "It's nothing. Go on, go on. Out of my kitchen."

She tried to shoo them, but de Guise took her firmly in hand and led her back to Anne's room. Jacqueline followed, and she showed Marthe the bruises on Anne's neck. Marthe blinked and frowned. Then she shook her head.

"Too much work to do."

She swayed as she turned to leave. De Guise wrapped his arm around her waist. Although she protested vociferously, she didn't fight him as he escorted her to the other bed in the room.

"I haven't made up these beds yet," Marthe mumbled. "More work for me."

"Not so, madame," Mr. Smith assured her. "More time to become friends, you and I."

Jacqueline chewed the inside of her cheek. How could she open her château to a gathering in the midst of an epidemic?

Two people does not constitute an epidemic! Jacqueline could almost hear her twin Angélique scold her. *Stop exaggerating, Jacky. You'd drown in a glass of water.*

But it could not be a coincidence that Marthe exhibited the same symptoms as her niece after a mere twelve hours, both of them suffering overnight. There was no fever, so it wasn't an infection. Spiders? Hover flies? Vipers? All of those were far more extreme than a simple puncture and a lewd love-bite.

How would Jacqueline manage if Marthe fell ill? Invitations had already gone out, with guests expected within the next two days. Marthe had been preparing for over a week, laying in stores for the gala and hiring extra kitchen workers, servers, and attendants.

But more than that, Marthe and her husband Luc had raised Jacqueline and her sister Angélique with stern hands, hard wisdom, and firm common sense. They were more than housekeepers: nursemaids, teachers, guides, and surrogate parents when Monsieur Duval was away, which he often was. Reception or no, Jacqueline couldn't bear the thought of losing Marthe.

And now the King of the French sat beside one of the sick, soothing her brow and telling stories although the girl was barely awake.

"A bit of protein, I think," Mr. Smith said, nodding. "I'm sure you have goat's milk. Eggs. Some beef tea. And much water."

Jacqueline's brow knit. "Monsieur, do you think it's wise to stay, given the circumstances? If this is an infection—"

He waved. "No, I don't think it is. Other than fatigue, they show no signs of extremity, no fever." He smiled at Jacqueline. "If it will ease your mind, I will have de Guise visit the village to inquire if any others are in similar distress."

"I was going to suggest the same," de Guise said. "Madame Duval, if you would, see to breakfast for Mister Smith?"

He was gone before she could reply. Jacqueline sighed and returned to the kitchen. Reception preparations would have to wait, and let the King's choice to risk infection be on his own head.

Jacqueline spent the morning making broths and boiled eggs for the two invalids. Marthe complained about her confinement, but was no less grateful for the ministrations. By noon, Anne could sit up on her own. When Mr. Smith brought a set of checkers from the salon, the girl was soon laughing over games, giving Jacqueline the confidence to head to her forge's workshop for a few hours. She had a spark of an idea to assist de Guise's efforts in keeping the King safe. She hummed happily as she braided fine copper wire while the resident black cat strode in and out of her legs and leapt to the worktable for caresses, closing its crystal blue eyes in delight.

De Guise returned in the late afternoon and joined Mr. Smith and Jacqueline in the salon where they had retired for refreshment, since Anne and Marthe were both sleeping. Jacqueline had ordered all curtains to be drawn over the open windows and doors, so the heat of the day made the spacious room stuffy and humid. De Guise's grim expression only added to the oppressive ambience.

"Forge-à-Bellesfées is secure, but two villages over, a young girl died of a wasting disease a few weeks ago."

"The bruising? The bites?" Jacqueline asked.

De Guise nodded. "Now, this wasn't sudden. Over the past few months since spring, she would sometimes awaken too weak to get up and around. They feared at first she was phthisic. She seemed to be better when her parents returned from the fields at evening. Then one morning, they found her body pale and cold."

"How horrible! Marthe—"

He calmed her. "Marthe and Anne are both in our care, and we won't let them languish. I think you might want to insist any maids and farmhands stay on, though, rather than returning to their homes at night, at least until this passes."

Mr. Smith cleared his throat. He seemed ill at ease. "I don't wish to alarm you overmuch. Only, what you say about the dead child... In my youth—that is, my sister—"

He paused, and they waited anxiously as he organized his thoughts. Finally, he drew a deep breath and released it in a sigh, his eyes no longer lit.

"I have a sister. Dear to me. Very dear. When she was about your age, Madame Duval, she went to reside with our aunt, and together they moved to Bratislava, on the border of Austria and Hungary. Our aunt was a devout woman, and they made many visits to the local convents, doing works of charity with the good sisters there for a few years. The sisters told a tale, one repeated throughout the region, of someone who stalked women during the night. Young women, young girls of the villages, would fall ill, weak and listless. Then they were found dead, and deathly white rather than blue or mottled, as if they had been drained of their blood. They said — and I am only repeating my sister's story — they said it was a vampire."

Jacqueline wrinkled her nose. Ghosts. Revenants. Sorcerers. Now a vampire. More dire myths and legends come to life, invading Jacqueline's ordered world of science and logic. She sighed and rubbed her brow. De Guise gave a quiet grunt of agreement.

Mr. Smith glanced from one to the other, confused by their lack of horror. "Perhaps you have already heard this tale. I counted it as peasant superstition, as did my sister. But superstition aside, something has killed a child and attacked two women here in Forge-à-Bellesfées."

"Only women." Jacqueline glowered. "I'm *sick* of attacks on women!"

Mr. Smith startled at her vicious tone. De Guise leaned closer and explained, "Madame Duval's sister was the victim of a heinous assault."

"Poor dear," Smith murmured. "Well, de Guise, we have our work laid out before us here. These attacks occur at night. Therefore, you and I will take our rest during the daylight hours and serve as the night watch."

Jacqueline and de Guise exchanged sly smiles.

"That won't be necessary, Mister Smith," she said. "We have Monsieur Claque and our porters. Claque will stand guard over the servants' wing, and I will keep my porters by my chamber window and door."

She rose and strolled to the windows to peek out across the vale to the orange rooftops huddled beyond the forest. "My greater concern is safeguarding the villagers. They may not be our tenants, but Bellesfées needs them. If the villagers suffer, we all — "

She caught herself before she offended her so-called "Citizen King," who, despite his outward preference for simplicity and his history of plain industry, generally ignored the plight of the working class in favor of causes that benefited the wealthy elite. Turning back to the men, she continued.

"Vampires, then. Superstition would have it that garlic, silver, and crosses are efficacious in repelling the vampire. I'll head to the forge and manufacture a few batches of silver crosses. Monsieur de Guise, can you check our stores of garlic? We can visit each home and offer these as tokens against illness, lest we terrify them with tales of bloodsucking monsters."

De Guise added, "I should also inquire whether there are new visitors in the region. Has any nearby château exchanged owners? Has a cousin come from afar? Someone from Austria, Hungary, or Transylvania?"

Jacqueline snorted. "I think you'll find there are more Poles, Austrians, and Hungarians in France than there are in all the rest of Europe, including Poland, Austria, and Hungary."

"My only concern is Bellesfées at the moment."

"Mine as well."

"I'll see what I can learn. May I make use of your Chappe telegraphic system?"

"Of course." She caught his arm. "But you haven't slept."

He kissed her brow. "I'll sleep soundly once I have more information." He excused himself with a nod to each of them.

Mr. Smith poured himself another sherry. "I must say, Madame Duval, you have taken this tale of terror in stride." He offered to refill her glass, but she shook her head.

"Perhaps Monsieur de Guise has not told you all there is to know about Bellesfées since last you visited," she replied distantly. "Or even how Monsieur de Guise and I met."

"He has alluded to vague details, although I would like to know much better the woman who has so changed my friend."

Thinking back to that first day, she blushed: Knocking de Guise's hat off his head as she stepped from the Paris-Orléans train. De Guise putting his arm around her waist. Untying her corset so she could breathe more easily as she freed the ghost from the bronze automaton. Kissing her hand, carrying her packages, taking her into his arms, dancing her through the Catacombs...

She stifled the rising warmth her memories evinced. "I will say only that we have both learned that there are many forces in this world besides those explored by da Vinci, Descartes, Kepler, and Newton—laws we have not yet discovered."

Shaking off further thoughts of the Draganov affair, she turned her focus to Mr. Smith. "But you, monsieur. I believe I can assist you in your current predicament. First, a disguise."

His brow rose and his merry eyes danced once again. He downed his sherry and followed her.

A pair of mud boots, a broad-brimmed straw field hat, and one of Luc's barn coats still smelling of muck adequately covered Mr. Smith, but Jacqueline had to keep reminding him to slump his shoulders and walk with less martial bearing as they made their way along the drive. Attached to the forge, an old outbuilding the size of a small barn served as Jacqueline's workshop, an organized clutter.

"Mind your head," she warned, ducking the chains of overhead winches.

She picked up a large crucible from a workbench and set it back on the shelf along the wall with others of varying sizes. As she led Mr. Smith past workbenches, she pushed chisels, tongs, or fullers out of the way. He paused to admire a collection of highly burnished brass cogs and sprockets along with large wheels punched in irregular designs.

"Oh, my, what are these beautiful pieces?" He ran a finger along the punches and cried out when he came away with a slice in his fingertip.

"Careful!" Jacqueline warned belatedly. "My clockwork music. Those punches catch the teeth of the sound board."

He popped his finger into his mouth to ease it, and he nodded toward the dressmaker's model.

"I use that to form my androides," she explained. "Come along where it's a little safer."

She beckoned him to the side wall near the back, where another dressmaker's model stood beside a worktable featuring two torso frameworks, vests fashioned from fine copper wires woven and twisted around one another to form grids of hexagons roughly a centimeter across. She shooed away the cat and took one of the vests to wrap around the mannequin.

"Something I discovered quite serendipitously. I was returning from my dressmaker in Orléans one day last spring. I had a bundle of new dresses of Persian silk brocade. I had paused in the lane to rest my horse, Bisou. On impulse, I opened my bundle to admire my purchases, gathering the dresses to my bosom to savor the luxuriant feel of them. As you might guess—" She indicated her attire. "I rarely indulge in fashion in the course of my work. Suddenly, I heard the thunder of a hunting rifle. A moment later, I was struck in the chest with such force that I was thrown back into my carriage, where I lay quite stunned."

"*Mon Dieu!*"

"Stunned but unpierced by any shot."

His eyes widened. "You were fortunate, madame. I have known several times the brush of a shot. Your dresses saved you?"

"More than that, Mister Smith."

She opened a chest beside the workbench and drew out the re-shaped bodices of three silk dresses. These she placed over the brass mesh and covered it all with the second meshwork vest, forming a heavily padded waistcoat.

"The hunter, you see, was quite a distance from me, which would undoubtedly have slowed the shot before impact. Here at Bellesfées, we hope to keep any stranger at such a distance as well."

She went to the far wall and pulled down a rifle. Mr. Smith, his eyes bright with intrigue, took it from her.

"May I?" he asked.

Fetching a flask of gunpowder, a patch, and a ball from the firearms cabinet, she gave these over to the King. He loaded expertly, but she stopped him when he took aim, drawing him back to the doorway of the workshop, a good twenty meters, and then indicated the mannequin. He fired. The mannequin slammed against the back wall and dropped.

"Oh, dear," Mr. Smith said, setting the rifle aside.

Together they went to inspect their experiment. Jacqueline removed the outer mesh and handed it to Mr. Smith.

"It's quite light," he said in surprise.

She then pointed to the mannequin. The ball embedded in the silk left an indentation three centimeters deep, but the silk remained intact.

"Success! I hoped I was right. A few centimeters isn't enough to kill a man, and the silk will serve to stanch the wound until medical help can arrive. But more importantly, there is nowhere on the estate closer than four hundred meters that would provide cover for an assassin's shot. Now, monsieur, what do you say to a new silk waistcoat?"

He examined the brass bodice, then assessed the indentation. "Perhaps a doubling of this technique, though it might make me appear too plump."

Laughing, Jacqueline took the rifle to clean and oil, while Mr. Smith inspected the rest of the workshop.

"You've done all this yourself?" he asked on their way back to the château. He nodded with appreciation at the gas lamps that lit their way in the evening dusk. "And apart from the Benets, you have no servants? De Guise tells me you have no assistants, apprentices, protégées."

She pointed to the forge beyond the workshop. "The forge is too small. I can't take on apprentices; it would be dangerous to have more than one in there. We have a few servants who come in from the village to help at the château and with the animals and gardens, but I'm quite capable of cleaning my own house when I'm not at work. Each day a different room. I'll hire more villagers on occasion. For example, to help with the reception. Otherwise, Marthe, Luc, and young Jean-Paul have always been all we needed. Although—" She paused with a sad smile. "I do miss my sister."

"I understand completely. I would be quite lost without dear Adélaïde to keep me in line."

For a moment, Jacqueline was willing to forget her antipathy for the monarch and appreciate the sentiments of the man.

When they reached the château, Mr. Smith bowed and took his leave, and Jacqueline turned her attention to the kitchens for dinner. To her surprise, she found Marthe already at the hearth, where a large cauldron bubbled with fragrant herbs and meaty beef bones. The housekeeper leaned against the mantel with one arm and stirred with the other. Jacqueline slipped her arms about her and kissed her brow.

"I want you sleeping here tonight, where I can keep watch," she said. "It's my turn to take care of you."

The housekeeper didn't answer. She yawned.

Jacqueline looked in on Anne and found the girl awake, so she sat beside her on the bed. "Anne, do you remember anything biting you here?" She touched the girl's throat. "A bug, perhaps, or a bat?"

"No, madame." Anne lay back on her pillow. "I just had bad dreams. In my dreams, a giant cat sometimes scratched me."

"Tell me."

The girl rubbed her freckled nose and pursed her lips. "Once I dreamed fairies played outside my window, and they kept calling me to play with them. I opened my shutters to shoo them. I told them I'm not a child anymore, but they flew at me, and they had terrible faces. I was frightened. Then a black cat came and chased them all away. A big cat, like a lion, not a kitty-cat. Then the other night, I dreamed the cat woke me up. The cottage was on fire and I couldn't get out my door. I threw open the shutters, but more fire came in through the window. I couldn't move, couldn't run, couldn't call out. And the cat was on fire too. That's when I fell out of bed."

"How terrified you must have been."

"And last night, the cat had a honeycomb, and it called my name over and over, so I invited it in for a saucer of milk. We drank tea and honey. But it scratched me." Anne's eyes welled with tears. "It's just— the cat keeps calling my name. Sometimes even when I'm awake."

Jacqueline froze. Her face must have reflected her thoughts, for the girl's eyes widened in fear. Jacqueline quickly smiled again and brushed Anne's hair gently.

"I know someone who can keep cats away, day or night. Would you like to meet him?"

Anne's face lit up again. "Monsieur Smith? He's very nice."

Jacqueline chuckled. "He is indeed. Very nice. But have you met Monsieur Claque?" She reached into her pocket and took out a small tin whistle. "Watch."

She blew a shrill note. Marthe growled something from the kitchen. Soon they heard the heavy tread of the autonomaton running through the château, metal ringing on stone. As footsteps stomped closer, Anne pressed to Jacqueline. Then Monsieur Claque himself appeared, halting in the doorway. He tooted a response to the whistle and tilted his head in curiosity. Anne giggled.

"There you go," Jacqueline said. "Monsieur Claque will stand guard in the hallway all night." She set the whistle on the table beside the bed. "If you hear that cat call you, you just whistle. Monsieur Claque won't let any cat give you bad dreams again."

"Out of the way, you clanking tin-pot," Marthe said, entering with a tray of supper for Anne and herself. "I'll be keeping an eye out tonight, thank you."

Jacqueline left them together, but she got no farther than the kitchen, where she sat with her head in her hands.

The girl had invited the cat into her dreams. Now it would haunt Jacqueline's as well.

3.

DESPITE JACQUELINE'S FEARS, EVERYONE SLEPT PEACEFULLY THAT NIGHT. By morning Marthe had fully recovered, and Anne was bright-eyed and anxious to get out of bed, even if it meant helping in the kitchen. Jacqueline insisted the girl be given tasks she could complete sitting down, so Marthe had her trim vegetables and season meats. After breakfast, a small army of village youths Marthe had hired for service arrived, and she took up her rolling pin to command them.

Jacqueline went to the workshop to complete the shot-deflecting vest, supervised by the cat sauntering in and out of her workspace, flitting its tail along Jacqueline's face at inconvenient moments or rubbing against her legs as she tried to walk. Jacqueline then fired up the forge and began the task of fashioning small silver crosses, two hundred of them. She hoped no one would complain they were not crucifixes. As a measure of precaution, she stamped them with a symbol of conjoined wedding rings, so she might present them as tokens of celebration rather than demonic wards. She showed one to the cat.

"What do you think? Does this scare you?"

The cat eyed her with disdain, then turned away to lick its paw and preen.

She chuckled. "I guess if you were about to bite me, you'd run."

The day began to feel normal, and Jacqueline settled into an easy complacency.

In the early afternoon, she returned to the château to find Mr. Smith relaxing with a book in the library. He stood and bowed, then showed her the book — *The Fencing Master* by Alexandre Dumas père.

"He served as my clerk in my youth," he said. "The fellow can talk your ears off. I directed him to writing, mostly to keep him from his endless chatter."

She chuckled, knowing full well what he meant. "My sister Angélique adores his works, as well as his company. He's one of the invited guests, but I don't know if he'll attend."

"If you're serving good wine, I'm certain he'll be here. I will enjoy surprising him."

"According to Angélique, he prefers a treat called dawamesc. It's an Algerian confection far more powerful than wine, I'm told. Angélique will have none of it."

"No, you do not want Algerian poisons in your house."

He settled back and she left him to discover the tale of the Decembrist Revolt in Russia.

As she passed through the hallway, she saw de Guise riding up the drive. With a rush of relief, she ran to greet him. He hopped down from Bisou and handed the reins to Jean-Paul so he could embrace Jacqueline, then hugged her until she squealed and laughed.

"Maman says there's a Bedford luncheon ready inside, whatever that is," Jean-Paul told them as he led the mare away to the stables.

They strolled into the family dining room, where Marthe had laid a board of charcuterie and fresh cheese, sliced fruits, and a pitcher of beer. Mr. Smith, in his disguise but without the filthy mucking coat, rose to welcome them.

"What news, de Guise?"

"A mixture of good and bad." De Guise seated Jacqueline and poured beer for the three of them. "No property has changed hands in this region for over two years, so I doubt we need worry about your neighbors, Madame Duval. There is a visiting cousin from Austria, but he's a congenial fellow, and unafraid of the sunlight, as I found him fishing by the Loire. Whoever this predator is, if we're to believe our theory of a vampire, he's not a public figure, probably no one we know. A vagrant, perhaps, whom we can fend off with preventative measures. I've warned the prefecture and the innkeeper to be wary of newcomers."

Jacqueline bit violently into a chunk of cheese. "I'd rather hunt him down and pierce his heart with a stake." She pondered the cheese, her mind elsewhere. "I could fashion a weapon, like a crossbow but to carry a heavier projectile."

"You design weaponry?" Mr. Smith's eyes narrowed. "Are you familiar with that infernal machine Fieschi constructed for my demise?"

She shuddered, avoiding his gaze. "I am. I was at the Polytechnique at the time." She suppressed an inappropriate smile, for the King of the French had no idea how she herself had been involved in Fieschi's failure. "I'm very thankful the monster knew so little about weaponry that he overcharged the barrels somehow. Still, such devastation. Twenty-five rounds firing simultaneously, a veritable one-man infantry. The horror of that slaughter. If the timing had been any different..." She glanced at the scar on his scalp he still sported from the attempt on his life. Then she caught his meaning. "Ah, yes, I could replicate something along that order."

"I am also thinking of de Guise's weapon of choice," Smith continued. "A repeating firearm rather than a cannonade. Mister Colt's patents should provide some inspiration, n'est-ce pas?"

Jacqueline thought back to her early days at the École Polytechnique and the designs of Jean Pauly she had studied. Although Pauly's quirky fish-shaped thermal airship was the focus of her interests, the man had done intense work on the concepts of automatic weaponry, designs improved upon much later by Casimir Lefaucheux and, of course, the American, Colt. A revolving mechanism of multiple chambers, cartridges, firing pins, self-contained, perhaps steam-powered —

"We've lost her now," de Guise said with a grin. "Come back to me, my love! But let me continue with my report on another matter, the upcoming rendez-vous at Eu. I've learned there are those in western Europe who are not pleased at the thought of a cordial relationship between the two parties involved in next week's meeting."

Mr. Smith tugged at his whiskers. "I can understand. The Habsburg Monarchy has already been greatly diminished in its struggles with the Ottomans. The Coburgs do not want my son to marry the Spanish princess. Neither does England, for that matter." His smile was tense. "Hence, the meeting at Eu."

"And once more, we hear of a threat from the Danube. Twice in as many days. I'm not fond of coincidences." De Guise sipped his beer and sighed appreciatively. He examined the golden beverage. "How have I not tasted this before now? Madame Duval, did you brew this here, or is this from the village?"

"This is ours, though the recipe is from Plzeň, in Bohemia — actual Bohemia, not Paris." Jacqueline smiled at the memory. "I discovered it last year while consulting on a new foundry in Prague. Doctor Škoda treated a burn," she said, showing a thick scar on her forearm, "and we became fast friends. He knew I don't care for heavy, dark beer, so he introduced me to the brewer who developed this recipe. Saaz noble hops, a lighter malt, cold fermented. It's not heavy, and it's such a simple brew."

She pried open a roll, stuffed it with chunks of cheese and slices of meats, and shoved the whole thing into her pocket. "Messieurs, you must excuse me. You've given me much to think about, and much work to do before the Duke and Duchess arrive. It seems to me that the reception would provide propitious opportunity for either assault or assassination. I want to be prepared to prevent either. Mr. Smith, I do apologize, but I think it wise you remain indoors until we learn more about our enemies, both political and supernatural."

"I agree," de Guise said. "Perhaps we can relax in the concert hall with the balconies open."

"Splendid idea!" Mr. Smith's eyes gleamed. "I'll have a chance to preview your project."

With a brief curtsy, Jacqueline trotted down the hill and around the pond to the lawn where Luc and Jean-Paul had finished erecting four of the five huge pavilions. She hoped four would be enough, for she needed the Benet men to help her defend the château and her guests before they set about on a fifth.

Luc, a tall, imposing man with a quiet demeanor, complemented his stout and voluble wife. Jean-Paul favored him, with sandy hair and brown eyes, and an instinct for making himself useful to the mistresses of Bellesfées, a fact in which he took great pride. The Benets had taken the twins' eccentricities in stride, showing particular patience with Angélique's unique nature. Jacqueline knew she could rely on them to accept her alarming news with equanimity and would follow her instructions with meticulous care.

"The garlic and the crosses must be presented as gifts to the village in celebration of Angélique's marriage. Everyone should be instructed to wear the crosses and keep the garlic under their pillows. Tell them it's a Welsh custom, a special blessing for sweet dreams for the happy couple."

Jean-Paul asked, "Do you think it will be enough?"

She had no answer, but her doubt only encouraged the boy.

"I could gather some of the fellows to help. Then Papa could stay here and help you with the windows."

"Wonderful." Jacqueline dug into her pocket and brought out some coins for him. "This should secure you a small cohort, eh?" Clapping him on the shoulder, she sent him off to the workshop to collect the sack of crosses.

She turned to Luc. "I'll fetch the chisel, blow lamp, and iron. You get the silver and stamp from my workshop. Let's make sure nothing can invade the château."

Bellesfées, with its chapel, servants' wing, and music conservatory, featured forty-seven windows and twelve doors, including the balconies. Jacqueline and Luc finished embossing each window casing and door lintel with a silver cross except in the chapel, which Jacqueline judged would not require such attention. She stamped wedding rings into the last cross over the balcony doors of the concert hall and set the tools on the porter. Disappointed that de Guise and Mr. Smith had already departed the hall, she mopped her brow with a sigh of weariness.

Luc had worked silently at her side, but now he cleared his throat to draw her attention.

"Yes, Luc?"

He pressed his lips tightly together. "Not my place to ask, I know, but—" He hesitated. "It's Mademoiselle Angélique. Only, she's married now, so Madame Laforge. Or is it Madame Llewellyn? Anyway, we wondered—not our place, but helpful to know—that is, when one marries, one expects—"

"Children." Jacqueline blew out a long breath. "I don't know, Luc." She rested against the balcony rail. "We have no idea the extent to which her lycanthropy—or Llewellyn's for that matter—will adapt to such changes. Would a child in the womb take on the same powers? Or if Angélique is in her other form when they… Well, further, can we expect a litter of four, or will she have twins like our mother, or will that skip a generation? Wolves only need eight or nine weeks to deliver pups. Will that be a factor? We simply don't know how their condition will affect the whole process, Luc."

Luc stared at her without expression. He blinked a few times, shrugged, and said, "I just wondered if you wanted me to convert any rooms to a nursery any time soon."

Jacqueline giggled. Her whole body gave over to laughter, shedding weariness. She was still chuckling throughout her bath, and the smile remained with her as she dressed for dinner. Her good humor turned to joy when she heard the commotion below and footsteps running up the marble stairs.

Angélique flew through the door into Jacqueline's arms and kissed her until Jacqueline squealed.

"You're home!" "I'm home!"

They spoke at the same time, then giggled and hooked little fingers in a childhood tradition, teasing, "Twinicism!" They held one another, laughing.

"Mon Ange! Mon Ange! There's so much to tell you," Jacqueline began.

"I know there's a stranger in the house," her sister replied, tapping her nose. "Is Papa away again?"

"He said he'll be home for the reception, if the weather holds."

Angélique held her at arm's length to look her over. "You're positively glowing," she declared. "De Guise has been good for you."

Jacqueline pouted. "In fact, he's been gone for the past ten days. I nearly went mad here by myself."

"*Bof.* You do best when you're by yourself. Unless…" Angélique pinched her sister's nose. "Ah, yes. Love! I forgot what it's like, that wonderful drug of adolescent infatuation."

"I'm hardly an adolescent."

"Well, late-bloomer infatuation then. But he's here now."

A smile tugged at Jacqueline's lips. "He's home. He calls Bellesfées home."

Angélique hugged her again. "You still need me to clean and coif your hair, though, don't you?"

"Absolutely. But first tell me about the wedding."

Angélique grabbed Jacqueline's hands and the two swirled like a whirligig. "It was so simple. Gryffin has no family, although he has dozens of servants. I've never seen so many people scurrying about a house."

Jacqueline released her and Angélique flopped back on Jacqueline's unmade bed. "So, the two of us sent for his estate's vicar, presented ourselves at the altar, and it was done that quickly. But, oh, that night!" She curled her legs up in delicious memory. "That was slow and lingering and… Oh, my! I never knew how wonderful love could feel!"

Jacqueline cast a doubtful eye. "All those years of shameless bacchanals, and you waited for the wedding night? You?"

"We did." Caressing the pillow fondly, Angélique said, "He treated me as a gentleman would treat a lady, even when I was a wolf. And I wanted to be the woman he saw in me. So, yes, we waited. And it was wonderful. And it's been wonderful every single night. And sometimes even in the day. Sometimes even as wolves! Mmm."

She sprang up, laughing at Jacqueline's blush. Pushing Jacqueline to sit at the vanity, Angélique took up a hairbrush to begin the task of taming her sister's wild hair. "So how goes your own romance, m'amie?"

Jacqueline pouted. "Not without pitfalls."

"Your sheets and pillow tell a pleasant enough tale." Angélique tucked her head next to Jacqueline's and met her gaze in the mirror solemnly. "He was gentle, yes?"

"Angélique!"

Her sister nudged her. "You don't fool me. I know you were a virgin." She tapped her nose again.

Sudden flashes of memory of that first night in de Guise's bed ignited a fiery arousal Jacqueline tried to hide, like a child caught stealing cakes. "It's none of your business."

Angélique snickered. "You don't have to say anything. I can guess. You were absolutely terrified. You probably tripped getting into bed, and if I know you, you turned down all the lamps and wrapped yourself so tightly in the bedclothes he couldn't see you at all. You then proceeded to give a lecture on the Latin names of all the parts of the body as he tenderly, lovingly, kissed each and every one."

"Stop!" Embarrassed by her own naïveté before her worldly twin, Jacqueline buried her face in her hands, then drew a deep breath. "Besides, our romance involves a bit more than—that."

"'That'?" Angélique mocked lightly. "Oh, I know. There's games of cribbage and chess, reading aloud to one another in the library, discussing the latest designs in your workshop, the worrying over finances. All the things that make for a boring marriage."

Angélique resumed brushing, working a rose pomatum into Jacqueline's locks so they took on a golden sheen. "All right, keep your secrets. Tell me about these pitfalls. If he dares break your heart, I'll eat him."

Jacqueline leaned back against her twin, savoring the familiar luxury of having her hair done while she described her woes of the past three days to Angélique.

"Louis-Philippe, of all people. Yes, he's very sweet, and he's been quite congenial in all things. Of course I don't want to see him assassinated, but you know how I feel about politics, his politics in particular. And now the possibility of a vampire? A nightmare out of peasant lore, who perhaps has been in our valley since the spring? What am I supposed to do with that?"

"My dearest Jacky, there's nothing easier." Angélique plaited Jacqueline's hair as she thought aloud. "I can keep the King entertained, and if not, Gryffin can discuss the plans for Eu with him; Victoria's his queen, after all. Then tonight, when you're all tucked into bed, Gryffin and I will go on the hunt and make certain neither the vampire nor any strangers are on the grounds or in the village. We could find the creature's scent at Marthe's sister's home, if you think that's where this began."

"No," Jacqueline insisted. "You've been traveling for, what, four days? Five? Marthe will want to fuss and spoil you. I want to spend time with you and Llewellyn, as will de Guise. And honestly, I would like just one night of rest before guests arrive tomorrow."

Angélique finished her plaits and wrapped them around the remaining curls atop Jacqueline's head. She grinned a wolfish grin.

"But Gryffin and I have not run out our legs, and he's anxious to explore his second home. Now come, turn-about. Help me get ready for dinner. Marthe's setting the formal dining room, and I've grown quite accustomed to wearing curls now that I'm a duchess. It involves heating an iron rod, and you're so good at that."

All talk of vampires and assaults and assassins was put aside for the evening. Anne assisted Marthe, with Jean-Paul acting as footman, replete with livery that had not been used since the girls' début ball. He caught Jacqueline's eye and winked to indicate his mission in the village had been fulfilled. When she slipped him an écu, he puffed up with pride, filling out his jacket with distinction. After the meager repast de Guise had presented the previous evening, Marthe made up for the lapse with a roast leg of lamb, pommes dauphines, and green beans amandine, with a subtle garlic and rosemary seasoning and accompanied by hearty Bordeaux from Médoc. All anxieties fell away before the conviviality of the newlyweds' tales of their joys and their travels of the previous weeks.

"Your sun-glasses, Your Grace," Mr. Smith commented, pointing first to Llewellyn's and then Angélique's blue-tinted spectacles, restructured from Ayscough spectacles by Jacqueline in such a way they hid their wolf-eyes, the physical manifestation of their lycanthropy. "Is this the fashion in England now? I have seen some in Paris wearing them as well, but I thought them a whim of students, fops, and the Incroyables."

Llewellyn cleared his throat. "Ah, yes, you see, both my wife and I are afflicted with astigmatisms, and tinted glasses afford a measure of comfort." He took Angélique's hand in his. "I'm very thankful for them. God bless Mister Ayscough."

Mr. Smith seemed satisfied with that answer, while Jacqueline glared at de Guise to dispel his smirk.

After dinner, they retired to the salon for brandies. Angélique delighted the company by playing two new sonatas she'd composed while in Glamorgan, along with some of her older compositions, on the Pleyel. Mr. Smith was enthusiastic in his applause, but Jacqueline treasured the adoring look on Llewellyn's face as he watched his bride perform, and she mused on their brief history together.

A scant six weeks ago, Jacqueline encountered de Guise on the Paris-Orléans Chemin-de-Fer, unaware he was an agent of espionage for the King when he assisted her in dealing with the automaton that had halted their train, the automaton that was now Monsieur Claque. That very night, de Guise's companion Llewellyn had tried to steal the automaton, whereupon Angélique had dropped a winch on his head, taking him prisoner until she and Llewellyn were carried off by the nefarious Count Draganov, whose plans for world domination Llewellyn and de Guise conspired to thwart. When Draganov shot Angélique and Llewellyn, their blood mingled, and Llewellyn revived with Angélique's gift—or curse—of lycanthropy.

Was that all only a month ago?

And did Angélique ever confess her role in that lump on his head?

Still, to see Angélique performing at the piano again brought happy tears to Jacqueline's eyes, and her heart swelled with contentment. Her sister had finally returned to her, at least for now.

Angélique sighed and flexed her fingers. "*Bof*, it's stuffy in here. Do we really need to keep the windows and doors covered? Alas, it stifles the Pleyel's timbre. These will sound better on the Érard. Perhaps tomorrow."

"Oh, but guests arrive tomorrow," Jacqueline hastened to argue. She didn't want Angélique ruining her surprise. "I'll need your help, if only to identify half the people on your list and get them into the right rooms. Besides, I haven't cleaned the concert hall yet. I've kept the piano tuned, but the dust covers haven't been removed."

Angélique pouted. "I see. But I'll wager the airship is polished and ready to sail?"

"Ben, oui. How else should we transport so many arriving from Paris on the train tomorrow?"

Mr. Smith's twinkling eyes brightened. "Airship?"

4.

THEY BOARDED JACQUELINE'S COLOSSAL AEROSTAT ESPRIT JUST AFTER lunch. While Jacqueline started up the boiler and opened the hydrogen tanks to inflate the massive envelope, de Guise gave a wide-eyed Mr. Smith a tour of the airship.

Unlike any other aero or thermal airship, Esprit was designed in the conceit of a modified galleon at three-quarter scale: thirty-six meters in length and a beam of eight meters. Rather than sails, a series of masts supported a vast iron ring that served to secure the envelope to be inflated by hydrogen tanks controlled from the deck. Four propellers on outcropped "wings" provided forward drive. Jacqueline had installed new machinery beneath the raised forward deck, or fo'c'sle, and a new capstan on the aft deck controlled the keel. Here she also kept the gauges that monitored speed and power. Smith was especially impressed by the aerostat's ability to mirror its surroundings. Whoever originally designed it had coated both the ship and its enormous envelope with a reflective material. The envelope shimmered a lovely blue while the hull of the ship mirrored the green of the field where she moored.

After touring the main deck, Mr. Smith was about to climb to the fo'c'sle, but de Guise stopped him. "I agreed to allow you this trip," he said, "but even with you looking like a farmhand, I'd rather you stay out of sight and out of range of anyone on the ground." He bowed slightly. "Mister Smith."

Mr. Smith acquiesced and took a seat on a bench beside the companion door, fanning himself with his straw hat. "Madame Duval built this marvelous airship?"

"No, Mister Smith, I appropriated it," she called as she wrapped a cable around her arm and swooped down to the main deck.

He laughed and clapped at her swashbuckling. "A true pirate vessel, then."

De Guise whispered in his ear, and Mr. Smith grew serious. "Draganov, eh? Monstrous affair."

"A monster indeed, resurrecting French souls to harness for his disgusting army." Jacqueline headed to the keel capstan and set gauges for their course, then returned to set the wing capstans. "But 'all's well that ends well,' as the English Bard has said. Better, in fact. I've streamlined the mechanics and technology, made her dirigible, and redesigned belowdecks to accommodate more elegant occupants than his putrid revenants and minions."

"It's beautiful, Jacky," Angélique exclaimed as she and Llewellyn returned from belowdecks. "How many are we expecting in Orléans?"

"Thirty-three, I think, including the children. I have—" She patted her coat, then her vest, then her hips. "—somewhere—" Then she smacked her derrière and dug into the back pocket of her work trousers to find the slip of paper with the list of guests expected by train. She handed it to Angélique and climbed to the fo'c'sle again.

Angélique's face pulled to a pout as she studied the list. "Thalberg declined?"

"He's off on his own honeymoon in Italy, but he sent gifts, and I sent gifts to them in your name. And the Polish Corpse claims he's too ill, but I know he's still at Nohant having a miserable time with Madame Sand. Liszt will not attend without Marie, and I know how well you get along with her, so Liszt is off the list," she quipped. "I'm just disappointed Flora Tristan could not attend. I think I would have liked her voice among so many tavern babblers."

Angélique joined her above, lowering her voice. "Jacky, there are a number of—well, Republicans and Socialists among my friends. Aren't you afraid one of them might be—" She nodded back to indicate their monarch, who chatted blithely with de Guise and Llewellyn.

"De Guise thoroughly investigated and approved the list. It will be up to us to keep everyone engaged enough in other matters to forestall revolution before its time. Some good music, some storytelling. According to Mr. Smith, Dumas alone can entertain through all hours, and didn't you promise Charles an evening recital of his poetic prose? A grand concert tomorrow evening. Two sopranos, a clarinetist, four violinists—certainly no one will dare argue politics through recitals."

"Have you hired an orchestra?" Angélique demanded indignantly. "Or did you count on me to accompany everyone?"

Jacqueline grinned and kissed her sister's cheek. "I have thought of everything, mon Ange." Then she frowned again. "Except how to fight off a vampire or European assassins." She chewed the inside of her cheek, a nervous habit. "The timing could not be more inopportune."

Slipping an arm around her, Angélique said, "We're together again, m'amie. What can we not face when we're together?"

They landed the airship at a park close to the Gare Orléans. De Guise accompanied Jacqueline to the station, where they secured diligences to transport their guests' bags and servants to the château. After so long a time seated on the train, the guests, especially the children, were eager to walk the short distance to the park, marveling at the shimmering, elusive image of *Esprit* as they drew nearer. On the main deck, Angélique and the men had set out an array of refreshments, for the train did not make post stops and the passengers were hungry.

Rather than create a stir among so many who would recognize him, Mr. Smith hid himself belowdecks. He bowed to Angélique and Llewellyn, saying, "This day is for you, mes chers amis," as he descended the ladder. They showed him to the great cabin to pass the journey home, and de Guise made certain no one left the main deck other than some of the women who complained of fatigue, although Jacqueline suspected they planned to loosen their corsets and relax their tortured frames. Not for the first time, Jacqueline gave thanks that her lover accepted her own unorthodox manner of dress.

She removed herself to the aft deck to weigh anchor, surveying the skies as *Esprit* rose while her sister held court, receiving the gifts and compliments of *tout Paris*. For the first time in many years, life was as joyous as when they were young: Jacqueline in the wings playing with her machines while Angélique scintillated on the stage.

Once they were airborne, Jacqueline was glad to see the wind was with them. She took a moment to go belowdecks to make certain Mr. Smith was comfortably settled, but she needn't have worried. She found him in the captain's chair, writing. He didn't even look up when she peeked in.

The women who had gathered behind a closed door giggled as Jacqueline looked in on them. One inquired how long the journey would take.

"As long as you wish, if you wish." Jacqueline winked broadly, and the women giggled again, toasting her with champagne.

Topside, Jacqueline slipped along the rail, avoiding the company. Dressed as she was, she was ignored as a servant, so she wasn't caught up in any of the conversation, which suited her. She had no love of politics and despised the verbal jeu-de-paume between would-be philosophers and "left-wing" activists fresh up from the taverns of the Boul'Mich. She checked the gauges controlling the keel, adjusted the course accordingly, and leaned back to study the horizon.

Her moment of ease was short-lived. She drew her spyglass from the inside pocket of her coat to get a closer look at an odd dark spot in the distance east of Orléans. De Guise was suddenly at her side.

"*Ohé matelot!* Or as Llewellyn would say, 'ahoy matey.'" His teasing tone belied his concerned look. "What do you espy, ma belle capitaine?"

Jacqueline passed him the glass, then cranked up the pressure to effect more forward drive. "A thermal airship. It appears to be a simple Montgolfier balloon, not dirigible, but I'm not taking any chances."

De Guise focused the spyglass. "Two operators. Did you see it rise?"

"I think so. Close to Châteauneuf-sur-Loire."

"Too close to be a coincidence, too far to investigate just now." He applied the glass again. "But the wind could carry them to Bellesfées eventually if it holds."

"By then, we'll be under the pavilions."

He returned the glass to her. "At least we have a look at our enemy."

"Such as it is, if it is."

"It's enough. At least we can enjoy the flight home."

"Yes, and then keep watch for a vampire."

An explosion of laughter startled them. Dumas père and fils were performing a parody of the chaotic bedroom scene from the first act of *Hernani*, but with far bawdier rhymes than Hugo had ever set down. Dumas fils as Doña Sol sang out in falsetto while his father bombasted about the deck, menacing would-be invaders to his "beloved's" bedchamber. Jacqueline had never seen Angélique laugh so hard, wiping tears away and barely catching her breath before falling into more giggles.

De Guise pulled Jacqueline closer. "I wish I could give you all of this, chérie."

"Bof." She rested her head on his chest. "This isn't for me, Alain. Grand parties, fancy dress, constant blather, insufferable hours of pretentious discourse… My happiness is here."

Then her head bumped up against the Colt Paterson, a reminder he wasn't yet hers.

He kissed her neck and released her. "You may not remember, but you once promised you would build an airship and we'd fly away and we'd be together —"

"Forever and ever," she finished for him. "The day will come, Alain. But I'm content for now." Then her smile faded, and she gazed east. "I'll be more content when I know more about that balloon."

He held her hand. "You and I are of the same mind." He kissed her palm. "Chérie."

Esprit soared over the vineyards east of Bellesfées. On the hill beyond, the towers of Château Bellesfées gleamed rose-gold in the early evening sun, eliciting appreciative murmurs from the company. Jacqueline cut the hydrogen and released the lines on the envelope so it settled safely above the heads of those on deck as the aerostat drifted down. She and de Guise cast off the anchors, and below them Jean-Paul and his liveried cohort secured the ship to the ground at the top of the eastern lawn. Cries of "Bravo!" and the clanging of the ship's bell alerted the ladies belowdecks it was time to imprison one another in their corsets once again.

Jacqueline and de Guise shooed Llewellyn off and battened down the ship themselves while Jean-Paul and his fellow footmen distributed the silver crosses to each guest as they stepped off the gangplank. Llewellyn joined Angélique, leading their guests to the pavilions on the western lawn where other guests from nearby had already gathered to welcome them. Jacqueline had warned the servants to forbid entry to the château before they could ascertain the identity of every invited or uninvited guest. The makeshift privy near the pond would have to serve any immediate needs.

"Ohé Pirate Jacky!" called Mr. Smith from the ladder doorway. "A most blessed journey, I must say. My own sons could not have done better. What naval officer has instructed you?"

Jacqueline yanked the last of the crown lines and knotted it off. "It's all machinery, Mister Smith. Cogs and sprockets and steam. I know a little bit about those."

De Guise indicated the gangplank to Mr. Smith, but an anxious older woman waited at the bottom. Mr. Smith stepped back and de Guise went down to her.

"It's my mistress, monsieur," the woman said. "Countess Murkiewicz. The Count and the children all descended, but she hasn't appeared."

Jacqueline swung down from the fo'c'sle. "I'll fetch her. She probably fell asleep."

She took the ladder two steps at a time to check the salon. It was empty. Curious, she inspected the berths and other quarters. Her breath caught when she found a woman she assumed was the Countess unconscious in the tiny library with a book of Lamartine meditations in her lap. Spotting the three empty glasses beside the divan, she chuckled and gently tapped the Countess' shoulder.

The woman's head drooped to the side. Mottled flesh with two punctures colored her neck.

Jacqueline fought to breathe. She set the back of her hand to the Countess' cheek. It was cool. Powder and rouge came off on Jacqueline's hand, but she noted the Countess' skin was likewise pale beneath the maquillage.

Her eyes swept the little cabin for any sign of the monster. If the myths were to be believed, a vampire could become a mist. He could easily slip between cracks in the hull or under a door. A ship was not an abode; he required no invitation to enter, if that legend were even true. He could be anywhere aboard, even here, still, in the cabin with her.

Choking back fear, Jacqueline straightened. She needed to be stronger than she felt. She scooped the woman into her arms and carried her from the library just as de Guise descended the ladder.

"Sacrebleu!" He rushed forward and took her from Jacqueline. "How the devil could this happen?"

"He's on the ship. Somehow. I never thought to safeguard quarters within the airship." Tears stung her eyes as shame and anger stung her heart. "This is all my fault."

"This is *not* your fault," he argued as they climbed the ladder. "If the creature was already aboard, there's nothing else we could have done. It's what we do now that matters. Jean-Paul!" he called from the deck.

While de Guise seated the Countess on the bench and together with Mr. Smith tried to wake her, Jacqueline went to the gangplank to tell the lady's maid, "Your mistress is unwell. Please summon the Count."

The woman hastened away as Jean-Paul climbed aboard. When he caught sight of de Guise and the unconscious woman, he jumped down again.

"I'll get Monsieur Claque and tell Maman."

He took a few steps, spun about, and ran back up the plank to toss Jacqueline a silver cross from his pocket. Then he was off again. Jacqueline tucked the cross behind a brooch on the Countess' bodice just as the woman stirred and opened her eyes.

"Such a pretty kitty," she murmured with a smile.

A chill seized Jacqueline. *Kitty.* Not a lion, as Anne had described. An ordinary cat, such as the many that roamed the parc and outer buildings of Bellesfées.

Jacqueline sat beside the Countess and took her hand. "Pretty, perhaps, but he does bite."

Count Murkiewicz with his brood of children accompanied the Countess to their chambers, babbling animatedly more about the autonomaton that carried the countess than about his concern for her.

"Wonderful." The inside of Jacqueline's cheek was chewed raw. "Do we know this Polish refugee Murkiewicz? Is he perhaps our villain?"

De Guise shook his head. "He was on deck with his children the whole time. No, the monster hid within the hull of *Esprit*, I'll wager."

"And now the sun is gone, so we're all in peril," she replied, throwing up her hands. "We've lost sight of the Montgolfier as well."

"Montgolfier?" Mr. Smith measured the concern on their faces. "Ah. I suppose I should take myself to a quiet inglenook inside?"

"Mister Smith, I will no longer deny you the full bounty of pleasures my château affords." Jacqueline folded her arms. "The time for hiding is past, even if the time for caution is that much greater. Your cross is pinned to your lapel. You're wearing my doubled vest?"

He thumped his chest.

"Good. If you would, please?"

She offered her arm. His mischievous smile returned and he accepted. Together they disembarked with de Guise following, keeping himself between the King and the forest as they headed to the pavilions. When they entered, Angélique and Llewellyn played their roles in the charade while guests looked on in curiosity as the peasant farmhand bowed to the couple before taking a seat at a table with the two Dumases.

For the first time all day, Dumas père sat in stunned silence as his former employer greeted him with a handshake and a finger to his lips. The author's dusky face reddened and his jowls shook with mirth.

Mr. Smith waved to de Guise and indicated the seat beside him. "De Guise, come meet an old friend."

As the hired musicians tuned, Jacqueline checked the guest list against the numbers in the pavilion. Satisfied, she gave the cue. The orchestra began with a Viennese waltz. Angélique and Llewellyn opened the dancing to applause. Then couples joined in. A full cotillion swelled into spinning couples filling all the pavilions.

Jacqueline would have liked to learn the mazurkas the Polish immigrants requested, or the reels called for the groom's sake. They looked like enjoyable dances, although she probably would have only tripped over her own boots. She concentrated instead on faces. Introductions seemed to slide past her. She cursed her inability to hold on to names, but at least she was assured they had all passed muster with the bride and groom as well as de Guise.

The King was seated deep in the center of the crowd, surrounded by approved personages. De Guise was content enough to be at ease, even putting his name to a few unmarried daughters' dance cards — "for the sake of the couple's joy," he excused himself to Jacqueline as an older teen fluttered her lashes at him and extended her hand. A spasm of jealousy piqued Jacqueline when he waltzed away so gracefully with the charming girl on his arm.

A sudden flash of clarity, always too late, made Jacqueline realize she had no place at this celebration. She had planned every element except herself. Her boots, her sweaty work shirt, stained leather trousers and vest, travel coat, all filthy from the day's work…

She didn't belong. She made her way through the crowd and breathed a deep sigh of fresh night air as she left the pageantry of the pavilion and climbed the hill to the château.

She paused when someone called her name. Angélique's bohemian friend Charles caught up with her, panting. A would-be poet edging his way into the burgeoning literary industry in Paris, he was a bit of a dandy in his fashion, although his black curls, full beard, and mustache were often unkempt and his appearance disheveled due to his predilection for drink and various opiates.

"Jacky, Jacky, sweet Duval, you never explained your adventure in the Catacombs last month," he scolded her. "Did you find what you sought down among the blessed dead?"

Jacqueline answered with a grin. Charles had been obliviously instrumental in her defeat of Count Draganov, but he had been so drunk at the time, she marveled that he even remembered their encounter. She clapped his back familiarly, but she was in no mood to regale him with the full story.

"It was a spectacular expedition fit for Barnum's 'freak show,' dear Charles. But I have a better tale for you."

She indicated the pavilions with a sweep of her arm, full of laughter, splendor, music, and lavish delicacies. "You read Poe, n'est-ce pas? The American? If not, you should do. What if—and I'm not saying it is so—but what if, instead of keeping out the night, they've locked it inside with them?"

Slowly his eyes widened, and he considered her worried expression. "Jacky, you once accused me of having a morbid soul. You, on the other hand…" He blew out a long breath that smelled of Scotch whiskey and, of course, garlic.

Jacqueline felt a twinge of guilt for depressing him. "You're right, Charles. I'm feeling melancholy this evening. Perhaps you can cheer me up?"

Taking her hand, he pressed her fingers to his lips. "Consider, Jacky, that here among the beautiful fairies of Bellesfées, you traverse a temple fashioned from living pillars." He stretched his arms wide to take in the last crimson strip of sunset beyond the Loire, the meadows and gardens, and the forest beyond the western lawn. "Beneath a canopy of stars a million-fold, all of which call you to leave behind your ennui, the sorrow of your existence, and dwell instead in the rich, sweet, and joyous infinity of nature."

He gazed at her solemnly once more, and for a moment they shared a correspondence of mutual transcendence. Grateful, she managed a smile.

Then Charles belched. "That was rather good, wasn't it?" he said, surprised at his own eloquence. "But I'm going back to the gaslights, where champagne provides what nature cannot."

Jacqueline gave a mocking huff of indignation and let him go, laughing. But as she continued to the château, she caught the gleam of animal eyes near the pond, where the frogs had fallen silent. She fingered the silver cross pinned to her bodice. Anger and frustration piqued her melancholy once again. How could she keep them all safe?

5.

JACQUELINE MET MARTHE AT THE SALON DOORS. "HOW IS THE COUNTESS?"

"Hungry. I gave her a chicken broth with enough garlic to kill a cemetery full of—" Marthe caught herself, looking about in case Anne was in earshot. "Cats," she finished in a whisper.

"De Guise and Llewellyn verified the identities of all our guests. I made it clear Angélique is not to invite them into the château. The legends say a vampire cannot enter where he's not invited, and with the wards over every door and window, we should be secured. De Guise will toast Angélique and Llewellyn, and they will proceed hitherward. Our *cat* should not be able to pass under the crosses."

"Please, God." Marthe crossed herself. She sighed, and her whole stout body trembled with exhaustion. "The banquet table is laid. I gave orders, but—"

"Go to bed." Jacqueline pushed her inside. "Once the servants have gone to sleep, Angélique and Llewellyn will stand guard for the night. No cat or anything else will get past them. Ask Jean-Paul to gather the staff—all of them, including the visitors—in the servants' dining area. I want to address them."

Marthe toddled off. Jacqueline stood on the paved courtyard outside the salon. The unbridled gaiety on the lawn below and her own inability to enjoy it brought to mind Charles' words.

Did she have a morbid soul? She had not intended to. Jiggering with various systems of pipes, wires, gas, water, and machinery had kept Jacqueline happy since she was young. Her patented engineering designs had brought wealth enough to be able to live more than comfortably. Even Angélique's traumatic transmutation had not shaken Jacqueline's determination, despite her sister's abandoning her career.

But now Angélique had finally found herself, and in doing so had found a way to make her life complete. Despite what she had told de Guise, Jacqueline truthfully could not say the same.

Everything had changed when Jacqueline fell in love with de Guise. Since the morning he arrived at Bellesfées to stay, her carefully ordered world had turned to blissful chaos. The workshop forgotten, the forge cold, Jacqueline did not know how she had lived so long without breathing de Guise, tasting his skin, drinking his presence, molding her skin to his.

What had de Guise done to her? And what would she be without him if he ever saw her as she saw herself?

"You are happy for your sister," said a soft voice nearby. "Such a generous heart."

Jacqueline glanced at the woman who leaned against the ivied wall of the château a few feet from her. Her accent indicated she was one of the noble Austrian refugees from Paris Angélique had befriended in her years under Sigismond Thalberg's tutelage and Chopin's company. Her sleek black hair wove elegantly around a bejeweled tiara. There was a delicacy about her face that contrasted with the audacious display of her bosom, the sharp V of her wasp waistline, the ample curve of her hips. As she approached, the woman's perfume of jasmine made Jacqueline uncomfortably aware of her own body's odor of sweat, charcoal, engine fuels, creosote, and machine grease. She crossed her arms and stared down at her scuffed boot tips.

"Sometimes we see ourselves only in sharp relief, in contrast to all we are not." The woman's voice, low and soothing, like dark honey, seemed to amplify Jacqueline's thoughts:

I'm not stunning, alluring. Why would de Guise settle for me when he could have someone as beautiful as this woman?

"But as your friend has suggested, there is another kind of beauty, madame. One that is far more eternal." The woman reached out a graceful hand as if to caress Jacqueline's arm. "The music of Bach and Vivaldi. The grandeur of Venice or Rome. The majesty of Versailles. Your own creations, madame. Your own beauty, Jacqueline Duval."

Jacqueline met the woman's large eyes, half in fascination, half in doubt. Was the woman trying to reassure her, or entice her? She glanced away again.

"Beauty has never been one of my qualities, madame."

The woman drew closer to Jacqueline's cheek, longer than felt comfortable. "You are magnificent. You are loved. That is eternal beauty," she whispered in her ear.

The woman stepped back, nodded a farewell, and headed down the hill. She moved with seductive grace in each step. She looked back to Jacqueline and raised her hand in a regal wave.

Jacqueline drew a sharp breath. The stunning beauty had succeeded in making her feel as ungainly and unattractive as she had always suspected herself to be. At the same time, the sensuality of the woman's movements had awakened something in her, made her wonder if she could be desirable to anyone other than de Guise.

Assuming she was desirable to de Guise...

Jacqueline shook off the thought, and suddenly she was not merely melancholy, but downright angry the woman had made her doubt herself. She had no need to be universally desirable—de Guise loved her, utterly and passionately, as she loved him. There had been no real passion in that woman's eyes, only a kind of lust Jacqueline did not share.

"Someone in that company must be a very unhappy husband," she muttered.

The small army of servants Luc and Jean-Paul had hired for the event, along with the company's various footmen, valets, lady's maids, nursemaids, governesses, and ladies-in-waiting descended upon the kitchen where Jacqueline waited. The younger ones, curious, pressed around her while the adults waited at the back. A hush fell over them when she held up a louis d'or.

"A gold piece for each of you, beyond your pay, if you all swear to lock yourselves into your rooms this night once your duties have been completed, and not stir from there until summoned by your bells. Understood?"

Excited cheers from the younger ones resounded as they scattered to their tasks. Older servants exchanged quiet mutters, but they seemed equally content with the arrangement. Jacqueline chuckled and tousled Anne's hair. The girl yawned.

"To bed, Anne. You've only just recovered, and I want you rosy-cheeked tomorrow for the grand concert."

The girl obeyed, and Jacqueline heard her call goodnight to Monsieur Claque.

Jacqueline passed into the banquet room, where footmen, hired from the village, had just taken their places. They made an attempt to come to attention at her entrance; some of them had served the Empire, but military bearing had given way to age and good provincial cooking. She inspected and approved the banquet fare of roasted pigs, lambs, hens, and goats, with beets, beans, artichokes, salsify, cauliflower, and potatoes—all seasoned with garlic, of course—before plucking a few strawberries from a platter on her way to the doors.

Angélique and Llewellyn were just leaving the pavilions with a crowd following in procession. Jacqueline could not see de Guise. She paced anxiously, keeping her eyes on the line of guests. As Llewellyn and Angélique neared, Llewellyn lifted his wife in his arms and carried her over the threshold, the two of them laughing. Jacqueline supervised as each guest merrily entered the château, none of them hesitant, no one repelled by the crosses on the doorways. She wished she could share in their enthusiasm. She tried to find the woman whose intimations had so disquieted her, but then she realized neither de Guise nor Mr. Smith was among the company.

Fighting off panic, Jacqueline trotted down the hill. As she reached the pond, de Guise emerged from the pavilion, accompanied by Mr. Smith and a young gentleman who leaned heavily on an ornate walking stick. She hurried to embrace de Guise.

"You frightened me!"

She kissed him desperately, and he pried her away with reluctance when Mr. Smith coughed lightly. The other gentleman waited, his face drawn. De Guise introduced him.

"Baron Vordenburg of Styria." De Guise calmed her before she could react. "Yes, Austria. He has news."

She turned to him hopefully. "Good news?"

The young man slowly shook his head.

Although he limped and relied on his walking stick, Baron Vordenburg strode through the warded doors of the salon without invitation. That much gave Jacqueline some relief. The guests had taken their seats and were engaged in lively discussion while the musicians set up at the far end of the hall. For form's sake, the three sat and participated in the festivities despite the anxiety they felt. Jacqueline realized she was famished. Her concern for Baron Vordenburg's news gave way before the platters of roasts, vegetables, fruits, and cheeses. She declined the wine, knowing she might need her wits about her within the hour.

An hour turned to two, nearing midnight, but this was not Paris or the royal court. Everyone had risen at dawn to take the train, and weariness and wine were taking their toll. As children grew sleepy or cranky, Jean-Paul and Luc ushered them out with rides to their rooms on clockwork porters and automated lifts, producing giggles and squeals of wonder. Mothers joined their children. The tables cleared, the orchestra dismissed, and the brandy poured, the rest of the women excused themselves and retired.

Jacqueline's impatience and fear mounted with the delay. She caught Angélique's eye across the table. Her sister grinned. A moment later, a smile spread across Llewellyn's face as Angélique sent her thoughts to him in the silent telepathy afforded by their lycanthropy. The two of them rose and bid goodnight to their guests, then left the banquet hall amid quiet salutations, sly intimations, and amused nods. Jacqueline knew better. The plan was for the happy couple to slip away not to the bridal bed, but to the cellars, where they would remove their clothing and assume their lupine forms for the night watch.

The men with families soon took their leave as well. There remained only Mr. Smith, Dumas père, Baron Vordenburg, and Charles, although Charles was snoring in a corner. Jacqueline dismissed the footmen. The château fell quiet. She hoped Dumas would take the hint and go. Instead, he poured himself another brandy and took a seat beside the King. The two tipped glasses before Mr. Smith turned to Vordenburg, his eyes narrowed.

"Baron Vordenburg, I believe we are related."

The Baron smiled. "I believe all the nobility of Europe are related, Monsieur — *Smith*."

Dumas guffawed, startling Charles, who snorted, mumbled, and fell back asleep.

"Which is why I feel it is so important to keep cordial relationships with our royal counterparts," Mr. Smith continued, holding the Baron's gaze.

Vordenburg waved. "You have no argument from me, monsieur. Nor from our crown. No one else matters."

"Hmm. Except those who would take up arms to subvert my intentions."

"I know nothing of that, Monsieur Smith. I do, however, bring a tale of another nature."

Charles suddenly jumped up, gaping out the open doors. "Mon Dieu, was that a wolf?"

Jacqueline caught her breath, but Dumas laughed again and rose.

"You're drunk, Baudelaire. Or have you been nibbling on my cache? To bed with you." He tossed back his brandy, saluted his king with the empty glass, and took Charles' arm. "To bed with us both, my friend."

Charles blinked, confused, as he was led away. "I'm sure it was a wolf."

"Do you know the legend of the Wolf-Leader? Let me tell you the tale."

The pale, slight Charles leaned to the dark-skinned mountain that was Dumas père, and they stumbled away, pausing only to ask directions of Luc to their individual rooms.

"Now to *your* tale, Baron," said Jacqueline, finally allowing herself a glass of wine.

The Baron sat back in his chair. In stilted French, he recounted: "It begins with my great-great-grandfather, which is to say, a very long time ago, in Styria. He was engaged to a woman of good family, noble breeding. Countess Karnstein. Their engagement was not simply a matter of finance or fortuitous marriage; he loved her deeply. One day, Mircalla — that was her name — fell deathly ill, and within the week she expired. My ancestor was distraught with grief. He would not leave his chambers. A few nights later, as if in a dream, Mircalla came to his window. He could scarcely believe the miracle, and he hurried to the window to throw it open. To his horror he saw his beloved floating in mid-air, two storeys up, still clad in her funeral gown, barefoot, covered in the dirt of her tomb. 'Bid me come to you,' she said to him. 'Or do you come to me.' And so he would have done if not for his valet, who entered his room at that moment and saw the apparition. He seized the silver candlesticks from the mantel shelf and formed a rude cross to expel the creature, whereupon it shrieked and changed its form to a preternaturally large black cat that dropped to the ground and fled."

He paused to refresh his voice with water before concluding, "My good friends, it has been the sworn duty of my family since that time to seek out this creature and all like her, to destroy them. We have encountered many vampires, but I have never been able to find news of Mircalla until now."

A *woman* vampire. Jacqueline hadn't considered the possibility.

"Good God, I cannot believe this woman dares stalk my realm," Smith cried. "How can we track her, if you haven't been able to find her in all these years?"

Vordenburg calmed him. "This is precisely the reason I have come to France, here, to the Loire valley. My father, his father, and his father before him pursued vampires indiscriminately rather than pursuing only Mircalla. They followed the rumor of illnesses and deaths across eastern Europe, and while they have vanquished many of these demons, they have failed to find the accursed Countess Karnstein. After several years of the same pursuit, I decided to take a more enlightened course of investigation. I recently returned to Vordenburg and visited Castle Karnstein. There I discovered Mircalla's tomb had been removed. I retraced the steps of my great-great-grandfather. I consulted his notes and his letters. That was how I learned the full tale that has driven my family. I learned, too, how to find Mircalla herself. It has been my task to discover the many Roman burial grounds here in the Loire valley, for I am certain that is where she has concealed herself. I have located three thus far, to no avail. But my search is not complete."

Jacqueline frowned and tapped the table. She snatched up a brioche and bit off a piece to keep from blurting her thoughts. She studied the Baron quickly. He was clear of eye and earnest in his expression. He hardly seemed old enough to command so worldly a breadth of arcane knowledge. Then again, she recalled that she herself had entered the Polytechnique at the age of thirteen, so she couldn't fault him his youth. Still, one fact nagged at her.

"Baron Vordenburg, how did you contrive to get an invitation to the wedding celebration? I don't recall your name on the list."

He flushed and tried to look away, only to meet de Guise's keen eyes and cryptic smile. "Hmm. That is, I did, in fact, receive an invitation, directed to my cousin, the Conte d'Assier, who is at this time of year in Vienna visiting our grandmother. I have been staying with him since May, on the trail of this fiend. I met Mademoi—that is to say, the Duchess of Singlebury—while fishing the backwaters of the Loire one afternoon in the summer. We spent some time—I mean, we know one— that is…"

He paused with a guilty blush.

Imagining the scene—wild Angélique and the proper young baron—Jacqueline had to chuckle. "No, no. That was my sister before she met the duke. Go on."

"When your invitation arrived, I thought it an opportune time to better make your acquaintance, along with all my neighbors', and Monsieur de Guise assured me I would be welcome. I hope you will forgive the presumption. It was not my intention to deceive you."

She nodded, but still frowned. "And now explain how you came to broach the subject of vampires with de Guise."

Mr. Smith laughed. "Parbleu, what a mind. Are you quite certain I can't enlist you in the Sûreté Nationale?"

Vordenburg reached into his pocket and showed the silver cross Jean-Paul had given to the guests. "I knew of the dozen or so girls falling ill in the villages in the surrounding environs. It is the reason I am certain the villain that stalks them is Mircalla. Unlike young vampires, Mircalla is not interested in slaughter, nor in spawning other demons like herself. She rarely consumes the girls she preys on. Rather, she tends them, as a farmer might keep sheep, a kind of larder, to keep her in her strength. This poses no danger of creating rivals to her unless she feels a need for a minion of her own. You see, the victim may be made to drink the vampire's blood. If Mircalla has bitten that victim at least three times, then upon that girl's death, she becomes a vampire herself. But Mircalla has rarely groomed a minion. She prefers—"

"A larder." Jacqueline shuddered with revulsion.

"I came here tonight wondering if perhaps Mircalla was posing as one of our neighbors and would find your gathering worth her interest. When I was handed this cross by your young footman, I knew I had found a kindred hunter." He pointed to the tops of the doorways and windows, where Jacqueline had embossed similar crosses.

Satisfied, Jacqueline finished the last sip of wine. When she stood and stretched, the men stood as well. De Guise took her arm, but she hesitated. "Have I done enough?" she asked Vordenburg.

The Baron said, "You have done all you can for now. Within these walls anointed with silver and blessed with the cross of the Christ, we are all safe. Tomorrow we will find a moment to discuss further steps toward our prize."

Monsieur Claque's orders were simple: Allow no one into the halls of the music conservatory. As usual, however, Monsieur Claque's execution of his orders caused an early-morning calamity.

"Ja-a-a-ack-y-y-y!"

The piercing scream startled Jacqueline awake. She winced in the sunlight streaming through her window. Metallic *bongs* echoed through the château, a sound she recognized as someone beating on Monsieur Claque's bronze torso.

"Jacky, get your merdique tin-pot out of my way!" Angélique shrieked.

Jacqueline leapt from her bed, throwing her peignoir around her and foregoing slippers. She followed servants and children running downstairs to find the newlywed Duchess of Singlebury in her chemise à la reine, peignoir and slippers, beating on the chest of the massive autonomaton, which seemed massively amused by her efforts.

"Jacky, you've gone too far! This is *my* wing, *my* conservatory! You can't keep me out!"

Tiny *poots* of steam showed Monsieur Claque's dismissive nonchalance. The children squealed their delight, further enraging Angélique. Luckily for Jacqueline, Llewellyn reached his wife first and tugged her away from the clockwork guard, who continued to thrill the little ones.

"Anyel, my love, you promised," Llewellyn reminded her as he wrapped his arms around her. "No conservatory until Jacky readies the room."

Angélique fumed, calming only when Llewellyn nuzzled her neck.

"Shoo, allez, allez," Jacqueline said, pushing the children back to the château and ordering the servants back to the kitchens. She heaved a sigh and pulled her hair back out of her face, confronting her sister's fading ire with a patient frown. Jacqueline held out her hand. Releasing his wife, Llewellyn headed back to bed. As Jacqueline led her sister to the kitchens, Angélique took a final thump at Monsieur Claque.

Marthe set out two bowls of coffee and tipped in freshly clotted cream from the boiling milk as the twins took their seats—the same seats they had occupied at the kitchen worktable for the past twenty-one years since Marthe first hoisted them up on chairs and their feet dangled high above the floor. Angélique pouted, but before long she smiled ruefully. Jacqueline grinned. The two of them broke into giggles.

"And I thought things would change," Marthe said. She set down two plates of brioches with blackberry preserves, and went off to corral her workers to prepare the banquet hall for breakfast. The twins sipped their coffee and munched in silence broken only by snickers and happy sighs.

Finally, Jacqueline relented. "I wanted it to be a surprise, but come with me. You can test it."

They took their brioches and strolled to the music conservatory wing. This time, Monsieur Claque bowed and let them pass. Then he clanked off to patrol the grounds again, soon followed by flocks of little ones.

As the twins climbed the staircase to the concert hall, Jacqueline explained, "I had to program everything remotely, but I did commission the finest virtuosi in all Paris to assist in the punchwork. In theory, it should be perfectly synchronized for you."

Angélique looked askance. "I have no idea what any of that means. Tell me you haven't touched my Érard."

"Only to have it tuned last week. Ever since you left for Wales, I've been—oh, mon Ange, I hope you love it!"

She threw open the doors. Angélique stood shocked. The eight elegant brass, leather, and velour musicians sat on their Louis XVI chairs, poised with their fine matching instruments, all glittering in the morning sun in an arc behind the Érard grand piano, awaiting their conductor. Beyond them ranged five rows of ten chairs, with a central aisle. Jacqueline rushed forward to open the balcony doors. Then she came back to the entrance and pressed a portion of the wainscoting, releasing a section of wall that slid back to reveal a control panel. She threw all eight switches with a sweep of her arm and closed the panel again.

Click. Click. Click. Click.

Cogwork set a tempo. In a moment, the left foot of each clockwork musician tapped in time, setting other gears in motion within their frames. They continued to tap, winding, waiting.

Jacqueline turned to Angélique, hardly able to contain her excitement. "How is your Beethoven *Piano Concerto No. 5*? Or would you rather Mozart *Concerto 21*? Or—I know. Chopin. Always Chopin-ski-winski with you."

Jacqueline grabbed Angélique's wrists and drew her to the piano. "*No. 1 in E Minor.*"

She stepped back and indicated the bench. Moving as if in a dream, Angélique sat. Jacqueline took her sun-glasses from her. Angélique's amber wolf-eyes glinted. Her hands hovered above the keys, flexing and waving as she prompted her memory. Jacqueline scurried to the first chair on the aisle on the left side of the audience and sat. She depressed a large brass pedal with her bare foot, and the panharmonium commenced the opening of the Chopin concerto.

Angélique's eyes lit up at the opening strains. Allegro maestoso indeed! Imposing strings. Sweet flute. Commanding clarinet. Building tension through the legato as the violin floated along the minor melody. Tension mounted as volume and power grew with the insistent pounding of the semiquavers. The floor of the concert hall trembled with both clockwork under the floor and resounding bass along the marble.

Angélique straightened, threw her shoulders back, and poised. She entered on cue, equally commanding with the opening flourish, then almost playful in the response in the upper register. She pursued the song as it soared, or marched resolutely, or cascaded down chromatic scales. Her fingers danced along the keyboard, and Jacqueline's heart danced with them. The clockwork strains were perfectly tuned, producing a bright reverberation along the floor. Angélique shimmered, her tawny hair aglow in the daylight, her wolf-eyes gleaming. A golden aura filled the room.

Mr. Smith appeared in the doorway, breakfast in hand. He slipped inside and took a seat, followed by de Guise and Llewellyn, now decently dressed for the day. Then one by one, as they awakened and dressed, other guests were drawn to the music conservatory, keeping a reverent silence while Angélique played through the concerto, then Beethoven—the pedal by the second chair—and Chopin's first piano concerto, *No. 2 in F Minor*—the first chair on the right of the aisle—with the clockwork orchestra accompaniment.

The last chord finished, but the marble held onto it for a few seconds more. When it finally fell away behind the birdsong and the chatter of the children outside, the enraptured audience rose and crowded to Angélique to congratulate her. Llewellyn spun her about in his arms and kissed her, to the cheers of their friends.

De Guise took the seat beside Jacqueline and offered her his handkerchief to wipe the tears of joy that glistened on her cheeks.

"My brilliant, brilliant love," he said.

6.

WHILE ANGÉLIQUE RECEIVED THE COMPLIMENTS OF THE GUESTS, Jacqueline returned to her vexing concern of the vampire, a fear the daylight could not dispel. With the château overrun with so many strangers, she found herself flinching when she rounded each corner or encountered another unknown face. Ashamed at being terrorized in her own home, she decided to take further action — any action — to further safeguard her guests.

She visited Count and Countess Murkiewicz's chamber and was not surprised to find Vordenburg at the Countess' bedside. The woman was propped up on several pillows, but she looked well and her cheeks were full of color that didn't come from powder.

"Such a fuss," the Countess demurred. "I always feel a malaise aboard sea-going vessels. It should not be surprising that an airship would produce the same effect."

"Of course, madame," Jacqueline agreed. "I should have been more considerate in my grandiose plans."

"Not at all, my dear. I would not have missed it for the world, although apparently, I missed quite a bit." She blinked in confusion.

The Count patted a baby on his shoulder, and the little one produced a burp. "There, now, you see?" Murkiewicz declared. "Kaja blupped. Now everyone is in fine fetters."

"I think you mean feathers," the Countess mis-corrected him. She turned back to Vordenburg. "Do you still think some stray cat on the airship was the cause of this rash? I've never had such a reaction to cats before."

Vordenburg took a flask from his inside pocket and doused a linen from the side table. "Allergies can arise at any time of life, Frau Murkiewicz." He daubed the mottling and the two puncture wounds, where a small bit of foam sprang up at the application, although the Countess didn't seem to sense it. "I am certain you will feel yourself by dinner," Vordenburg assured her.

He rose, bowed with an awkward click of his heels, and took up his walking stick to leave. Jacqueline also excused herself. Vordenburg descended the stairs with some difficulty, but he waited until they were in the library before speaking.

"It is as I feared, as you feared," Vordenburg said. "Mircalla was aboard your airship in the guise of a cat."

Jacqueline tapped on the table, measuring her thoughts and forcing them to settle into logic. "Are you so certain it was your Mircalla, and not some other vampire? Not that it would make any difference in our fight, but—"

"Male vampires prefer to manifest as dogs, wolves, rats, or even bats. A large black jungle cat called a panther, or felis melis, is Mircalla's preferred animal form, but a house cat is small enough to slip aboard the airship and hide."

He set his hand on her arm. "I know vampires, and I know Mircalla. We can expel her from the airship, but in truth I doubt she is still there. She would not walk abroad in full sunlight, which would set her flesh aflame and destroy her. I only hope none of the children has invited any stray cats into the château."

"They've been instructed," Jacqueline said, "but what about cats in the barn, the stables, the mews?"

Vordenburg's grim frown upset her.

"There are dozens of cats throughout the parc, monsieur," she cried. "One of them practically lives in my workshop, always on my workbench, tail in my face. How can I—"

She stopped herself, swallowing bitter frustration. She pointed to his vest pocket, where he had hidden the flask. "What was that medicine you applied to Countess Murkiewicz?"

"Water blessed by the Archbishop of Tours. I cannot say if it will be efficacious in her healing, but it may avert further assault."

Jacqueline pursed her lips. "Alas, if only Angélique had courted a priest or two among her coterie. We could bless the whole plumbing system."

Vordenburg chuckled as he eased himself into a chair and rubbed his impaired leg. "I would like to see a vampire tossed into a sanctified cistern."

She sat opposite. "If I may ask, what happened to your leg?"

He grimaced. "A vampire. I was young, fearless, bold, and stupid. I was not prepared for the superhuman abilities of the demon. We fought on the parapets of Schloss Reubenkirche. As I threw myself at him, he flew into the air some ten meters to perch atop a spire while I— alas, I also flew about ten meters, but downward." He shrugged at her look of horror. "I was fortunate it was so close to daybreak that he did not stay to make an end of me."

Jacqueline's courage ebbed. "Baron, I can build machines that give the artifice of life. But demons and curses and blessings of God... I can't fashion a machine to harness such powers. I feel powerless."

"On the contrary," he assured her. "You have safeguarded your home and each of your guests." He tapped the cross pinned to his lapel. "Countess Murkiewicz alone is now susceptible to Mircalla's call, and I have insisted her husband not leave her side, so Mircalla should not be able to use her to cause mischief."

Jacqueline shook with a frisson of apprehension. "What do you mean, susceptible to Mircalla's call?"

Vordenburg hemmed uncomfortably. "A vampire's bite leaves a victim open to a hypnotic call, summoning them."

"Ah." She pressed her hands to her pounding temples. "Anne and Marthe have both been bitten. What if Mircalla calls them?" *As if Marthe would leave the kitchen in the middle of all her work!* She sighed. "I suppose I should have someone watch them. I'll alert the Countess's governess to keep an eye on her as well."

"Very good idea," Vordenburg said. "Now, madame, if you would give me leave, I would like to explore your parc and the environs a bit further and consult my ancestor's notes on the matter. Afterward, I will explain my thoughts and we will devise a plan to be rid of Mircalla."

"Only if you take Monsieur Claque with you." Jacqueline brooked no argument. "No one is to wander these grounds alone, and that includes you. If you wish, you can ride a porter to rest your leg, or take one of the gentler ponies. Luc can assist you."

He brightened. "That would be a great relief indeed." He stood and bowed. "I'll have some luncheon and be on my way."

"Happy hunting," she said with a smile.

But after he left, the loneliness of her predicament closed in on her. There was only one place Jacqueline could ever feel truly herself. Although she had donned a bright floral day dress and silk shoes for the sake of the guests, rather than her usual outfit, she strolled down the drive to her workshop nestled in the cool of the forest.

If de Guise's enemy navigated that thermal balloon, she could design offensive weaponry for *Esprit*. The airship could transport the King to Château d'Eu more securely than if he were to travel by train or over main highways. The "infernal machine" Fieschi had used in his attempt on Louis-Philippe's life had fired a volley of twenty-five rounds in a series, or at least it would have done if she hadn't helped engineer its malfunction. Jacqueline was certain she could adapt the design to operate much like de Guise's Colt Paterson, with a rotating chamber advanced by pins, cogs, and sprocketry, all powered with steam drawn from *Esprit's* systems.

She kept fresh drafting paper glued across her table, secured with steel bands, so it was always dry, flat, and ready for use. An etui attached to the side of the table contained her engineering tools. As she spread these across her table, the black cat sprang up to peruse them, then batted the ivory compasses to the floor. With a pang of suspicion, Jacqueline booted the creature outside and closed the door.

She began with a basic representation of the Colt revolving mechanism. From there, her imagination took over and she was lost to the world and time. When she finally straightened and examined her work, it was late afternoon, the magical hour when the sun dipped below the trees and Bellesfées glowed. Satisfied with her progress, she tucked her instruments away, stood, and stretched out her back and shoulders. The scent of jasmine wafted over her. She spun to find the beautiful guest from the evening before watching her from the open doorway with wide-eyed fascination.

"I'm sorry. Did I startle you?" The woman came forward. "I tried to keep very still so as not to disturb you at your work. May I?"

Still consumed by thoughts of her machinery, Jacqueline blinked to refocus on the woman—so beautiful with her ebony hair braided casually into a knot at the back of her head, her delicate face like a marble Venus, and her large, heavy-lidded blue eyes gazing into hers with both invitation and challenge. Even in a simple blue day gown, the woman's sensual beauty emanated a siren's call. Llewellyn had once described Angélique as "hypnotic"; Jacqueline now understood what he meant. In the presence of the exotic woman, she felt just as lost as she had been these past hours.

When Jacqueline didn't answer, the woman paused. "I should introduce myself. Lady Carmilla Pierre, Countess Laroche."

"Your Excellency." Jacqueline curtsied reflexively at the title, but she made no move to allow the Countess any closer. Instead, the instinctive gesture freed her from the spell of the woman's beauty. Jacqueline reached behind the table and drew an oiled leather to cover her work. "I never show my designs until I'm ready to exhibit them."

The Countess stepped behind her, and again murmured close to her ear, her breath fragrant. "I understand. I can wait until you are ready."

Jacqueline shivered. The woman's velvet-soft voice sent warm chills through her. She tied the leather down and knotted it. "Some things, madame, I will never exhibit."

She stalked out of the workshop and held the door. The woman's inviting smile never faltered as she sauntered down the path into the forest. Jacqueline locked the door, angry all over again. She considered asking Angélique to disinvite this Countess, but it was, after all, her sister's celebration.

"Excellency," she called after her, "you shouldn't wander the forest alone."

Just then Charles appeared on the path and took the Countess's arm. Jacqueline smirked; she should have guessed.

Why then had the woman sought her out? Why so seductive an approach? And why did Jacqueline care so much that Carmilla Pierre, Countess Laroche was so extraordinarily beautiful when Jacqueline was not?

Jacqueline needed no reminders that the reflection in her mirror held no prepossessing features. At the twins' début cotillion as young teens, it had been made clear to her that although she and Angélique were identical, Angélique was the graceful embodiment of art and ephemeral beauty, while Jacqueline was an avatar of the new industrial frontier: muscular, strong-willed, enduring. Such a derogation would have insulted most girls, but Jacqueline was always too wrapped up in her work to care whether anyone courted her. At school, she was "Duval," just as the young men were known by their family names. Most of them never even realized she was a girl; those who did disdained her headstrong (some would say blunt) manner, her imposing intellect, and her lack of feminine qualities. That suited her purpose as well. She enjoyed complete autonomy to pursue her own ends, and those ends had never included love.

Until de Guise.

At first, she was flattered, then infatuated, then suspicious. But what other purpose could he have to lavish his tender affections — his love — when she hadn't sought him out, had made no pretense of seduction, and so obviously didn't deserve him? Ruggedly handsome and well-formed, yet elegantly so, de Guise could have any woman he desired, as was made plain by the many who had offered themselves to him at the reception.

De Guise had chosen Jacqueline. It shouldn't matter why. And yet...

She suddenly had a desperate hunger to see him.

Jacqueline couldn't find de Guise or Mr. Smith in the château. Lively games of cribbage and whist were going on in the banquet hall. Several of the governesses had gathered the children on the front lawn for games of ring toss, stick ball, tag, and statues. In the concert hall, Angélique and the invited soloists were rehearsing, presenting contrapuntal variations as they explored the panharmonium's repertoire and generally improvising pieces, while Lewellyn and other partners watched in amusement at their interplay. When Llewellyn caught sight of Jacqueline, he followed her from the conservatory.

"I haven't yet told you how extraordinary you have made our return, Jacky." He embraced her warmly. "I've never seen Angélique shine more beautifully than here in the halls of Bellesfées. You are indeed the two beautiful fairies of this valley."

Jacqueline beamed as he kissed her cheeks and took her arm on their way to the salon.

"As you no doubt have presumed, we found nothing untoward on the grounds of the château last night," he continued. "And should we scent anything new, we'll know it, now that we've personally greeted all the guests. I've enjoyed meeting some of Angélique's more *interesting* companions from Paris, and the musicians are spectacular. Whatever will we do to occupy ourselves once our festivities have ended?"

"Aren't you still in the Queen's service?"

He shook his head. "I'm resigning my commission. I've found my purpose. Angélique wants to return to the stage, to her music. That brings me great satisfaction. I remember the first time I saw her perform in Vienna, the winter of 1837. I think I fell in love with her then and there. This slight young angel bringing so much beauty and energy to her music. To think she came into my life again. To think she will perform again! And I want to be by her side. Every moment of every day, every night, for the rest of our lives."

His infatuation cheered her. "But your own estate, in Glamorgan?"

"It will make a pleasant summer home. For all of us, Jacky." He gave her a quick squeeze. "And wouldn't you love designing a second forge? I can have one built to your specifications so you don't waste a day in absolute leisure."

She laughed, but her humor was strained. "We shall see, Llewellyn."

"Please. Gryffin. We're family now."

"Gryffin," she agreed. "We shall see what this week brings us."

Turning her to face him, he removed his tinted glasses so she might read his olive-green wolf-eyes. "Jacky, you've taken this all upon yourself, but you're not alone. How much more prepared are you to face such threats, after all you've been through? All *we* have been through together? You stood against the dead. Iesu mawr, Angélique and I died! Yet we triumphed. Are we not the stronger for our adversity?"

Charles staggered around the corner. Llewellyn quickly replaced his glasses.

"Died?" Charles repeated, his eyes wide and dark with dilated pupils. He grinned. "You've visited that 'undiscovered country'? My dear Duke, you absolutely must enlighten me. As Jacky has refused me her tale, I must, *must* hear yours."

Llewellyn kissed Jacqueline's cheek, turned on his heel, and returned to the conservatory. Charles looked at Jacqueline with hopeful eyes, but she shook her head.

"Don't you understand? They belong to one another, not to you. Or to me. Their hearts, dear Charles, are two torches that can't be extinguished but by consuming each other. What could their tale do for you? Our tales are not for others' souls. You must find your own, just as I must find mine."

He tugged his mustache, unusually thoughtful. "Bah, you tease me with overblown poetry. I may steal it. You're cruel but wise, Jacky. But I adore you, for I'm in love with another Duval, as exotic as you are native, and as harsh as you are generous. This I will say: femina simplex. That's your tale. You're frank, honest and open; in a word, unembellished. And for that, I love you all the more."

He folded his hands behind his back and bowed to her, retreating. Jacqueline hoped he would take up with Countess Laroche again and keep the woman away from her.

The evening deepened. Jacqueline followed the sound of the King's laughter alternating with the frogs' raucous dusk concert of quacks and barks unique to the vale. De Guise and Mr. Smith huddled together in one of the pavilions. Smith wiped tears from his eyes and breathed deeply to stop his hilarity.

"I searched the whole grounds for the geese and ducks. De Guise tells me they're frogs! I've heard frogs peep and croak. I've heard the deep bellow of a bullfrog. I've never heard them quack, madame. Why didn't we hear them last night?"

Jacqueline put a finger to her lips, and Mr. Smith hushed. The frogs resumed their concert. He shook with silent laughter.

"They're shy, Mister Smith," she whispered. "You won't hear them when a crowd is about or if there's any smell or noise to frighten them off. Angélique and I often hunted for them when we were children, but we never found them. You can enjoy them as long as we keep our voices down."

She wrapped her arms around de Guise's neck. "Where have you two been hiding all day? I've missed you."

"Here and there," he answered. He freed himself to keep her from distracting him from his sentry between the King and the line of trees. "Luc reported foreigners in the village tavern inquiring about rooms. How have you spent your day?"

Jacqueline sat. "I've got a working design for the weapon we discussed. I can have it finished in the next day or two. Once I mount it, we can fly *Esprit* to Eu. I wouldn't mind taking in the sun at Mers-les-Bains myself. I think I've earned it after this summer."

Mr. Smith patted her hand. "I will not forget your kindness or your concern for my welfare. You are most welcome at Eu."

She swallowed the retort she wanted to make, that she would be satisfied if her efforts went toward a measure of consideration when his friend Armand's suit came before him.

Changing the subject, she pointed to the château. "Angélique and her fellow artists have been preparing a concert for us. We should go up for some dinner before they begin. I can see the gathering in the banquet hall from here."

"Ah," Mr. Smith said as he got to his feet. "Is that why the frogs have stilled?"

Jacqueline caught her breath. When did the frogs stop barking? What had frightened them? Her heart skipped, then pounded in the ominous silence that continued.

"De Guise," she whispered.

Two dark forms streaked across the lawn from the servants' wing toward the far end of the pond and the forest path.

"My God, I believe those are wolves," Smith cried. "That Baudelaire fellow wasn't dreaming."

De Guise drew his revolver while Jacqueline hurried to close the gas lines, dimming the lanterns in the pavilions. As her eyes adjusted to the dark, she saw Angélique and Llewellyn racing into the trees.

"Jacqueline, take His Majesty to the château," de Guise ordered. His tone was sharp, demanding—a voice Jacqueline had never heard him use. "Wait for me. I'll follow the wolves."

Mr. Smith spluttered. "Surely there's no danger from them? Wolves generally avoid people. See. Already they've vanished into the parc."

"Go." De Guise's fierce command was not to be gainsaid, even by the King.

"Come, Majesty."

Jacqueline dragged Mr. Smith unceremoniously out of the pavilion and uphill to the rear of the château. He didn't protest any further, but as they entered the kitchens, he forced her to stop. His face was red and he puffed heavily.

"I'm not so young as I once was," he excused himself, taking a seat at the worktable. He drew his handkerchief and mopped his brow. "Please explain our urgency."

She opened her mouth to respond. The report of a gun stopped her. Shot through with dread, she cried out.

Mr. Smith frowned. "That was no revolver. Now I know why the frogs were silent."

He stopped her from racing away, shaking his head.

"But de Guise—"

"He commanded us to wait. We will wait. If I, his king, heed his orders, so should you, Madame Duval."

Jacqueline flounced into a chair, then leapt up again to pace the kitchen. Who was shooting? What if someone had shot de Guise? Or Angélique or Llewellyn! Chatter from the banquet hall had not ceased; evidently the ebullient conversation had covered the gunshot. Where was de Guise? And why did the King seem so unconcerned for the man risking his life for him?

After a few tense minutes, Marthe came in followed by Anne, both of them carrying empty platters. Marthe swatted Jacqueline with a towel.

"Ma fille, you know how I feel about guests in the kitchen."

"How can I help, Marthe?" Mr. Smith intervened with a broad smile. "Surely we are old friends by now."

"Hmph!" Marthe stood arms akimbo, but relented and pointed to the spits of lambs cooling at an unlit side hearth.

Humming a distracting tune, Smith expertly retrieved the roasts and spilled them onto the platters. "Now how about if you two ladies take a brief respite while Madame Duval and I bring these out? I myself will probably have an entire shank for my own, and what's the best way to get what I want if not to be the one holding the platter, n'est-ce pas?"

Jacqueline's angry eyes argued, but he placed the laden platter in her hands, took up the second platter, and nudged her out of the kitchen. They made their way without speaking and deposited the platters on the banquet table. Mr. Smith again stopped Jacqueline from heading to the doors by handing her a plate as he took one for himself.

"Patience," he told her, "is rallied more easily on a full stomach." He indicated the table.

Jacqueline furiously stabbed some meats and vegetables and left the hall with Mr. Smith to go to the salon in solitude. How could she eat with de Guise out there, possibly dead? The wolves would not have manifested this early in the night unless some grave danger threatened the château. She dropped her plate on a side table and went to the open doors of the salon. The barking of the frogs once more filled the night. That meant neither de Guise nor anyone else was near the lawn.

"Eat, madame," Mr. Smith said, as he followed his own advice. "The evening has begun badly, and we may have a long night ahead."

His words were more than prophetic. Before she could rebuff him, a scream cut through the quiet outside.

7.

"YOU STAY HERE," JACQUELINE SNAPPED AS MR. SMITH TRIED TO FOLLOW her. "You're my guest, but you're also my king."

Slamming the doors on her way out, she followed the screams coming from outside the kitchens. When she rounded the back of the château, she found Countess Murkiewicz's governess shrieking beside the nursemaid's limp body on the bricks of the courtyard.

"Zofia is dead! Dead! The wolves took Kaja! God save us!"

Jacqueline knelt beside the nursemaid and felt for a pulse. The young woman still lived. Jacqueline lifted her onto a table, then turned to seize the governess by the shoulders.

"She's not dead, you silly woman." Her voice shook, but she tried to sound dismissive. "And if the wolves had wanted the baby, they would have devoured her on the spot, not carried her off. No doubt Zofia fainted at the sight of wolves, and Kaja crawled away. Go look for her."

She turned the maid around and gave her a firm shove. The woman ran off shouting for Kaja, smacking her lips as if the baby were a dog trained to come when called. As Jacqueline watched, panic threatened to paralyze her. Could the baby have crawled so far, or had Mircalla made off with easy prey?

Upon inspecting Zofia's neck, Jacqueline found the marks she suspected would be there. The girl must have forgotten to wear her cross, or perhaps it had come undone in nursing the baby. Jacqueline scooped her up across her shoulder and carried her toward the salon. As she rounded the turret of the château, she almost collided with Countess Laroche. The countess dandled a cooing Kaja in her arms.

"Oh, dear. That explains why this little one wandered off," the Countess said with a wry grin.

Jacqueline blinked in surprise, a rush of relief burning through her limbs. She had not wholly expected the child to be found. "You are a lifesaver, Your Excellency." Jacqueline pointed her elbow toward the kitchens. "The governess is around back, out of her wits, looking for her. If you would be so kind."

"Of course." The Countess tipped her head. "Is that woman all right?"

Jacqueline shifted the nursemaid to her other shoulder. "She will be, thank you."

"And are you? All right?" The Countess smiled. "Of course you are. You are magnificent, ma chère."

Her coquettish grin sent a shudder through Jacqueline. She nodded an uncomfortable response, then continued toward the salon. In a few moments, she heard the governess' cry of joy. One tragedy averted, she got inside and set the nursemaid on a divan. Mr. Smith hurried to assist her.

"Another victim?"

"I'm afraid so." Jacqueline patted Zofia's face to rouse her. "Would you ring for the kitchen, please?"

He did so. Anne appeared; he sent her for fresh beef tea. When it arrived, he brought it to Jacqueline and together they managed to wake Zofia. She mumbled incoherently, then startled.

"Kaja!"

Jacqueline hushed her. "Safe and well. What happened, Zofia?"

Since Zofia spoke no French or English, Jacqueline translated. "She says she was suddenly very tired and fell asleep. She's never done that while nursing the baby. Kaja jest bezpieczna," she assured the girl. "Safe."

Relieved, Zofia fell back again. When Mr. Smith pushed the beef tea on her, she didn't protest, but she was nonetheless distraught that she had been so neglectful of her charge. Jacqueline told her she had likely succumbed to the same malady that had taken her mistress aboard the airship. The explanation seemed to assuage the worst of the girl's anxiety, although it only deepened Jacqueline's because of its veracity.

"This may be to our advantage," Jacqueline murmured to the King. "If the rumor of an illness hastens our guests' retreat, we can concentrate on containing this creature, as well as safeguarding you."

Just then, she heard heavy tromping heading their way from the lawn. Monsieur Claque entered the salon. He too carried someone: Vordenburg.

"No, no, I'm all right." Vordenburg allayed her dread by disengaging himself from Monsieur Claque with an embarrassed laugh. He gained his feet unsteadily. "The porter ran out of steam and I found myself at a disadvantage a great distance from here. Thankfully, your Monsieur Claque obliged." He spotted the nursemaid and his humor faded.

Monsieur Claque bowed to Jacqueline and turned to leave again.

"Claque."

He turned back at Jacqueline's call. She didn't know how to form the words, but he waited. She had to say it.

"De Guise hasn't yet returned. Can you—that is, do you have the fuel to go find him?"

For answer, he pooted a sparse puff of steam.

She sighed. "Can something, anything go right this night? Mister Smith, I need to tend to Monsieur Claque. Will you lock the doors behind me?"

She hooked arms with the autonomaton and left. She heard Mr. Smith complete her orders. She and Monsieur Claque took the shortcut to her workshop, down the hill to the pond and around through the woods a half kilometer. To her great relief, she met Angélique and Llewellyn, still wolves, on the path. She stooped to welcome them into her arms, and they both whined.

"She was at the château all along," Jacqueline told them. "She took a nursemaid."

The wolves shook themselves. Angélique huddled down and shuddered. Her back arched, then stretched. Her fur retreated into her skin. Her tail withdrew. Paws gave way to hands and feet, and the lupine head shifted smoothly to Angélique's delicate features. Her tawny mane shook itself out, and she arose… nude.

Jacqueline hurried to embrace her sister and scold her. "Of all times for me not to have a coat."

Angélique patted her back. "Modesty has never been one of my best qualities. Listen. It was not the vampire that drew us out." She fondled Llewellyn's ears as he nudged her legs. "A band of six men entered the parc and stirred the deer. They seemed to be searching the forest. The men smelled… well, sour, bitter, all wrong. Nervous, angry. They had guns. One fired on us. Anyway, they're gone now."

Jacqueline took Angélique's hands. "De Guise hasn't returned."

Angélique lifted her head. She and Llewellyn both sniffed the air. "He's safe. No blood scent. No fear. Where are you going?"

"The workshop. Claque—"

"Claque can wait. Gryffin and I need a distraction so we can return to the cellars and dress without being spotted again. Can you gather everyone into the concert hall? They would all be safer inside anyway with that thing about, and so will you. We'll watch you."

Jacqueline hesitated, torn. Angélique hugged her again.

"Stop chewing your cheek. I promise you he's safe right now. He's probably in stealthy pursuit of the band we chased off—who, by the way, were speaking German."

Angélique kissed her. Jacqueline caught her back as she was about to return to her wolf shape.

"Mon Ange, why couldn't you sense the vampire?"

Llewellyn whined and gruffed annoyance. Angélique's brow furrowed and she growled.

"You tell me she prefers the cat form, and we have too many cats to know each individually. And in her human form—Jacky, there are so many people about right now. We sensed no one new. Perhaps if we'd been there tonight when she attacked…" She squeezed Jacqueline's hand. "We'll visit this nursemaid and Countess Murkiewicz both. We'll find her scent."

Angélique folded into herself again. In a moment, she was the lush, tawny wolf. She and Llewellyn mawed each other lovingly.

Jacqueline blew out a weary breath. "I'm sorry, Monsieur Claque. Get to the workshop, and I'll find you again before the end of the night. I need you to keep watch over Anne and Marthe, especially."

Monsieur Claque bowed and stomped toward the workshop while the wolves accompanied Jacqueline to the edge of the woods, keeping watch as she climbed the hill once more, this time toward the banquet hall.

Les Dumas and Charles along with a few others she didn't know were gathered outside at a table, smoking and arguing good-naturedly as if they relaxed in a Latin Quarter tavern, debating the great philosophies of the period with all the weight and wisdom borne of too much wine.

"Madame Duval," Dumas père called to her, waving a large cigar.

"Messieurs," she answered, "the concert is starting soon. Will you not come inside to the concert hall?"

"Of course, but first, I need a woman's opinion, please."

She bit back a profanity. As if there were a difference between men and women's opinions! "I am all out of women's opinions, Monsieur Dumas," she replied. "Call me when you want mine."

Dumas guffawed. "Why, this night is young," he insisted. "And I have such esteem for your intellect. As a fellow creator, I must hear your thoughts on this argument of man and nature. Is man's creation superior to nature, or is the natural man the ideal to which we should all aspire? Do we not show ourselves superior to the noble savage when we emulate our Creator, lift ourselves out of the base scrabbling for mere existence, and—"

Jacqueline groaned and leaned on the table, hanging her aching head. Pretentious Paris philosophizing. "I know no noble savages, monsieur. Therefore, I have no gauge by which to measure or weigh the balance. Please, the bride asks us—"

"But surely, as a creator yourself?"

"Superior to nature? Bof, if my next creation is superior to the one I've just completed, I'm happy."

One of the other men slapped the table enthusiastically. "Well said, Fräulein, very well said. In this age of industry, it is our work that will redeem us. That thermal airship of yours, for example. What could be superior to such a creation?"

Charles belched and tried to straighten, his nose already far into the cups. "The flight of an albatross, for one thing. Endless miles, soaring far out to sea, borne up by the winds alone."

Another man laughed at him. "And then, like you, Baudelaire, it comes down to earth and flops about with its head too big for its feet."

Charles combed through his beard and stared glassy-eyed at the one who offered this image. He nodded with a sad moue.

"Whereas," Jacqueline finished, "with enough fuel, you could soar as long as you wished."

A champagne bottle popped behind them and the cap hit the German in the head.

"See it soar?" said de Guise as he stepped from the shadows. He proffered a flute glass to Jacqueline. "Some fuel, my love?"

"De Guise!" She threw her arms around him and kissed him desperately, to the hoots and applause of the men at the table.

"There's my argument," Charles commented. "What can any man possibly create more wonderful than such a profound love? Nor roses increase its fragrance. It's beyond both creature and creator."

Jacqueline buried her face in de Guise's lapel, drawing strength from his firm arms around her and forcing herself to hold together for the sake of company. Why did she feel so much less than herself when she was apart from him? It annoyed her, but she had far too many other worries at the moment.

He tapped her shoulder with the champagne flute. "My love?"

Sheepishly, she took the glass, let de Guise fill it, and saluted the men. She drained the glass to their cheers, then suppressed the bubbles that repeated on her.

"Messieurs, I believe the musicians await us in the hall," de Guise said, "and it would be rude to refuse Madame Duval's invitation to attend at once. Allons-y."

"Herr Heine, please see that Monsieur Baudelaire makes it there," Jacqueline added, shooing the others inside. She watched them enter the château and close the warded door behind themselves. She then wrapped her arm around de Guise's waist, accepting another glass of champagne.

"Our *friend*?" De Guise asked, again in that tone she did not recognize, the voice of the agent of the King's Sûreté.

"No." She drank. "Another woman has fallen prey." She trembled, and silently cursed her trembling. "I can't keep them all safe, de Guise. I can't be everywhere. I want them to leave. I want them gone. I hate crowds and I hate all this social pretentiousness. Yes, your king can be charming, but considering all else… If we could just focus on one thing at a time. I do wish Papa were here. He could handle Mr. Smith so much more ably."

De Guise kissed the top of her head. "I followed the intruders to the road. They were headed to the village. I'll look into it tomorrow. We'll use the rumor of wolves to keep everyone inside the château for now, perhaps tomorrow spread the rumor of illness. Why don't you go to bed? Vordenburg, Mister Smith, and I, along with Llewellyn and Angélique, will discuss all we've learned, and the newlyweds will safeguard us tonight."

Sleep was tempting, but it felt wrong to leave her guests. She was mistress of Bellesfées, la Belle Dame. Since she had invited them to enjoy her hospitality, she ought to see the night through to the end.

"Go," de Guise insisted. "Go now, and I'll join you later."

Jacqueline accepted those endearing terms. She held up her flute for a third champagne. He poured, and he kissed her lightly before offering his arm to take her inside and escort her to the stairs.

"You've done everything you can, and more, chérie. Rest. I mean it. I want to find you fast asleep when I come up."

She kissed him deeply. "Mmm. What fun would that be?"

He answered with his beautiful smile. Jacqueline released his hand reluctantly and trudged up the steps, tipping back the rest of the champagne and enjoying the sweet bubbly sensation in her nose. She'd had so little to eat all day, her thoughts bubbled as well.

"Not enough fuel," she mumbled. Then she gasped. *Fuel!*

She had left Monsieur Claque to puff away the last of his fuel in her workshop. She couldn't leave the servants' wing unguarded, no matter what de Guise promised. Whether Anne blew the tin whistle or Mircalla decided to "call" her victims, Monsieur Claque had to be ready to defend them. The guests had brought so many servants, governesses, attendants whom she had promised gold if they stayed locked in, but only because she had counted on Monsieur Claque to safeguard them.

De Guise and the wolves had chased off the assassins. The sooner she got Monsieur Claque refueled, the sooner everyone would be protected. Luc or Jean-Paul could do it, but Jean-Paul was seating guests in the conservatory hall, and Luc would be out at the barns bedding down the animals.

She descended the stairs and headed into the night.

A lovely solo violin filled the air. Jacqueline was no connoisseuse. She had no idea who was playing since she had invited four different violinists; nor could she name the piece. Still, the serene melody that soared from the concert hall's open balconies and drifted across the valley to echo from "the temple of living pillars," as Charles described the parc, settled her anxiety, reminding her of the joy her endeavors had evinced thus far. It was possible three glasses of champagne had softened her spirit, but she preferred to think it was the violin. She hummed along, and at the same time laughed at herself, her awful sense of pitch, her low, almost baritone voice.

"Ah, de Guise, de Guise. What can you possibly see in me?" she whispered to the gas lamps.

The very mention of his name brought to mind the previous night in her bed, and she pirouetted in delight, giggling, before returning to the violin's song. Her fantaisie was interrupted by a retching noise near the pond. In silhouette, she saw a man bent double. A woman stood beside him, rubbing his back while he emptied his stomach.

Jacqueline snickered. "Too much fuel."

How many times had she done the same for Angélique, during her twin's years of decadence and dissolution. Before Llewellyn. Before Angélique could put a name to the void in her life. Before she had learned that *what* she was, was not more than *who* she was. Before she had become the agent of her own destiny, avenging herself against the ones who had wronged her. Before she had learned to love herself, and to love another even more.

Perhaps that's what the poor fellow at the pond needed. She hoped the woman beside him could help him find it.

"You two should be inside," she called to them. "The concert has already begun."

The fellow straightened and waved. "I love you, Duval!" he called.

Charles. She should have known. And Countess Laroche, no doubt. She waited until she saw them walk away. Her anxiety returned. She would have to check the grounds after finishing up the fueling to be certain they made it safely inside.

Jacqueline followed the drive past the Benets' cottage down into the woods, gas lamp posts illuminating the path to the workshop. Seated at the third table along, Monsieur Claque raised his head as she entered and lit the phosphorus lucifer lantern beside him, bathing the workshop in blinding white light that reflected and refracted off every polished metal in the shop, creating a dazzling fairyland of sparkles. She breathed in the magical scents she loved: sawdust, hardwood, machine oils, burnt metals. If only she could spend these hours here rather than among tout Paris.

"Sorry to keep you," she told Monsieur Claque, patting his arm.

She went to the fuel storage cabinet and removed a canister of a liquid fuel she had developed from coal extracts. She brought it to the worktable next to Monsieur Claque, then went back for two other canisters. When she opened his breastplate and removed his fuel tank, the autonomaton's head dropped and the lights of his indicators went dark.

"I never meant for you to get so low," Jacqueline said, "but if it's any consolation, I'm operating on zero myself." Then she hiccoughed and chuckled. "Unless you count alcohol. I have some of that for you too."

She measured out portions of the three liquid fuels and poured them into Monsieur Claque's tank, then returned the canisters to storage. She closed the cabinet, but as she shut the lock, the workshop went dark.

The utter blackness after the brilliant phosphorus blinded her. Instinctively, Jacqueline seized a claw hammer from its hooks beside the cabinet. She whirled. "Who's there?"

She heard nothing, saw nothing but the faint glow of gaslight from the forest walk. The pond frogs barked and quacked, and cicadas buzzed, unalarmed. As her eyes adjusted, she sidled toward Monsieur Claque. Something large, soft, and furry tripped her. She landed hard, slamming her brow into the claws of the hammer.

Her vision exploded in fireworks. *Futter that damned cat!* She couldn't breathe. Her pulse pounded against her skull, and blood streamed into her left eye. Groaning, she managed to get up to her elbows to flip over and sit, brandishing the hammer in one hand.

Jacqueline snatched the hem of her dress to mop blood from her face. Pressing the fabric to the gash on her brow, she waved the hammer around wildly. Her head throbbed, pain and blood blinding her. As terror mounted, her thoughts raced.

Angélique. Angélique will smell fear. Angélique will smell the blood. Llewellyn will —

Talons seized her shoulders from behind. Sharp teeth pierced her flesh. Jacqueline choked on a strangled cry. Then…

Sweet, sweetest euphoria overtook her senses. The dusk of the workshop enfolded her in delicate warmth and she gasped in wonder. The very air caressed her arms, her legs. Jacqueline nestled into it with a sensual moan.

Utter peace filled her, in the way hydrogen might fill the envelope of an aerostat, and she floated up to follow the song of the violin. It carried her beyond the forest, above the vineyards, up into the night sky of myriad stars. She reached for them and kept reaching and kept rising.

A shot tore away the envelope, and Jacqueline fell to earth.

8.

JACQUELINE WOKE TO HUSHED ANGRY VOICES. SHE LAY, EYES CLOSED, ON brocade, rough on her cheek. Furniture. A divan. She wanted to sit up. Her body denied her. She didn't argue. Her head pained her just above her left eye. Her wet hair dripped down her face, icy cold, but she couldn't fathom why.

Too much champagne? No, I only had two glasses. Didn't I? Or was it more? Must have been too much. Can't remember. Can't remember ever being this drunk…

She decided to stay where she was rather than face her hangover. She turned her attention to the voices instead.

"What am I supposed to do, chain her up?" That was de Guise. Bellowing. De Guise was bellowing. Another sound she had never heard. Someone shushed him.

Chain who up?

"My task is the King. I can't—"

"No, of course not." That was Llewellyn. So calm, soothing. "You must pursue your mission. Bellesfées is ours to guard."

"You were too late!"

Why is de Guise so angry? Too late for what? The concert? Oh, de Guise, de Guise. Calm yourself. My head hurts.

"We were in time." A different voice. "Two tonight. She has never done so. Not in my records." One of the guests. Baron something. With a V. Like the V waistline of the alluring Countess Laroche's gown.

Oh, to be that beautiful. To be truly desirable. Alluring. Hypnotic. Not that it mattered. No, it didn't matter. Still…

"But she has not visited the same woman more than once, as she has done in the villages. I think she merely sustains herself. She is searching for something."

The conversation no longer made sense. Too weary to puzzle it out, Jacqueline tried to go back to sleep, but her head pounded like a hammer.

Hammer!

Her eyes flew open. At least, her right eye did. A bag of ice set on her brow secured by a bandage around her head kept her left eye closed. The room was blurry, and a large shape blocked her view of most of it.

"There we are," Mr. Smith said with a sigh of relief, and backed away from her. "She's awake."

De Guise dropped to his knees beside her with such a dark fury in his eyes, she flinched.

"How could you be so reckless?" he roared in her face. "Going out by yourself with a vampire on the grounds! I sent you to your room. You were supposed to be safe in bed."

He reached for her, but his arms tensed. For a moment she feared he would throttle her.

"Why did you not take precautions? For once! Do you *want* to throw your life away? How could you? Damn it, Jacqueline, you are so damned headstrong."

Jacqueline had never seen de Guise angry. Ever. Angry at *her*, piquing her own temper. Unable to form a response, she stared stupidly at the fierce stranger he had become. The blurred shapes surrounding them took on their identities as vision cleared: Llewellyn, Vordenburg, Smith, Luc, Marthe — all frowning at her. Tears streaked Marthe's face. Outside the closed doors, the night was dark. Music drifted faintly through the windows.

De Guise snarled as Mr. Smith tugged him away. "Before you hurt someone," Mr. Smith warned.

Tucking himself beside Jacqueline on the divan, Llewellyn removed his sun-glasses and peered into her open eye. She recalled the first time they had encountered one another. His eyes had been deep blue, like the Caribbean Sea. Now his wolf-eyes were a soft green as he studied her face and, she supposed, sniffed her for tell-tale scents of her condition.

"She has no concussion, just a mean gash and a lump." He grinned at her and winked. "A lump on the head in the workshop? We come full circle, don't we, ma'm'selle."

Jacqueline tried to return his grin. "Did I fall down the stairs?" She tried to put a hand to her head, but she felt too weak to move.

"What do you remember?" he asked. He held out his hand to Marthe, and she came forward to give him a bowl of beef tea which he held to Jacqueline's lips.

"I went upstairs." She closed her eyes and sipped again. "Too much champagne?"

"Jacqueline!" de Guise barked.

Llewellyn held up his hand to silence de Guise. "You went upstairs, but then you came down again," he prompted.

"Oh. That's right." She nodded, then winced and decided she would not nod anymore. "Claque needed fuel."

De Guise exploded with an obscenity. A dishtowel snapped against his cheek to silence him. Marthe glared.

"Language! You aren't helping," she warned him. "And I don't approve of that word in this house."

He ramped about the room like a caged animal.

"No." Squeezing her eyes against the pain, Jacqueline sat up with Llewellyn's help. "You tell me what happened," she said, growing more annoyed watching de Guise. "I remember nothing else. What did I do wrong? Why are you angry with me?"

"I'm not angry with you," de Guise shouted. "I'm angry—ah, damn!"

He finally sat and pressed his head to hands. Jacqueline ached too much to even frown at him.

Llewellyn fed her more broth while he explained, "At the concert, Angélique and I smelled your sudden fear, then blood, then something else. Something dead. I signaled to de Guise, and together we ran to the workshop as swiftly as we could. We heard a shot. You were on the floor, and Luc was holding you."

"Luc?" She turned to her groundskeeper.

Luc tossed his big shoulders. "I saw you go to the workshop as I came out of the barn. I thought you shouldn't be alone out there."

"Exactly," de Guise snapped.

Luc continued, "The light went out and I heard you call. I ran. There was someone else with you. I shot, but whatever it was disappeared." He scratched his chin. "Odd, that."

Vordenburg said, "No bullet would have stopped her. You expelled her, and in time to save Madame Duval's life."

Jacqueline put her hand to her throat. She felt the punctures. She slowly looked to de Guise. His rage had turned to—what? Loss? Regret?

"De Guise?"

He bowed his head. His voice was ragged. "I couldn't get there in time."

"But Madame Duval is safe for now," Vordenburg said.

"For now. For now. I keep hearing that. I'm sick of hearing that!" Jacqueline got to her feet, then dropped to sit as her head pounded.

"Where's your cross?" Llewellyn asked.

She put her hand to her bodice where she had pinned it. It was gone. "I must have—when I carried Zofia—" She was about to curse but thought better of it, with Marthe's towel so near at the ready.

"That's what I mean. Careless," de Guise grumbled.

Marthe swatted him again.

Luc folded his arms and scowled. "I don't call it careless when the mistress works into the night to see to the welfare of the household, monsieur."

"I quite agree, Luc," Llewellyn said. "De Guise, why don't you accompany Luc back to the workshop to finish what Jacky started so Claque is ready for duty. I'll take her to her room."

De Guise's glare softened when he looked at Jacqueline, and he followed Luc meekly from the salon. Llewellyn helped Jacqueline stand.

"Llewellyn. Gryffin." Jacqueline took his arm and leaned to him. "It grieves me to say this, but we have to bring the festivities to an end. I can't risk any more women being attacked, and I can't—" She swallowed the lump in her throat. "Well, now that I've been bitten, I can't trust myself to protect anyone."

Llewellyn tenderly brushed her hair back to check the bandaging on her brow. "Nothing will be easier. I have the ideal excuse. We'll employ every carriage in your mews to convey everyone to Orléans. Those neighbors who rode in will be importuned to carry a few passengers. If needs must, we will borrow a few wagons from the village. Our guests will be on the train tomorrow."

"But how?" she grumbled. "How do we convince them to leave without being ungracious?"

He grinned slyly. "I have just spoken to Angélique. I've asked her to feign sudden and severe fatigue at the recitals. She'll swoon, be revived, and excuse herself to bed."

The wolves possessed that mental ability to share thoughts, Jacqueline knew, but the meaning of Angélique's fainting eluded her.

Llewellyn's grin widened. "After all, we've been married several weeks now," he said with a wink.

Marthe threw her hands up with a sharp, indignant cry and left the salon. It took Jacqueline a little longer to appreciate the intimation. She chuckled, then winced.

"What's wrong with my head?"

"We were hoping you'd tell us. You were clutching a very bloody hammer when we found you."

Jacqueline searched her thoughts, though her skull felt like it would crack open with each attempt at finding a memory. "The lights went out, and I reached for the hammer..." She grinned. "Just like the night you tried to burgle us." Thoughts scattered again, with one clear thought breaking through. "Why is he so angry at me?"

"His temper will abate," Llewellyn assured her. "He's angry at himself, not you. Although, I must tell you, Jacky, it was thoughtless of you to go out into the night by yourself. You should have asked for assistance."

"But Claque—the servants—I just—" With a sigh, she admitted, "Reflex. I've always managed on my own. I just didn't think about myself."

"No, you didn't. But that's you, Jacky."

"*Bof.* Yes, thoughtless."

"No, *selfless.*"

"No, stupid."

She had only herself to blame. Perhaps de Guise was right. Too headstrong for her own good. Caring more about Claque than common sense. Little wonder he was angry. She'd been stupid. She couldn't tolerate stupidity in others; why should de Guise tolerate it in her?

"I'm going to bring you eggs, more beef tea, and cheese and bread. And you'll eat all of it before you go to sleep," Llewellyn told her. "If nothing else has come of this, we have the creature's scent. She can apply all the powder or perfume she wishes, but we'll track her if she appears again."

When they got to the marble staircase, Jacqueline's steps faltered when she pondered the spiral. Llewellyn lifted her into his arms and carried her. He swept her into her room and laid her on her bed. "I will not presume to undress you. Angélique will be here any moment to do that."

He locked the windows shut and verified the wards there, then at the doorway. He was about to shut the door again when Angélique rushed in. She leapt onto the bed beside her sister and embraced her, weeping.

"Mon Ange, mon Ange," Jacqueline murmured, caressing her sister's back. "I'm so sorry. So sorry."

"For what?"

"The party. The concert. I had such plans." She hugged her sister. "I've ruined everything. Everything."

Angélique choked on a sob. "Idiot. That's not why I'm crying."

She sat up and signaled Llewellyn to leave. He blew her a kiss and closed the door behind him. Angélique tossed her glasses aside and wiped her tears.

"I nearly changed when I caught the scent of all that blood, right in the middle of Jean-Delphin's performance. I could almost *feel* your anguish, and the pain. But when you just vanished from my senses, I was beside myself."

Jacqueline managed a smile. "I remember the violin. So beautiful."

"Good. Maybe you'll remember more as we go along."

"I remember I wanted to engage Jacques d'Île and his flügelhorn, but he's in England just now."

"Oh, Jacky, that's not what I meant."

Angélique gently tugged off her sister's bloodied dress. She tossed it in the corner and fetched a chemise à la reine. As she slipped it over Jacqueline's head, she took a moment to examine the wound on her neck, sniffing for the scent of the creature that had left the marks.

"I will find the bitch," she said fiercely.

"I'm more concerned about my head," Jacqueline lamented. "I have so much more work to do."

"Which you'll only accomplish once you've eaten and slept."

A light tap at the door indicated Llewellyn had returned with the promised plate. He set the tray on the bedside table and leaned over to kiss Jacqueline's brow. Then he kissed Angélique.

"Dumas père is joyfully spreading the rumor we desired him to spread," he said, "and everyone but your closest friends have agreed to depart tomorrow."

"Meaning?"

He pursed his lips. "Meaning we still have Charles, the Dumases, someone named Custine and his—companion? And those crazy Germans."

"Ooh, merde, don't let any of them near the King!" Angélique laughed. "I'll get rid of them tomorrow."

Llewellyn wagged his finger at her. "I'm not sure how much more of your past I wish to know, fy nghariad."

"Mon amour." Grabbing his finger playfully, she kissed it, then shooed him away.

"Nighty-night," he called in English on his way out.

Jacqueline dropped her head on her sister's shoulder again. "I've lost him, mon Ange. I lost him already. I was so stupid. He was so angry, I didn't even know him."

Angélique quietly laughed as she rubbed her back to soothe her. "He wasn't angry with you, and he could only be so angry at himself if he loved you, my silly sister. He'll learn."

Jacqueline could only see the fury in his eyes, hear the rage in his voice. "I've lost him."

"I know these things, Jacky. Trust me." Once again, Angélique tapped her nose. "He loves you. Now, eat your dinner, and go to sleep." She took up the beef tea and made her drink.

Jacqueline dutifully ate her light meal and drank the broth, but nothing could make her feel satisfied or complete. She had lost de Guise's respect, a blow worse than any vampire could deal her.

Angélique unfastened her reticule from her belt and withdrew an ampule. "This will help with the pain."

"Not any of that North African poison Charles takes?"

"Belladonna only. Dawamesc is too extreme. We'll save that for when you're dying. Open." She poured the ampule's contents into Jacqueline's mouth, then caressed her face and kissed her bandaged brow. "Voilà. The kiss of an angel," she said. Angélique replaced the ampule and put her reticule on the side table. Then she began to undress.

Jacqueline eyed her curiously. "What are you doing?"

Angélique didn't answer. When she was fully nude, she changed to the wolf and jumped up on Jacqueline's bed to lie down at her feet.

"Mon Ange."

Jacqueline lovingly stroked Angélique's silky pelage until the belladonna took hold, stilling the pounding in her head. She fell asleep with her fingers entwined in the fur of her sister's ruff.

The wolf was gone when Jacqueline awoke the next morning. She debated going back to sleep, but then noticed Angélique had left a small porcelain bell on her side table. She rang it, knowing one of the wolves would hear. Sure enough, a few minutes later, her sister came through the door with a basin and fresh cloths.

"How are you?"

"I can't say yet." Jacqueline sat up with a grunt and winced.

Angélique carefully removed the bandages. She wagged her head. "You look awful."

"Thank you."

"Two black-butter eyes, a swollen, gaping slash, and a lot of grey, which I assume is purple."

"I've had far worse. Please tell me no one else fell victim last night."

"Thankfully, no. Charles tells me he and some woman were down by the pond last night. He saw nothing amiss, but he was probably too drunk to notice anyway." She gently dabbed at the gash. "Baron Vordenburg claims to have discovered information that may lead to this Mircalla Karnstein's tomb. Something about a Roman burial ground west of Bellesfées. He and Gryffin will go together to investigate."

"And de Guise has gone to track down the intruders?"

"No."

"Why not?"

Examining the gash again, her sister tsked. "This will leave a terrible scar. It stopped bleeding, but we should have a surgeon close it. I'll fetch Sédillot before he leaves."

"One of your friends is a surgeon?"

"Indeed." Angélique sat back and grinned. "You know, if you and de Guise would join Gryffin and me, you'd never have to worry about these kinds of accidents. In both your lines of work, it would be an advantage."

"Yes, yes. Magic blood. No wound can kill you. No scars. New mercies every morning." Jacqueline waved her away. "But I need to distinguish colors for my work, thank you, and I need my calluses on my hands. I *don't* need my looks. It's not as if I had any looks to worry about."

Angélique caught her chin with a stern frown. "Don't say that. Don't ever say that. Not to me, not to anyone, especially not to yourself. You are Jacqueline Marie-Claire Duval de la Forge-à-Bellesfées. No one is more brilliant or more magnificent. And no one is more beautiful to me."

"Or to me," said de Guise from the doorway.

Jacqueline flinched. De Guise hadn't shaved; he hadn't even brushed his hair. His eyes, bloodshot and dull, wouldn't meet hers, and his shoulders sagged. He carried a bed tray with a bowl of coffee, a creamer, and her favorite pastries, croissants chocolats. Setting the tray over her lap, he sat beside her on the bed, careful not to jostle her.

Angélique took the basin and headed to the door, turning back a moment to flash a wicked smile. "Kiss and cuddle, you two," she said. "I'll send the surgeon."

De Guise handed Jacqueline a croissant to distract her while he examined her face and her throat with clinical concern. She ate silently, unwilling to engage him. She still hadn't reconciled herself to the ferocity of his anger the night before. She had always wondered how the gentle, gentlemanly, disarmingly charming "railroad agent" who had first courted her could be an agent for the King's elite espionage forces, fighting off assassins, killing enemies of the Crown. The raging man she had seen last night was that agent. She was afraid to look at him. Which man would she see?

De Guise poured cream into the bowl of coffee. He proffered it, and she took it from him. "Good," he said. "You're much stronger."

But he looked at her hands, he looked at the remaining croissant, or he watched her replace the bowl. His eyes were everywhere but on hers.

And why should he look at her? A swollen lump and open wound and purpled eyes from a headstrong act of defiance, recklessly stupid. He deserved so much more. Coffee couldn't ease the tightness in her throat. The pain in her heart surpassed the pain in her head.

Just when she could bear the silence no longer, he suddenly gripped her hand and pressed it to his lips.

"Forgive me," he said, in slow, measured tones. "I was—deranged. I'm not easily frightened. But you—"

"I'm sor—"

"I was terrified, Jacqueline. No, I shouldn't have shouted at you or lost my temper. I can't recall when I've been so angry, and I was angry because — because you put yourself in danger."

He wrung her hand. "As I've told you many times, I'm not given to outbursts of emotion. Now you see why. I can't afford to lose control of myself, Jacqueline. It could cost me my life, or the King's. I'm sorry, Jacqueline. I know you're an independent woman. I love you for that. I can't remember a time when I didn't love you. I love your single-mindedness, your passion for your work, your incredible intellect, your devotion to your sister, your dedication to the people of the village, your absolute generosity without a thought to yourself. But —"

Her heart dropped, heavier than iron. There it was: "*But...*"

She wasn't compliant enough, not feminine enough, not deferential enough. She was always too engrossed in her plans to make time for him. Too headstrong, too determined to get her own way, too impulsive, thoughtless. Lavishing more attention on Angélique or Monsieur Claque than on the man she said she loved. Flouting rules of a society he was sworn to protect.

Which "but" would he claim was too great an obstacle to any future together? Which flaws of her nature would he claim he could no longer tolerate?

With a groan, de Guise shoved the charger to the floor. Coffee and cream splattered everywhere. Jacqueline gasped as her bowl flew from her hands. He seized her, clutching her head to his shoulder as he rocked her side to side.

"I've watched men die. I've killed in cold blood. But —"

Another 'but.' Jacqueline was confused. His embrace said one thing, but that voice, that tone — demanding, angry...

"I live a solitary existence, Jacqueline, fraught with danger and deceit. Hiding who I am, becoming whoever I need to be for the sake of the King. Crawling among the worst — But you! You're infuriating!"

He crushed her in his arms. She squeaked a protest.

"Intelligent, open, direct. You struck me like a thunderbolt. The more I watched you, the more I lost myself in you. Those idyllic days we spent here after the Catacombs... Everything was new again. You, so pure, so open. But, Jacqueline —"

He squeezed her again. Her struggling finally eased his hold enough that she could speak. She rested her head on his shoulder, wondering if this would be the last time the spice of his skin would touch her innermost thoughts.

"But, but, but." She ran her hand along his stubbled cheek. "I understand."

She couldn't be angry with him. He had his calling, and she was a distraction. He should not be asked to divide his attention between the King and her welfare. Should he lose his sang-froid, he could never again be an effective agent of the King in the underworld of Europe. Better to surrender him than risk his life with her stupidity.

Again, he crushed her to him. Again, he demanded, "Think what would happen if you — if —" His voice broke. "Damn it, Jacqueline, I could have lost you. The only woman I've ever truly loved. Did you not think of me in the least? Don't you love me enough to share your life with me?"

Stunned, Jacqueline couldn't move. This wasn't the farewell she had expected. She mumbled incoherently into his shoulder. He released her, sitting back to search her face in hope and trepidation. She wasn't sure how to answer him. She held his hands, trying to will away the ache in her head.

"I can't change who I am," she said plainly. "How can you ask me to share my life?"

She waited for him to leave her. He didn't. His gentle, pleading eyes filled with tears. "Jacqueline —" he whispered.

She met his eyes — the eyes of the only man to whom she'd ever surrendered any measure of her self-control. The keen, penetrating eyes of the King's bodyguard, yes, but also the sweet brown eyes in which, night after night, she had seen her true self reflected as she gave herself to him, and he to her. How could those eyes have not seen the truth?

"Alain, you *are* my life. Did you not know that?"

He caught his breath. Before he could speak, someone tapped at the door and opened it. A heavy-set man wearing a white powdered wig peeked in.

"Someone needs patching up, I hear?"

De Guise laid his head in Jacqueline's lap and she stroked his wild, unkempt curls.

9.

JACQUELINE COULD HEAR MR. SMITH AND OTHER MEN ARGUING LOUDLY in the salon as de Guise escorted her downstairs for a Bedford luncheon that afternoon. They broke off their argument to stand when she entered, but their anger smoldered so bitterly Angélique had to cover her nose at the smell of so much inflamed passions in the suffocating heat of the salon. Jacqueline tried to hide her disappointment that the most outré of her sister's friends had ignored the social convention of departing when hosts were indisposed to guests. She frowned at Angélique, who pressed her fist to her head to indicate her own frustration.

When they sat, Mr. Smith declared, "I will still insist such acts are disgusting and unnatural. An offense against God. Scripture is quite clear."

The King's peremptory tone vexed Jacqueline. The hours of tender, luxuriant caresses she had passed in de Guise's arms had restored a portion of her sense of self and self-mastery. She wished only to return to her role as head of the household, and would suffer no usurper, not even the King of the French. She lounged on the divan, assuming the pose of a queen of Egypt.

"Scripture is rarely clear, Mister Smith," she admonished. "If it were, we'd have no need of faith. What have you encountered these past few days that you could *possibly* consider unnatural?" she asked, gently teasing him. "I will warn you, though, messieurs," she said to the room at large, "I'm in no mood for discussion. I prefer to deal with physics, not metaphysics. One plus one will always be two."

De Guise poured her a glass of Bellesfées wine and took a place near her. "Except where two will forever be one." He touched his glass to hers, holding her in his gaze still warm from their hours of reconciliation.

Angélique agreed. "I am further not inclined to hear any protests about what one believes God *should* have created over what *has been* created, and therefore is obviously God's design and perfectly natural." She shrugged when Llewellyn snickered.

Mr. Smith shifted and cleared his throat to reassert himself in the presence of the formidable twins. Madame Heine rose to pour herself more wine and focus on the light fare of fruits and cheeses, having little interest (nor sufficient intellect, Jacqueline noted) in the argument. Seated around a small table off to the side of the hearth, the Marquis de Custine and his companion wore angry frowns, while Heine refused to engage in any discussion with Mr. Smith, whose rise to the throne he had endorsed but now felt betrayed by the King's response to the Damascus Affair.

Yet, they all perked up to listen to Jacqueline. Les Dumas père and Charles seemed particularly heated by whatever topic had set off the disagreement, the flame of anger tingeing their cheeks as they glowered about the room waiting for someone to pursue it further. Jacqueline suspected they had even surreptitiously laid wagers. Little wonder Angélique could not nudge them away.

"What say you, Jacky?" Angélique prodded with wicked glee. "Let la Belle Dame de Bellesfées be heard, so we can put an end to this once for all. Tell us your thoughts."

Jacqueline's first thought was to curse her sister for cultivating bohemian habits like these intellectual scrimmages, and with such irrational creative sorts who would likely amount to little beyond their fanfaron, with the exception of les Dumas, of course. No one of any significance cared for Heine's angry pessimism; and while Charles had occasional moments of insightful lyricism, his poetry was, for the most part, jejune, and she feared his newfound love was leading him into darker meditations. Dumas's supplying of haschich and dawamesc didn't contribute to Charles' well-being either, and he would likely come to a poet's tragic but unremarked end.

Still, Jacqueline could never refuse Angélique, nor a chance to assert command of the situation.

"Honestly, messieurs," Jacqueline said with a vicious smile, sipping her wine slowly, making sure she had their attention, "I say, I've just had my head sewn back together like Madame Shelley's creature. It aches with every word I speak. Look into my black-butter eyes and tell me you don't sympathize with my anguish. Therefore, if you demand I play these silly Paris parlor games with you, I will suffer no counterpoint. Once I've had my say, you will take your leave, *as you have been requested to do.*" She emphasized the phrase with a stern wagging of the finger.

"Soit," Charles agreed. "As you wish."

"So I say this. First, I'm hungry. Would someone please bring me something to eat before I give you all something to ruminate upon?"

Charles complied, eager to hear the forthcoming speech. He brought her a plate of peach slices, figs, and cheese, and retreated with a bow. She dined between declamations.

"Now then, natural versus unnatural, that old bone. Honestly, Monsieur Dumas, haven't we moved on?"

Dumas grinned and nodded an apology of little remorse.

Jacqueline clucked. "The church would have us believe we're born tainted, while philosophers would argue the natural man is utterly innocent from birth. Personally, I don't know what it is to be a natural man, for I was born a woman. I *am* a woman. A natural woman, and a woman by nature. I hope I need not substantiate that claim, but should you need a witness, Marthe has bathed me enough since I was a child to testify to the veracity of my statement."

The men chuckled, and Vordenburg rapped his walking stick in approval.

"Yet, because I wear clothing that's comfortable and suitable for my work, I'm often accused of not being a natural woman, even of attempting to be a man. Is that fair, to deny my God-created nature based on the man-made creations that adorn me? Man-made rules dictate clothing must be worn, but should man-made rules determine which clothes I can or cannot wear?"

"Femina simplex, I say," Charles responded, thumping the table.

"Thank you, Charles," she acknowledged, "I think? Now, if we wish to drag Scripture into our arguments, I would have to confess, I know of no natural law of physics that explains how water can be transformed into wine, nor by what force of gravity a man might walk on the sea without breaking the natural surface tension. Reach out your natural hand, messieurs, and reshape the bones in Baron Vordenburg's leg, would you? No? Indeed, those are unnatural behaviors, yet according to Scripture, those are the behaviors of the Christ, who has insisted we follow his example. Or is the Christ also an unnatural offense against God?"

When Mr. Smith opened his mouth to protest, she cut him off. "My home, my discourse, no counterpoint." She smiled primly. "Ah, those pesky Scriptures. St. Paul, for example."

When Custine and his companion steeled themselves, Jacqueline confirmed that this was the bone of contention: intimacy between two of the same gender. The Marquis de Custine was a registered homosexual in the Paris police records. It was only by the grace of his social standing and his generous salons that he kept company with the artists and intellectuals of Paris.

Regardless of social mores, however, any accusation of sexual immorality from the King of the French, a man who had more mistresses than children, Jacqueline considered nothing less than hypocrisy.

"St. Paul speaks of God abandoning sinners to unnatural passions. What are *natural* passions, if not the ones with which we are born? Or, as in some cases, re-born?" She winked at Angélique and Llewellyn, who smiled at one another. "Natus. Birth. The root of the word 'nature,' n'est-ce pas? The passions with which we are born define our nature; so, if we believe we are created, we must believe we are created to be what we become. Naturally."

Raising her glass, she saluted Custine, who beamed at her and gripped his companion's hand — a hand much more finely manicured than her own, she noted with a touch of chagrin. Mr. Smith glowered, but kept silent.

Then she dropped her teasing tone. "Consider the legend of the vampire, or the werewolf. Those re-born against their will."

Certain ones around the room sat up, and though Vordenburg bristled, Angélique and Llewellyn leaned forward, amused yet intent. Dumas père folded his hands in delight and nudged his son.

"The Wolf-Leader," he said. "It's an old werewolf legend, but a fascinating study in the loss of one's soul, the loss of one's self. I've been working on a novel—"

"But those are demons," Mr. Smith interrupted with a note of finality. "To be consumed by the Devil is not to be reborn."

"Let us say, they are given a new life," Jacqueline amended. "Creation, re-created. Therefore, they have a new nature. It is the vampire's nature to feed on blood, the wolf's nature to hunt and devour. We all need our fuel."

She held up her empty glass, and de Guise replenished it dutifully, his eyes twinkling.

"What's the difference between the human and this re-born creation?" she asked. "Only this: those re-creations do what our teachings—which are man-made creations—have *told* us is unacceptable; therefore, we're *told*, they must be evil. Or as Mister Smith would have it, 'disgusting and unnatural.' I tell you, it is what it is, we are who we are, sumus quod sumus. And if we are to claim the Holy Scripture as our basis of judgment upon others, let's remember a few alternative verses. I wear a linen chemise, leather pants, and woolen hose. I can't recall if Scripture dictates I should be stoned for that, or simply banished. Les Dumas are dark-skinned due to their West Indies African blood; Scripture tells us Africa was settled by the sons of Ham, cursed by God to serve. What do you think, my friends, are Dumas père et fils to be made our slaves for the curse of the color of their skin? Scripture further states, most emphatically, 'You shall not commit adultery.' Do you consider adultery unnatural, Mister Smith? Or is it simply a natural passion, the taint of which our priests wash clean in the confessional like so much dust on the altar, then provide the appropriate indulgences in exchange for some specie, only to repeat the ritual from week to week? No, no. Scripture is clear on the topic of adultery, at least, and far more equitable than French or ecclesiastic law: Death for both parties."

She sipped her wine as the guests guffawed and Mr. Smith squirmed.

"So now tell me, monsieur," she pressed. "Which of our many *natural* tendencies on display here are you condemning?"

When the King made no answer, she concluded, "The Christ has also said, 'Judge not.' That is all. Now, everyone, go home and leave me alone. I came down here to rest and munch in peace, and you have sorely vexed me."

A stunned silence reigned. Then Dumas père chuckled. "You are playing with us, madame."

Her eyes flashed in subtle anger. "You invited me to play, monsieur. Quod erat demonstrandum. I win."

After a moment, Charles stood and applauded. The others joined in, laughing, and she exaggerated a modest bow. Only Mr. Smith remained unmoved, although his mischievous smile did threaten to appear. He accepted his chastisement with a good-natured dip of his chin.

De Guise commented, "Chérie, if you made such discourse two hundred years ago, you would have been burned at the stake."

"*Pfft*. My heresy will still be heresy two hundred years from now, I've no doubt."

He clinked his glass to hers. "To heresy then." He turned to the guests. "My friends, Madame Duval came to the salon for a well-deserved afternoon of rest, and instead you drew her into a most taxing exercise in patience and oratory. Shame on you. May all your disputes be settled by such Solomonic wisdom."

"Indeed," cried Charles, clapping Dumas père on the back.

Angélique added, "If you need further views on the topics at hand accompanied by piano, please, by all means, betake yourselves to Nohant, where Madame Sand would be thrilled to oblige you, while Chopin will rally his sorry frame to entertain you, as he usually does."

De Guise stood and inclined his head with a formal dismissal. "But now I insist you observe her request. Since both mistresses of Bellesfées have found themselves indisposed, Madame Duval has begged us to bring the festivities to a close, and with regret we must send you on your way. We secured rooms for you all in Orléans, and Jean-Paul will be happy to convey you there as soon as you can be ready."

De Guise ushered the hangers-on out of the salon. Smith, Vordenburg, Angélique, and Llewellyn accompanied him.

Alone in peace at last, Jacqueline lay back on the divan with a heavy sigh. The five stitches in her forehead pulled, and her head burned, but at least the blinding throb was gone. The quiet of the salon was enhanced by children's giggles and squeals out on the lawn, where one of the hired village boys had pulled a pig bladder over his head to cover his eyes and nose. As if he didn't look silly enough, the boy began inflating the casing by blowing through his nose. Giggles turned to shrieks and howls of laughter. Jacqueline, too, chuckled at the sight of the little body weaving about with an inflated head, chasing his playmates until he tripped. The bladder flew off along a dizzying path. The children traced it down to begin the game again.

Images teased her. De Guise popping a champagne cap. The bladder zipping through the air. Air propulsion. Like water jets. Could steam alone create a force strong enough? Volume, pressure, the design of the jets, the weight of the freight…

"Ah, we've lost her again," de Guise said, returning. "Come back to me, my love."

The others filed into the salon behind him. They were once more just six.

"I think I've had as much of Monsieur Dumas as I can endure for a while, and I am not sorry to see Charles go," Jacqueline grumbled good-naturedly. "He may have been invaluable to us in Paris, but between his dissipation and his tendency to appear out of nowhere at the most inopportune times…"

She pushed herself to sit up, making room for de Guise to settle beside her. "I'm sorry for crossing you, Mister Smith, but discussion aside and rank notwithstanding, it was not your place to insult my guests in my home. I find nothing offensive in the intimacy between the good marquis and his companion. They hurt no one." She shivered. "Still, I'm very glad to be rid of your friend Countess Laroche, Angélique. When a woman's Sapphic attentions are neither sought nor desired…" She waved her hand in dismissal. "For that matter, anyone's persistent attentions when they're clearly not requited. I'm just glad she's gone."

The others looked at her, perplexed.

"And who is this Sapphic Countess Laroche?" Angélique asked.

Llewellyn said, "Was she the woman Charles spoke of last night?"

"You didn't see her?" Jacqueline looked from one to the other around the room. "Surely you noticed her. Stunning beauty and elegance. Sultry-voiced. Seductively graceful. Fragrant of jasmine." She wrinkled her nose. "Made me feel like an ox standing next to her."

"I'm sorry to have missed her." Mr. Smith tugged his whiskers.

But Angélique pursed her lips. "Is that what put you in this mood? Jacky, no one should ever make you feel less of a woman, especially another woman."

"As I've said," de Guise added, "you are never less than." He kissed her head.

"Jasmine?" Llewellyn caught Angélique's arm. "Fy nghariad, didn't you say —"

Baron Vordenburg exploded angrily. "Laroche!" he shouted. "French for 'rock.' What was her full name? Do you know?"

Jacqueline gauged the severity of his tone. Only one theme could have produced such a response. Realization struck her with a force that shamed her. "Carmilla Pierre. 'Karnstein' also means 'rock.' Oh, you should hit me in the head with that rock. Carmilla — Mircalla. How could I have been so blind?"

De Guise jumped up, spilling his wine. "You met her? You spoke with her? The thing that's been preying on — the thing that attacked you? Jacqueline — " He stopped and drew a deep breath to calm himself. He groaned, then chuckled forlornly. "I swear, Jacqueline. The day I met you, you knocked my hat off, but since that day, you keep knocking my feet out from under me."

Llewellyn tossed him a napkin to mop himself. "Because, dear fellow, you keep treading where you're not meant to walk. Didn't Monsieur Duval warn us? This is Bellesfées, and his daughters cannot be tamed. Stop trying."

Jacqueline lay back on the divan and closed her eyes. "Fine. It's done. Carmilla Pierre, the Countess Laroche, is Mircalla the vampire. Now that we know, let's move on. I've been bitten. Vordenburg, tell me what this means."

Vordenburg cleared his throat, but his voice still quavered with anger. "It means your mind is now vulnerable to Mircalla's call. You are under her control, and you must do as she bids you to do, feel what she forces you to feel. You are no longer your own."

Conversation at the dinner table was blessedly subdued, if tense. De Guise and Mr. Smith discussed returning to Eu safely and soon; de Guise wanted to be able to focus on Jacqueline, and Mr. Smith agreed. Vordenburg believed that on his excursion with Monsieur Claque, he had located the general area where a Roman burial ground might be hidden, so he and Llewellyn laid plans to locate it the next day and, if it proved to be Mircalla's resting place, defile it and destroy the creature. Angélique leaned on Llewellyn's arm listening in.

Jacqueline brooded in silence at the head of the table. When she closed her eyes, she could close out the voices around her and focus on the threads she needed to tie together.

Esprit was vulnerable to the assassins. A rifle shot from the ground or from the thermal balloon, if that was indeed their conveyance, would not endanger the envelope, but from the right angle it might strike someone on deck. If Jacqueline's repeating guns could outdistance the rifle, she would bring down the balloon in a fiery crash before they could fire a shot. Would the assassins be smart enough to realize these facts?

The gondola of the Montgolfier only held two, while Llewellyn and de Guise were certain there were at least six involved in the conspiracy; she had to admit she could be leaping to the wrong conclusion about the role of the balloon. However, the coincidence of its rising at the same time as *Esprit* ate at her. Angélique always scolded her for over-dramatizing circumstances, but such usually proved Jacqueline right. She had to find a way to defend against the balloon. Once she destroyed it, there were still others to be reckoned with. Perhaps she could rig the revolving guns on a kind of ball turret whereby she could shift the aim from the balloon to the ground. Slay them. Slay them all.

"Absolutely not!" Vordenburg said sharply, bringing Jacqueline's attention back to the table.

Angélique giggled while Llewellyn suppressed his own laughter. They glanced up at Jacqueline.

"I merely asked if I might serve as bait," her sister explained in mock innocence.

Jacqueline smirked. "You're obviously the wrong flavor." She closed her eyes again.

Angélique sobered. She turned her chair to face Jacqueline and folded her hands over hers. Her wedding ring gleamed by the light of the gasolier. Jacqueline smiled sadly. For the first time in her life, she regarded her sister with envy.

"You're still hurting," Angélique observed. "Is it just your head, or is there more to it?"

Jacqueline measured her response. "I don't know if I can put it into words." She plucked at the tablecloth. "I feel childish thinking it. It's nothing rational."

In a quiet but firm voice, Angélique told her, "You curse yourself for allowing her to attack you. You think yourself stupid for not realizing this Laroche was our monster. You think it was your fault you were set upon. That you must have done something to encourage her, or that you didn't do enough to discourage her. You think you somehow deserved the violence visited upon you. Yes, you do," she stopped Jacqueline's protest. "What's more, you believe you now don't deserve to be loved for who you are because who you are could not prevent what happened to you."

Jacqueline immediately shook her head, but Angelique forestalled any response.

"No, no, m'amie, no argument. I know of what I speak."

She shuddered at the memory of Angélique in St. Petersburg, five years ago, when the shapeshifter Draganovich raped her, tore her apart, slaughtered her, and in so doing, made her the animal he was.

Angélique nudged her chair closer and pulled Jacqueline's head to rest on her shoulder. "Jacky, you've never thought of yourself as beautiful. You've said it to me often enough, and ever since you found love with de Guise, you've complained about your inadequacy. You feel you don't deserve him. Now on top of that, you feel shamed. Beaten. And you want someone to pay for all the anger inside you."

Jacqueline trembled. When had her wild sister become so wise?

Angélique set her tinted glasses on the table and lifted Jacqueline's face to meet her lupine gaze. "Do you think I don't know that anger? That shame? That desperate longing to find something to fill the unfamiliar rent in your spirit? What do you think has driven me to my imprudent behavior these past five years?"

"You got your revenge," Jacqueline observed.

"No. I got justice. But I never got back what was taken from me. That can never be replaced."

"Then what hope do I have?"

Angélique tugged Jacqueline from her chair and put her arm around her. The men stood, and de Guise started toward them, but Angélique waved him off.

"Jacqueline is exhausted," she said. "I will keep watch again. Your Grace, please do not go traipsing about holy grounds without me."

Llewellyn bowed; then he winked. "Your Grace, I would not dream of crossing you."

When they got to the bedchamber, Jacqueline began the task of undoing her evening gown. She paused in confusion when she saw Angélique grab pants, chemise, and a work vest and toss them on the bed.

"I know very well you will be miserable lying here alone, falling deeper into self-pity. Better to put your efforts into whatever project took your attention away from us earlier. Now hurry, before de Guise catches on," Angélique scolded. She untied Jacqueline's light bustle and corset knots. Then she had her sister undress her as well.

Jacqueline grinned at the shift in plans. Suddenly, her head didn't hurt so much. She donned her work outfit, making sure to transfer a new silver cross to her chemise. Once Angélique changed form, the two of them slipped down the back stairway and collected Monsieur Claque to head for the workshop. They passed Marthe on the way. The housekeeper glared in disapproval, then wagged her head and went on with her work. She knew better than to argue with the twins when they put their heads together.

On reaching her workshop, Jaqueline stopped abruptly at the gleam of silver at the lintel. She turned to her sister, tears pricking her eyes. "De Guise?" She *hmmph*ed. "I should have thought of that."

Angelique whuffed with a whine, then shooed her inside.

Jacqueline set Monsieur Claque to work gathering materials to build the type of weapon she'd contemplated at dinner. There was plenty of piping, and Jacqueline had already cast spare parts when she first re-designed Monsieur Claque. It was now a matter of welding, filing, and fine-tuning the timing mechanisms to build a revolutionary new weapon of defense for the airship. What she lacked, however, were sufficient shells to supply the ammunition. She would have to consult Luc in the morning before she could test her creation.

Angélique remained outside patrolling the area around the workshop and forge, poking her head in from time to time to check on Jacqueline's welfare. At some point in the middle of the night, Jacqueline noticed Llewellyn had spelled Angélique at sentry. She flashed a grateful smile but kept on working.

Esprit could now defend the King, but the concept of revolving guns nagged at her. She still required satisfaction for the vampire's assault. Guns had no effect on Mircalla. What then? Holy water and crosses?

"How did people fight vampires before the Romans turned the world Catholic?" she mused.

A wooden stake. Decapitation. A revolving rifle with enough speed to decapitate the countess. Not as effectively as a blade, though. A re-volving rifle of wooden stakes, perhaps? And for some reason, she kept returning to the idea of air jets, like water jets, as a form of propulsion. With enough steam pressure, she could fly. Better still, she could make Monsieur Claque fly; he'd be less likely to hurt himself on landing, though his mass would require more pressure. The design twisted itself around and inside-out in her mind, and the answer suddenly came to her. She called Monsieur Claque over to sit and bent to work anew.

A quiet, sultry voice intruded into Jacqueline's busy thoughts. *"Jacqueline."*

At first, she ignored the annoyance, as one would brush away a fly. Immersed in welding the final new steam tank onto Monsieur Claque's shell, she focused only on the bronze and the blaze.

"Jacqueline. Jacqueline!"

The voice persisted, like the workshop cat that constantly flicked her tail in Jacqueline's face in the middle of a project. Jacqueline growled.

"I'm working."

"I need you, Jacqueline. Only you."

"I said I'm busy. Go away and leave me alone."

"Never. Beautiful, exquisite Jacqueline. My own Jacqueline. Come!"

Like a bullet fired point-blank, Mircalla's call shot deep into Jacqueline's spirit. The workshop withdrew from her senses, supplanted by dark mists threading through her, stabbing like a needle to embroider her own words into her soul: *elegant, delicate, graceful*. The threads wove for her a reflection that could have been her own: *stunning beauty, audacious display of bosom, ample curve of the hips, hypnotic eyes*. Steam, coal, fuels, compressed gasses—these were powers Jacqueline commanded. Maths, science, and logic Jacqueline wielded with authority. Such power in femininity Jacqueline had never sought to master, but Mircalla offered it freely to her in a summons too strong to resist.

Her hands went numb, dropping the blow lamp. The sawdust on the floor ignited with a *fwoomp*. Turning from the flames, she walked out into the night, unseeing, unfeeling. As she plodded into the dense forest, the lamp exploded. Somewhere a wolf howled. She heeded only the call of Mircalla.

"Yes, Jacqueline. Come."

The cool darkness of the forest swallowed her, swallowed the sounds of alarm in her wake. Quickening her pace, Jacqueline slipped between the trees, heedless of the bushes and low branches whipping her leather pants, vaguely aware of a steady metallic tread behind her. A bell rang; not a church bell, not a single knell, but an insistent clamor, a tintinnabulation fading into the distance as she pressed on, following an instinct borne of sweet jasmine lulling her senses, pursuing an aura of pale green that drew her steadily forward until silence swathed her. Her heart raced, pounding in her ears. Closer. Almost there.

"Magnificent, my own Jacqueline."

She stepped into a clearing, into the fragrant mists, into the arms of the beautiful creature who had summoned her. She laid her head on Mircalla's bare shoulder, breathing in the sweetness of her pale flesh, listening for a pulse to answer her own, finding none. How could such sublime beauty be embodied in one undead? Overcome with awe, Jacqueline lifted her head to gaze into Mircalla's eyes, dark pools. Jacqueline longed to drown the reflection she saw there and be transfigured. Mircalla's alluring smile promised that much and more.

Mircalla removed Jacqueline's cap and brushed back her hair. Jacqueline tipped her head to the side, exposing her throat.

"No, Jacqueline. Remove the cross," Mircalla whispered.

The soft demand momentarily broke Jacqueline's thrall. Confused, she glanced down at the cross pinned to her work vest. A little thing. A man-made creation symbolizing a man-made religion. The Christ returned from death, called his followers to their great commission, then ascended. Mircalla too rose from the grave and called followers. Now she called Jacqueline to join her in apotheosis.

Jacqueline fingered the token, hesitant. God had created her as beautiful as her twin; she alone had contorted that beauty into the unappealing form she saw in the mirror every morning. She had no right to disdain what she herself had wrought.

No. She would not remove the cross.

She trembled as Mircalla traced the hem of her collar with her elegant nails, daring to tuck her fingers under the hem and caress her flesh. Jacqueline's will wavered at her touch.

Mircalla's hungry smile tightened. "Remove your vest, then," she said.

Jacqueline succumbed. No sooner had the vest fallen away when Mircalla ripped Jacqueline's chemise wide to slip from her shoulders. With a shocked cry, Jacqueline hastily crossed her arms over her breasts, staring into Mircalla's hypnotic eyes.

"Yes," Mircalla said, sliding her hands along Jacqueline's muscular arms gleaming with perspiration. "See yourself as I see you, Jacqueline. Feel what I feel. Such power in you, beautiful Jacqueline."

What power Jacqueline possessed leached from her with each touch of Mircalla's hands on her shoulders, her throat, her cheeks. Impotent, she suffered the vampire's claim on her body, unable to move, unable to protest.

The vampire pulled Jacqueline's arms away and cupped her breasts, squeezing them painfully. She pressed her mouth to Jacqueline's in a harsh kiss and pulled her closer, forcing Jacqueline to open to her. Her tongue wrapped Jacqueline's like a serpent and sucked it so tightly Jacqueline cried out in pain. Releasing her, Mircalla yanked Jacqueline's chemise down to bind her arms at her sides and expose her. Mircalla's alluring smile widened, displaying two sharp fangs. She dove down to savage Jacqueline's breast, gripping her in an obscene embrace like a wild beast clutching prey to feed.

Jacqueline felt nothing. No pain. No revulsion. No shame. Unable even to think, she stared at the night sky with empty eyes. Mircalla's will flooded into her.

Yes, she wanted this. Yes, she would surrender herself. Yes, she longed to be so loved.

Thus enthralled, Jacqueline melted into Mircalla's arms and watched herself vanish into Mircalla's whole being. Just when she thought she could surrender no more, Mircalla broke away, severing the blood tie connecting them, to run her talon-like nail along her own breast. A dark line appeared, then her blood oozed down. She caressed Jacqueline's brow tenderly, then seized her by her hair and shoved her face against the flow.

In the next instant, Mircalla screeched, hurling Jacqueline to the dirt.

Jacqueline lay confused, empty, as Mircalla scrabbled back, clutching a wooden stake embedded in her shoulder. The vampire hissed in fury and yanked it out. Shrieking, she dove at Jacqueline to feed again.

Llewellyn bolted into the clearing and leapt. Before he could bring her down, Mircalla dissipated into mist.

Jacqueline blinked away the vampire's will that had shrouded her mind. "W-where am I? What—"

Monsieur Claque hoisted her by her arms and set her on her feet, but she dropped to all fours, gulping air. "Claque. You shot her. New weapon—worked."

Monsieur Claque showed off the revolving stake gun Jacqueline had welded to his right arm. All the untested engines she had installed for wrist weapons and air propulsion chugged smoothly.

"You—you primed them..."

Llewellyn snarled in her ear.

"Llewellyn? I don't—"

The wolf nosed her. She saw the glow in the sky beyond the woods, at least a full two kilometers away. She had no memory of the distance she had traveled, but vague details rekindled.

"Claque, the gun!" she cried.

She foundered, unable to rise. Monsieur Claque got her to stand and she lumbered forward, trying vainly to command her arms to dress herself or her legs to pump. So tired. Her head buzzed. *Merde!* Monsieur Claque easily outpaced her. She pushed herself forward, tripping and faltering, dizzied, lost, following the lurid beacon, while Llewellyn harried her, snapping at her heels and nosing her when she paused.

By the time Jacqueline staggered to the workshop, the entire structure was engulfed in flames, but at least Monsieur Claque had retrieved the massive construct of revolving guns and turret. The rest of the household had mobilized the system of pump hoses from outside the forge to the workshop. Mr. Smith and Vordenburg manned two pumps, Jean-Paul and Marthe guided the hoses, and Luc and de Guise sprayed down the flames. Some of the neighboring villagers, summoned by the alarm, drove onto the grounds armed with buckets and formed a line from a third pump.

Acrid smoke burned Jacqueline's nose and throat as she gaped at the hellscape before her. Her eyes stung, streaming. She ripped away a sleeve and tied it around her face, then tottered forward a few steps before Llewellyn thwarted her, snapping and driving her back from the fire.

Vordenburg yelped. "Mein Gott, a wolf! Madame Duval, come away!"

Llewellyn kept Jacqueline at bay. She swayed, helpless, at the edge of the radius of searing heat, retracing her memory to the moment Mircalla had summoned her. Claque. The blow lamp. An explosion.

"The fuel canisters!" she cried, then coughed in spasms. "Claque!"

Monsieur Claque set the gun down and marched back into the inferno. He emerged wreathed in smoke, carrying the entire cabinet, the canisters within knocking against the steel-and-cement sandwiched doors.

"What else?" de Guise called to her.

What else? Tools, winches, pulleys, chains, cogs, sprockets, vises, clamps, designs, materials… *Everything!*

Her senses whirled. She collapsed on the soaked ground and clutched mud. The burning wood groaned.

"Back away," de Guise cried. "Everyone, back, it's going to— *Jacqueline!*"

Too late. The workshop listed and keened.

Monsieur Claque scooped up Jacqueline. Knocking his knees together, he ignited the jets she had installed on his back. His heated casing scorched her exposed skin. She screamed in pain as Monsieur Claque shot through the air and landed neatly to set her on her feet at the entrance to the château, where Angélique received her into her arms.

"You did it, m'amie!" Angélique crowed.

In the distance, the workshop fell in on itself in a conflagration.

Jacqueline's heart broke. Her spirit collapsed within her, leaving a void of despair. Dropping to the stones, she wailed.

"I've lost it all!"

Angélique knelt beside her, cooing soothing sounds, careful not to touch her burns. "Revolving guns, a flying autonomaton, and a wooden-stake launcher. I'd say that's a good night's work." She wiped tears from Jacqueline's face. "Now, let's go get that bitch."

10.

ANGÉLIQUE HALF CARRIED JACQUELINE UP THE MARBLE STAIRCASE TO HER chambers and helped her into bed. The pillows still carried the warm scent of de Guise from their morning reunion. Unbidden came the sensation of his careful caresses, now superimposed by Mircalla's bold, demanding touch. Shame welled up from the depths of Jacqueline's soul; with it, a cry of inexpressible despair.

Angélique folded over her, brushing back her hair. "What? What is it?"

She couldn't say, couldn't confess it. The brash obscenity of the vampire's will that consumed her, filling her head with such lusts as she had never felt or wanted to feel. The thrill that shook her being and aroused base desires. The syrupy thick voice demanding, "Feel what I feel."

Jacqueline curled away from her sister, clutching her torn, bloodied clothes tightly closed. "Go away, go away. Don't touch, don't look."

"Jacky, tell me. Tell me what's wrong. What happened?"

"I can't. Not yet. Go away." She buried her head under the pillow seeking to cover herself with de Guise again, to make her body belong to him.

The pillow wiggled and shifted, then Angélique's face appeared as she too ducked under and snuggled up close to her. She wiped Jacqueline's tears, leaving her hands smudged with soot. Angélique grinned as she pulled the coverlet out from under them and brought it over their heads.

"I remember this fortress against the world," she whispered conspiratorially. "Nothing could get us so long as they couldn't see us. Keep your hands and feet tucked in, m'amie, or they'll catch you."

Jacqueline groaned and buried her face.

Patiently persistent, Angélique gently rubbed her back. "Jacky, when was there anything we couldn't share between us?" she said. "When I thought my life was ended, you held me, carried me, brought me back. Every foul thing I've ever done, you took me in and nursed me. We're together. What can we not face when we're together?"

Her sister's words were not enough to ease Jacqueline's anguish.

"If anything, it's my fault for taking you out there." Her sister kissed her cheek and snuggled into her shoulder. "I thought if you were able to accomplish some measures against what we're up against, you'd feel like yourself again. When Vordenburg spoke of Mircalla 'calling' you, I didn't realize it meant drawing you away. We thought we could prevent her from getting near you. We didn't understand the extent of her power. It's our fault. *My* fault."

But it wasn't. They had sneaked out like two mischievous children defying their parents to play in the sandbox, ignoring the safety of their beds. Jacqueline carried the burden of guilt, knowing she was susceptible to the vampire's call, arrogantly believing herself strong enough to refuse Mircalla's demands. She had imagined confronting a monster and overcoming it with physical strength. She was very certain she could have slain a monster. She was not, however, prepared for Mircalla's seduction.

"She made me feel things," she said with disgust. "I didn't know she could do that. Ugly. Lust. Nothing I'd ever want for myself."

Not love, but a travesty of the tender love and sweet mutual surrender that enveloped her in her most intimate moments with de Guise.

Alain!

"How can I face him again?" she cried. "I'm so ashamed."

Laying her hands over Jacqueline's, Angélique said softly, "Gryffin told me what he saw."

When Jacqueline wailed and tried to roll over, her sister tugged Jacqueline's clenched hands around her waist and pulled her into an embrace. They were children whispering their confidences under a canopy of blankets. Their hearts beating against one another, Angélique's arms carried her to a place of safety, to a time when they needed only each other, two halves of a whole dreaming, giggling or grieving. Sisters.

Combing her fingers through Jacqueline's hair, Angélique told her, "You were not conscious, Jacky. He saw your eyes, and they were not yours. You were mesmerized. Whatever you think you've done, it wasn't you. Mircalla forced her desires upon you, forced you to experience them, hoping you'd share them."

Jacqueline gulped back a sob. "That doesn't mean I felt them any less. I disgust myself."

"Why?" Angélique's whisper, close to her ear, echoed her own anxious thoughts. "Are you so jealous of her beauty that you long to possess her?"

She gasped. "No!"

Again, Angélique calmed her. "Do you want her to possess you?"

"*Pfft.*"

"Good, then." Her sister hugged her closer. "You're still the indomitable, incomparable, brilliant Jacqueline Duval, my sister, my twin, overly innocent, infinitely naïve, and now grievously violated by an unnatural creature with unnatural passions. I have been where you are, m'amie. I know the way home."

A breeze through the window brought a waft of fresh air fragrant with roses to clear away the bitterness of burnt wood and ash. Holding each other — one to lend strength, one to draw comfort — they slept until dawn.

Marthe had laid out food for the villagers from the abundance of banquet leftovers, but she set a smaller buffet in the breakfast room for family and guests. The windows facing south were closed against the pervasive odor of the fire, but the west door was open, allowing a dewy breeze. As the sisters entered, the men broke off their discussion, and de Guise hurried to greet Jacqueline with a trembling embrace, mindful of the gauze wrapping her blistered left arm and shoulder.

"My brilliant, brilliant love," he murmured in her ear.

Jacqueline shied, but tugging her back to his arms, he lifted her chin and met the fear in her eyes with reassurance. "Llewellyn explained."

She grimaced. "Vordenburg warned me I would be under her control. I just didn't anticipate —"

"No one anticipated your walking off and torching your workshop behind you," he finished for her. "Llewellyn had a hard choice to make, but if the gas lines had blown, Bellesfées would have been lost, as would we all be. I'm just thankful he stopped her in time. And look at what you accomplished, my love."

Little solace, considering all it had cost. Pulling away, she sat, head bowed, digging the heels of her hands into her thighs until they hurt.

Vordenburg drew a notebook and pencil from his pocket, opened to a fresh page, and asked her, "Do you remember what happened to you this time? Did you hear a voice?"

Jacqueline worked her jaw, unwilling to confess her obscenity openly before Vordenburg and Mr. Smith. Mircalla's first attack had left her without memory of the assault. Why did she recall this one in such intimate detail? Revulsion clenched her stomach.

"I was aware of everything," she said bitterly. "I just couldn't stop myself. She called, and I followed. I heard the blow lamp fall. I heard Claque and Llewellyn. I heard the fire alarms. I just—followed. And I *wanted*—"

She glanced at de Guise, but she saw only worry in his expression.

"No, madame. That was not *your* will," Vordenburg assured her. He tapped his notes. "It is my theory that when the vampire bites, it leaves behind an infection that makes its way somewhere *beneath* the consciousness of its victim. Not unconsciousness, but I would say *unter*-consciousness. Mircalla forced herself on you. The more important question is this, madame: Did you drink her blood? Your wounds are still with you. That is good."

Jacqueline scoffed. "You think so?"

Vordenburg signaled to de Guise, who brought her brioches, eggs, and cheese from the side board. Grateful for the distraction, she bit greedily into the pastry, filling her mouth with sweetness and forestalling further interrogation. A smile came to Vordenburg's face.

"Good. Eat. If you had drunk any of Mircalla's blood, your wounds would have healed."

"Ah, well, perhaps I should have partaken," she said ruefully.

"No, *no*, madame. For if she bites a third time and you have her blood in your veins, you lose all appetite for food and soon—"

Vordenburg snapped the notebook closed. "Your Grace," he said to Llewellyn, "shall we execute our plan?"

Llewellyn halted, fork halfway to his mouth. "After some coffee? My night was somewhat longer than yours."

"You have only yourself to blame," de Guise said.

Llewellyn waved his fork in mock protest. "I swear it was all my wife's fault."

"The fault is entirely Mircalla's!" Jacqueline slammed her fist on the table, rattling plates and glassware. She glared about the room, brandishing a table knife full of red currant jelly. "If anyone is to share in it, it falls to me. Say what you will, Vordenburg, but if I were wiser, I would have insisted more people accompany me instead of sneaking off hoping no one would find us. Thoughtless, impulsive, and selfish. That's who I am, and that is why the blame lies with me. No one else."

Protests erupted but Jacqueline would hear none of them. She focused on her breakfast, making certain she indeed enjoyed the flavors and had lost none of her humanity. When the arguments grew too annoying, she broke in.

"Tell me what progress you've made on finding the German-speaking suspects," she said loudly enough to stop the other discussion. "I've done my part with Claque's new weaponry and the ball-turret revolving gun for *Esprit*."

After an embarrassed silence, de Guise said, "Truthfully, I'd like to see an end to this vampire horror before I return Mister Smith to Eu."

"But I can't help feeling a sense of urgency for his safety," Jacqueline argued. "The sooner we can get him away, de Guise, the sooner—"

He put a finger to her lips. "Alain," he reminded her, his eyes soft. He caressed her face, pulled her closer, and kissed her lightly.

A blush filled her cheeks as she murmured, "Alain."

The smile on his pretty bow lips warmed her to her toes, returning her to a true sense of womanhood. She didn't need to be beautiful if she could simply be herself and still be part of de Guise.

"Tell us your plan," he said.

She regathered her thoughts. "*If* your enemy employs a Montgolfier, and *if* they were mad enough to attempt a night flight, the burner that heats the air for the balloon would be highly visible in the dark. *Esprit*, on the other hand, is all but invisible at night. That's why I think we should depart this evening."

Mr. Smith's eyes widened. "I hadn't thought of that. Of course you can navigate by night. It's a ship, after all."

"And it's dirigible, whereas the balloon is not," Llewellyn added. "I think that's a splendid plan. What's our first step?"

"A visit to the village priest," Vordenburg replied. "We need a quantity of blessed water."

Jacqueline held up a hand. "On that subject, I was thinking I could fashion—" Then her face fell. "*Zut.* I don't know if—that is, the parts—a burner, tank, hose, gaskets, nozzle—"

"We could cannibalize Claque," Angélique suggested, and shrugged when Jacqueline glowered.

Llewellyn laughed. "I think she'd sooner cannibalize one of us, fy nghariad."

"But I could use one of the porters." Jacqueline munched another brioche, her thoughts tracing a design in her mind. "Yes, one of the steam tanks, a pump, nozzle. I'll dig out some tubing from the ashes. I'm sure not all of it was lost."

Mr. Smith clapped his hands and stood. "Splendid!"

He pitched face down on the table and fell to the floor. In the instant came the blast of a rifle shot from a distance. De Guise dove from his chair to protect the King, grunting mid-air as another shot followed the first. De Guise dropped on Mr. Smith's prostrate form, covering him from further harm.

"De Guise!"

Jacqueline threw herself to the floor as the breakfast room exploded in gunfire. Lllewellyn shoved Angélique under the table as the shots moved along the backs of the chairs, shattering plates and cups, tearing into the table linens and sniping chunks from the mantel. Keeping back from the range of fire, Llewellyn hurried to snatch the drapery tiebacks to cover the open doorway.

Silence fell. Llewellyn motioned Vordenburg back to a corner and carefully peered from behind the drapes.

"Nothing. They must be in the woods," he said. "Those were no muskets or mere hunting rifles. And all I can smell is the stench of burnt wood." He turned on Angélique fiercely as she crawled toward Jacqueline. "Stay down. No one moves."

"Your Majesty!" Jacqueline rasped, keeping her voice hushed as she bent over the fallen men. "Majesty!"

Mr. Smith coughed and drew a gulp of air. He answered with effort, "Alive, madame, thanks to your invention." He tried unsuccessfully to drag himself out from under de Guise, keeping to the floor. Blood covered his back. "I'm all right, de Guise. You can let me up. My God, they actually hit me this time."

Vordenburg squatted beside him. "They did indeed, Mister Smith."

"De Guise," Jacqueline urged. "Alain, my love."

When he made no reply, she wrapped her arms around him and pulled him off the King. De Guise was a dead weight. As she rolled him over into her lap, blood spread up his shirt from a dark hole in his side just below his ribs. His eyes, large and black, seemed to see nothing, and his breath came in shallow gulps. He gaped at Jacqueline, surprised, confused.

"No, no, no. *No!*"

Jacqueline pulled up his chemise and pressed against the bullet hole. Blood gushed over her hand. She snatched a napkin from Smith's chair beside her and shoved a portion into the wound, then leaned into it.

De Guise gasped. " — King?"

Mr. Smith tried to push himself up.

"Stay down, damn you!" Llewellyn ordered. "Anyel, get to the kitchens. I need clean linens and water. Tell Luc."

Staying low, Angélique left the salon. Jacqueline stared wildly about, then looked down at de Guise. A smile twitched his lips.

"King?"

She wailed and leaned harder on the wound.

Vordenburg also tried to press a linen to Mr. Smith's back, then backed away in surprise at the resistance. He peeled away the morning coat and waistcoat to discover the doubled copper-mesh vest. Mr. Smith grunted as Vordenburg pulled the outer vest mesh away. The lead ball popped onto the floor while the silk remained embedded in a small puncture in Mr. Smith's upper back to the right of his spine. He barely bled.

"Good. Ma chérie." De Guise closed his eyes. "So — brill — " His voice failed. His lips were turning blue.

Jacqueline couldn't find air. She pressed her weight behind her hands. All she could see was blood, de Guise's blood. "You can't. You can't. You can't. Alain. *Alain!*"

Someone pulled her away. She struggled, reaching for de Guise, her hands sticky and crimsoned. "No — "

"We'll take care of him, mademoiselle." Luc set her beside Angélique.

Colors blurred as she fell back into Angélique's lap. Many voices outside shouted and called to one another, "Over here!" "There! There they are!" "This way!" Then Marthe was washing Jacqueline's hands and arms. Talking to her. Words she didn't hear. Angélique tugged her into an embrace, murmuring in her ear. Jacqueline fought them both.

"Pincers. The porter —" Jacqueline sprang up and rushed from the salon, through the château, to the music conservatory. She dragged the porter from the lift and yanked the tool she needed out of the bag. She raced back to the salon. "We need to find the bullet."

She edged in beside Luc, setting steel pincers on the floor, and ripped de Guise's waistcoat and shirt from him to find a tear in the back of his shirt. She tipped his body slightly to see the shot had gone clear through him. More blood dripped.

"That's a good sign, isn't it?" She looked to Luc, pleading for the right answer.

Llewellyn took Jacqueline's place. He shoved a second napkin deeper into the abdominal wound and stuffed another into the hole at the back. Then he set his knee on the bandaging, giving it his whole weight. Jacqueline wailed in horror.

"I've years' experience with combat injuries," he insisted.

Jacqueline held her head, then winced when her hands pulled at the slash she had all but forgotten. "He's lost so much blood."

"I've seen far worse," Llewellyn assured her. "But we can do nothing until we stop the bleeding."

He glanced at Angélique, who then drew Jacqueline away to let the men work. She seated Jacqueline near the mantel and brought out brandy.

"At seven in the morning?" Marthe scolded, almost perfunctorily.

Vordenburg, meanwhile, slid Mr. Smith across the floor, keeping low and away from the windows until he could push him up onto a chair in the corner. He rolled Mr. Smith's shirt up to inspect the wound, eliciting a quiet grunt from the King.

"God was with you, Mister Smith," Vordenburg said. "A simple gauze and wrapping should suffice."

"Not God, Monsieur Vordenburg. It was Madame Duval's genius." Mr. Smith hissed in pain. "I wonder, Your Grace, Countess Llewellyn, if I too might have a brandy?"

"No," Llewellyn said. "No spirits. Not until it heals. Luc, is there anyone surveying the grounds? Not Jean-Paul."

"No, Your Grace."

"Will Monsieur Claque take your orders?"

"He'll take mine, the old tin-pot," Marthe said. "Where's that whistle?" She stormed out.

Angélique set the cordial glass to Jacqueline's lips and tipped it until she was forced to sip. "Jacky, listen. Listen! He won't die. We won't let him. Gryffin and I. We won't *let* him die."

The brandy burned all the way down, as searing as the conflagration in her workshop. Angélique's words, too, burned in her ears until they made a coherent thought and she realized what her sister was saying.

"No." Jacqueline shook her head. "Not without his permission. We can't—"

"But, Jacky—"

Jacqueline gripped Angélique's arm. "Don't you understand? Don't you remember what it felt like? To have this forced on you?"

Angélique knelt before her. "But he'll live. Gryffin—"

"Llewellyn had no choice," Jacqueline argued. "He was shot, you were shot. Your blood mingled with his. That could not be helped. This is different."

Llewellyn frowned at the two of them. "That's a discussion for another time," he said. "Let's concentrate on where we are now."

Mr. Smith huffed. "I don't understand the problem. The Duchess says she can save de Guise. I say—"

"Quiet!" three voices shouted in unison.

Vordenburg shook his head, unaware of the undercurrents. "Mister Smith, may I escort you to your chambers and there tend to this wound?"

Mr. Smith glared at the others. Then he waved, granting permission. Vordenburg crawled over to recover his walking stick. Mr. Smith had trouble standing, but he still hunched cautiously. He took Vordenburg's arm, and the two limped upstairs. From outside, the sound of Monsieur Claque's tread brought a measure of security.

Jacqueline got up and paced along the wall. "How do we convince these murderers they've succeeded? What would indicate the King is dead?"

Llewellyn grimaced. "Screaming 'The King is dead'?"

Jacqueline was about to argue when Angélique shrieked. "Dead? The King is *dead*?" She ran out the door to the west lawn, clutching her head and wailing. "My God! He's dead! The King is dead! What shall we do? It can't be! No! No! How awful! How terrible! He's dead!"

Her cries brought echoes from the villagers outside who had responded to the shots. Llewellyn nodded to Jacqueline. She followed Angélique's lead, though she had no need to feign her despair. The twins clung to one another, and Jacqueline wailed as they fell to the ground. She gripped the wet grass into her fists, desperate to hold onto de Guise. She couldn't let him slip away, now that she knew his heart as well as her own.

"Oh, God, he's dead. I couldn't—I can't—"

Angélique held Jacqueline and let her pour out her grief.

At last, as the sun rose above the treetops and brought the sky to bright blue, the villagers dispersed, taking the news with them. The twins also rose wearily and trudged back to the breakfast room.

"I need several more clean cloths and wrappings," Llewellyn said. "These napkins are drenched through. I shouldn't remove them, but I'd rather pack this with fresh bandaging."

Luc nodded and left. Once he was gone, Llewellyn turned grim.

"I want you to be certain, Jacky. If he doesn't wake, if it appears we will lose him, do you truly wish to let him go?"

Jacqueline knelt, then curled to the floor beside de Guise, stroking his hair and caressing his ashen face. "You've known him longer than I," she said. "What would you advise? You know what you're asking. Is this what he'd want? He's an agent of the King. His vision would change, but his senses would be heightened. Would lycanthropy help or hinder him? Would he welcome or resent awakening to discover he'd been changed without his consent? Should he move in international society wearing foppish sun-glasses? I can't answer these questions. I only know I have been changed against my will, and I'm filled with disgust and horror at what was done to me without my permission."

She laid her hand on de Guise's breast and felt his weakened pulse. She tucked her body closer and nuzzled into his shoulder. Her anguish melted as his familiar scent and the shape of his body next to hers transported her to a place of hope.

She kissed his neck, her tears soaking his collar. "Come back to me, my love."

It felt like hours before Llewellyn allowed de Guise to be moved to his room. Jacqueline had stocked rectified spirits for the reception to please their Polish guests; this served to cleanse the wounds.

"And if he wakes, pour some down his throat," Llewellyn quipped.

His good humor was not enough to convince Jacqueline that de Guise was out of mortal danger. "No spirits," she reminded him glumly.

Jean-Paul was dispatched to Beaugency to fetch a surgeon, since Angélique's friend Sédillot had left the previous day. Vordenburg was once again frustrated in his plans to hunt down Mircalla. Confined to his bed, Mr. Smith also fretted.

"We must maintain the illusion you've been assassinated," Jacqueline said as she tucked a light coverlet over him. "If you feel up to it, I'll transport you to Eu tonight. In fact, even if you don't feel up to it, I think that's what we must do." She fidgeted, scraping dried blood from her cuticles. "De Guise would insist on it. I know he would."

Mr. Smith surrendered. "I'm told I must not argue with la Belle Dame de Bellesfées." He calmed her hands, then shooed her away.

Angélique took Llewellyn's place at de Guise's side to give her husband some time to sleep. Jacqueline joined her, holding de Guise's hand.

"You should wash and change. You're covered in blood," Angélique observed. "You should also sleep if you're planning to fly out tonight. You're the only one of us who hasn't slept at least some of the night, and you're the one with that gash on your head."

Jacqueline stroked de Guise's clammy brow, twirling his curls. "What's a gash compared to this?"

"'This' is not preparing to take an airship to the coast, not after a vampire attack. You're weakened, whether you admit it or not, and it's more than two hundred fifty kilometers to Eu. That's more than eight hours at the helm. And I know you're preparing for war. I saw that thing you built."

Jacqueline growled. "Zut. I still need to install it before we take off."

When she closed her eyes, she felt herself falling off a cliff. Gently she set de Guise's hand on his chest. She longed to wrap herself around him and will him to live. Her whole body ached with a hollowness like a vast, black, empty ocean. She kissed him and left.

Jacqueline found young Anne in the kitchen kneading bread, herself dusted with flour. She told Anne to wake her at noon, then went to nap. Seconds later—or so it seemed—the girl woke her. In dismay, Jacqueline realized she had fallen asleep in her blood-drenched day dress, which had stained her bedclothes. She stripped quickly while preparing a bath, one of the amenities of the château even Versailles could not boast, as Mr. Smith had jealously commented: a full plumbing system, gravity fed, with heated water.

She dressed for work, then went to de Guise's room, where Angélique informed her that Jean-Paul had returned with the surgeon, who was with his patient, allowing no one but Llewellyn to assist him. Jacqueline gazed longingly at the closed door, blinking back bitter tears, then turned on her heel, Angélique calling vainly after her.

Jacqueline knew the only solution to her flagging spirits was to finish the task before her. She asked Vordenburg to assist in mounting the revolving guns on *Esprit*. By mid-afternoon she bolted the last nut on the turret, and Luc dropped a waterproofed case of cartridges on the deck beside the new gun. As they headed to the château, she was surprised to see Jean-Paul driving the cabriolet back from the village with the wizened curé on the seat beside him. Her buoyed spirits helped dispel the pounding at her brow.

"Llewellyn must have said something to him," she said. "Clever." She signaled Jean-Paul to go to the pumps and sent Vordenburg to meet him. "I'll be back soon with the proper vessel," she promised.

Once again, she raided the porter in the music conservatory. She found an appropriate capped tank she was sure she could modify into a canister with a spray device, and met the others at the pumps. The curé did not look happy with Vordenburg.

"What's wrong?" Jacqueline asked.

Vordenburg fumed. "He feels it is profane to bless a plain bucket of water."

"And so it is." Jacqueline showed the curé the polished tank. "This vessel has never been used for any worldly purpose. It is pure brass. It remains only for you to sanctify the container, then to sanctify the water that fills it, so evil will not prevail."

Her solution satisfied the curé. Within the hour Jacqueline had twelve liters of holy water for Vordenburg's use. She took the tank back to the porter and began to work, fashioning a usable sprayer with a vacuum pump and hand trigger, and a leather harness for Vordenburg to carry it on his back. She presented the finished canister to Vordenburg and he studied it in amazement.

"I suspect this will do some damage to a vampire if you get close enough," Jacqueline said, "or at least soak down the tomb to make it uninhabitable."

She hesitated, sighed, then laid her hand on his arm. "I'm being selfish when I ask this, monsieur, but I'm afraid to conduct the journey alone tonight. I have to admit my weakness is taking its toll. This creature has invaded *Esprit* once before, and may do so again despite my efforts. Mister Smith is wounded, so I can't depend upon his assistance if I should be—called away again. If you're with me, if you can wield that weapon, I will fear no furtive vampire in the ship's hull."

To her surprise, Vordenburg's eyes lit up. He clicked his heels and bowed deeply. "Madame, it would be my honor to escort you. I stand ready to defend."

She met his enthusiasm with a worried frown. "Understand, monsieur, Mircalla is not our only enemy. The flight may be fraught with peril."

He bowed again. "I am aware. And I shall be prepared."

Cradling the canister like a ten-kilo baby in his arms, he walked away.

11.

Marthe sounded the bell for dinner. Jacqueline wasn't sure if she was hungry or if the emptiness within her was something else. Mircalla's bite, lack of sleep, shock, exhaustion, terror, loss—fear of greater loss. She heard the others gather, but she wasn't ready to join them. Her life and the King's depended on Vordenburg's ability to defend her from Mircalla as much as her own ability to defend *Esprit* if the assassins pursued them. There was no good face she could put on their prospects, especially given the face she sported.

Jacqueline took the back stairway up to look in on de Guise. The room was dark, the drapes closed. The lamp on the mantel glowed faintly. De Guise lay still, pale as the linen of his pillow. The surgeon had assured them he would heal. Llewellyn had promised. But in that moment, the pall of de Guise's mortality blinded Jacqueline to any hope.

She climbed into the bed and lay beside him. His chest rose and fell evenly. His heartbeat beneath her hand was stronger than it had been that morning. She closed her eyes and dreamed of the mornings she had awakened just so, de Guise peacefully asleep, her hand on his breast, she breathing with his every breath, her whole body thrilling to the scent of him, the silvery-blond curls of his chest wrapping her fingers, her body wrapping his.

She had designed so many machines, so many devices, so many *things*; but she would never create anything as beautiful as the consummation of their two souls. And she could never create anything that would make it last forever.

Jacqueline awoke when de Guise groaned. She gazed at his face—drawn, tense. His eyes twitched and fluttered open. She hardly dared to breathe, hoping the pounding of her heart did not deafen him. He blinked and frowned, then slowly turned his head. He tried to smile, his bow lips flickering.

"Chérie," he whispered.

Relief washed over her. Her hushed voice quavered. "Mon amour."

He winced and swallowed. "I'm not dead then?"

Tears pearled in her eyes. "Not yet."

"The King?"

"We return to Eu tonight."

He startled, then grunted with pain. "No. Not—I—"

"You were shot, my love."

He relaxed again. "Ah. Not for the first time. How badly?"

She wiped her tears on her sleeve before they could fall on him. "The surgeon was here. You'll heal, but you must lie still. Rest. Sleep."

He murmured, "How can I rest if I can't keep you safe?"

She kissed his cheek as gently as she could, fighting the desperate urge to hold him tightly. As he breathed a heavy sigh, his whole body seemed to sink into the bed. His eyes closed. She waited, but he didn't stir.

Jacqueline rose from the bed and peered out the window. The scarlet band of sunset had turned to deep aquamarine beneath a sapphire sky. She had decided how to smuggle Mr. Smith aboard *Esprit*, in case their morning charade hadn't put off the assassins. She still had to safeguard Marthe and Anne against Mircalla's call in the event the vampire chose to stay and haunt Bellesfées rather than pursue Jacqueline. Either Monsieur Claque or Angélique and Llewellyn could serve as their guards.

She took one last look at de Guise. "Please, my love," she whispered. "Come home to me, and I swear I will come home to you."

Marthe thrust a laden plate at Jacqueline as soon as she appeared at the foot of the back stairway. Jacqueline sat in her childhood seat and hastily dined, eschewing wine for beef tea. "I'll take a few bottles with us, though," she said. "For the trip home."

"Good to see you eating at least," Marthe said as she tucked six bottles and a corkscrew into the basket she had already prepared with plenty of food.

Vordenburg must have said something to her. Jacqueline caught her arm and tried to find words, but Marthe swatted her away.

"You've a long night ahead and a long day tomorrow."

Jacqueline swallowed the lump in her throat. "You'll look after him?"

"What else have I to do?" The housekeeper hoisted the basket and swept away. "Much easier to look after him than the two of you."

Jacqueline chuckled and returned to her dinner. Anne watched her from the other end of the table. The girl still had flour on her apron and in her hair. Her eyes fixed on Jacqueline in awe.

"Does the cat still call your name?" she asked the girl.

Anne shook her head no.

"It's going to be all right soon, Anne. How do you like working with your tatie here at Bellesfées?"

Anne's head bobbed and she grinned. "I like Monsieur Claque. And I like the musicians. They're beautiful. So many amazing things here."

"If you like, I can show you how to make a musician of your own. Or your own Monsieur Claque."

The girl's eyes widened. Then they crinkled. "I don't think so."

"Why not?"

Jacqueline cast back to her own childhood. By the time she was Anne's age, she had already mastered the forge. It was probably too late for the girl to think about entering the Polytechnique, but she could still learn some mechanics if she wanted to.

Anne shook her head. "I'd rather work in the château. I can clean; I can help; Tatie Marthe can teach me to cook. I like being useful."

"Yes, I suppose cooking and cleaning are as useful as building things. Certainly safer." Jacqueline slid her empty plate aside and leaned her chin to her fists. "Would you like to be a lady's maid? I do need someone to help me."

Anne returned her gaze solemnly. "I didn't think you'd need anyone's help."

Jacqueline gave a rueful grin. "Oh, Anne. I never thought so either. But I was wrong."

Angélique entered the kitchen. "You, wrong? Never." She wrapped her arms around Jacqueline's neck and kissed her cheek as Anne scampered off. "Now you must decide," Angélique said, "who else goes with you besides Vordenburg? The correct answer is your loving twin sister, Angélique Aurélie Laforge, Duchess Llewellyn of Singlebury."

"Oh, mon Ange, I couldn't —"

"You didn't. So I'm telling you. Now, what's your plan?"

Jacqueline knew better than to argue when her sister was so close to choking her for a wrong answer. "We've done our weeping and wailing," Jacqueline explained, "and we've had the surgeon in. Now we need to return the body of our beloved king to his family. So, it must look like we are carrying a corpse to *Esprit*. Mister Smith must allow himself the indignity of being wrapped and enshrouded."

"Soit."

"If you're coming along, we'll need Luc and Gryffin to guard the château against Mircalla, especially Marthe and Anne, now that we know the extent of Mircalla's power to lure her victims away. Jean-Paul will keep a watch on de Guise along with the surgeon."

"We can do that too."

"And we —" She blew out a weary breath. "Well, we know Mircalla prefers women."

"She certainly prefers you."

"*Pfft*. But that doesn't mean she wouldn't attack the King en route to Eu, if she makes her way aboard the ship. And she can always come for me as well, equally putting the King in danger."

Angélique looked quizzical. "I thought you warded the ship."

"We did what we could. I placed a silver cross in every quarter, every cabin. But the ship itself is wide open, and she's already passed through it without being expelled, so I don't know if the wards will bar her. Besides, there are so many ways she could slip on board, I can't be certain we'll be safe." She shrugged. "For that matter, I can't be certain one of the assassins hasn't found a way aboard and is lying in wait for us."

"Ah, but I would know in either case." Angélique tapped her nose. "Shall we go? The sun is gone. The sky is dark enough."

Linking arms, they headed to the library. The others had already gathered along with Monsieur Claque. Mr. Smith had his bag. Jacqueline summoned Luc, then explained her orders to them all. Mr. Smith, rather than resisting, chuckled mischievously and rubbed his hands together. Luc arrived with two bed sheets, and he and Llewellyn loosely wrapped Mr. Smith as one would shroud a corpse before setting him in Monsieur Claque's arms.

"Don't worry, monsieur, he's never dropped anyone," Jacqueline reassured him. "Baron Vordenburg, you are ready?"

"I am."

Angélique gave Llewellyn a long and lingering kiss. He chucked her chin and kissed her brow. "Careful, fy nghariad Anyel."

"And you, mon amour."

A lump rose to Jacqueline's throat. She wanted one last kiss from de Guise. She wanted de Guise to give her his encouraging grin with those pretty bow lips. She blinked back tears and jerked her head.

Llewellyn caught her arm. "Come back safely. Come back for him."

The cortège proceeded slowly and mournfully out the back of the château to the field where *Esprit* was moored. Luc and Jean-Paul had opened the hydrogen canisters before sunset, so the monstrous envelope was sufficiently inflated, black in the night. With the château's windows all draped, no gleam reflected on the envelope's surface. The acrid smell of the charred workshop lingered, creating another kind of shroud.

Monsieur Claque led the group. Luc walked on Jacqueline's right, defending her from the dark of the forest. Vordenburg walked behind her. No one carried lanterns; nevertheless, Jacqueline felt exposed, fully expecting to be shot at any moment. Three hundred, four hundred meters. More. A thousand slow, pondering steps. Her heart pounded and her chemise was drenched with sweat. Almost there. She kept her head slightly bowed, leaning on Luc's arm as if grieving, but her eyes busily searched the grounds, the hillside, the edge of the woods.

At last, the group embarked, and as Vordenburg escorted Monsieur Claque down the ladder to secure Mr. Smith in the great cabin, the wolf Angélique slipped out of the shadow of *Esprit* and trotted up the gangplank onto the deck. She lifted her nose to scent the air. Slavering, she glared at Jacqueline and snarled.

Luc took in the exchange, and understood his lupine mistress sensed danger was near. "Mesdemoiselles?"

"No, Luc," Jacqueline told him. "Your task is here, at Bellesfées."

He glowered, unhappy to leave the twins in danger. He stomped down the gangplank and began the task of unmooring the great aerostat.

Jacqueline headed to the aft capstan and set the gauges. She threw the switch to initiate pulleys, locking the anchor rodes into place. The capstan slowly engaged and ratcheted up the cables. *Esprit* juddered, then left the ground, too slowly for Jacqueline's patience to endure. She kneaded the smooth handles of the ship's wheel.

When they cleared the treetops and she took in the nightscape of the Loire valley to the north, she breathed a sigh at last. Clouds floated high above them, but the skies were otherwise unoccupied. The ground below was nothing but open fields all the way to Chartres, a little more than an hour away. She checked their altitude and increased the hydrogen to take the ship up to a full thousand meters.

Angélique slunk to her side and nosed her. She whined and panted anxiously.

"Let me get us on our way first," Jacqueline answered, leaning over to scritch her sister's ears. "I'm so thankful you're with me, mon Ange." She then double-checked her silver cross was secure on her bodice, pressing against the offending bite on her breast.

Jacqueline visited the port and starboard capstans, and at the throw of a final switch the propellers engaged, nudging the ship forward. She climbed to the fo'c'sle and gazed out across the panorama. A glow on the horizon to the north indicated Chartres. Seizing a secured line, she wrapped it around her forearm and swung to the aft deck and the captain's wheel to make for those lights.

"Baron Vordenburg," she shouted. "Would you come on deck, please?"

In a moment, the Baron appeared in the doorway of the ladder, where he halted at the sight of Angélique.

"Yes, a wolf." Jacqueline beckoned him forward. "You'll have to get accustomed to her, for she may save our lives and help you accomplish your mission."

Vordenburg approached warily. Angélique eyed him, and Jacqueline suppressed a grin. Her sister loved to intimidate people.

"This wolf, Herr Baron, is my sister Angélique," she told him, and nodded when his look showed doubt. "The wolf you saw with me the other night when the workshop burned is her husband, the duke. You, who have pursued vampires, cannot be so daunted at the sight of other creatures out of legend."

Vordenburg stooped down to look into Angélique's eyes. She growled.

"Don't do that. She's a wolf. Wolves don't like being challenged." Jacqueline tapped his shoulder and made him leave off. "Angélique informs me Mircalla is aboard *Esprit*."

"What! But we—"

She held up her hand. "You and Angélique, go below and begin your task of anointing every inch of the hull, every passageway. Start at the great cabin and drive her forward. Angélique will know if Mircalla presents herself, and you must follow Angélique's lead."

"But you?"

"Send Mister Smith up to stand watch on my actions. Skies are clear and we're well away from any threat from the ground. My concern is that I don't bring you all into peril, and I think as the military mind here, the King is better suited to my plans."

He bowed and then followed Angélique belowdecks once more. A few minutes later, as Jacqueline had expected, there came a shout of horror. Mr. Smith slowly came on deck, visibly shaken by his encounter with Angélique.

"Now you may better understand my discourse on nature, Mister Smith," she said coolly. "We owe our lives many times over to what you have named unnatural, demon-born, re-created beings."

She gave him no time to reply. "You have two tasks, Mister Smith. If your assassins are not satisfied with our performance, one of those tasks should be simple: keep a weather eye out for that Montgolfier on the horizon. They couldn't attempt to pursue us, but they may have gone ahead to Chartres, Rouen, or somewhere between to intercept us. However, if they believe you're dead, the skies will remain clear."

She handed over her spyglass.

"And the second?" he asked.

Jacqueline held up a length of rope. "You are to tie me to the aft capstan to ensure I do not succumb to Mircalla's summons."

Mr. Smith measured the severity of her expression. With a sigh of misgiving, he secured her wrists to the bars she stood between, then wrapped the rope around her waist and tied it around the column of the capstan. He stepped back, and she tested her bonds.

"Well done," she said.

Mr. Smith remained uncertain. "I'm a military man, madame; my sons are the mariners. What is our contingency in the event you are incapacitated and *Esprit* requires navigation?"

"Monsieur Claque can keep us on course. I'm counting on Vordenburg and Angélique to keep me alive. But I do have a plan in the back of my mind should they fail."

She nodded dismissal. He gave a quick smile of encouragement, bowed, and climbed up to the fo'c'sle.

Esprit neared Chartres. Off to starboard, the gaslights of Paris lit the horizon, lending a dull gleam to the reflective envelope of the airship. A few minutes later, they could see Versailles. At the bow, Mr. Smith pointed, but since he had the spyglass, Jacqueline wasn't sure if he had spotted something amiss or was thrilled at the sight of the palace from this unusual vantage. He took the ladder carefully and joined her, his face a composed mask of determination; he was once again the indefatigable King of the French and not the whimsical Mr. Smith.

"There's something rising from the forest at Rambouillet," he told her. "I believe it's the Montgolfier. What is your plan?"

She chewed her cheek in frustration. "I'd hoped for more time. Go below and see how Vordenburg is progressing. Send Monsieur Claque to me."

She gazed toward Rambouillet, but the Montgolfier was still too far away for the naked eye. The breeze blew west. She doubted the balloon could be maneuvered accurately enough to intercept *Esprit*. Still, she wanted Monsieur Claque with her, second à la barre, since her own hands were tied.

"Jacqueline. Remove the cross."

Jacqueline snapped her head around. Mircalla's sultry voice awakened warmth. Unexpected hope filled Jacqueline's heart along with a hunger. Her arms jerked.

Ropes bound her to the capstan. She stared at them, confusion blurring her memory.

"Jacqueline, I need you. I'm coming for you."

"Yes." she murmured. "I know."

She must have anticipated Mircalla's rising. The bonds held her fast to her own plan to resist, for if Mircalla fed on her, the King might die, and de Guise…

Yes, de Guise. His voice only ruled her heart, and her heart ruled her mind. "Come back to me," she had pleaded, but first she had to return to him, safely, as Jacqueline, not as the minion of a rapacious monster.

Mircalla's command struck like the lash of a whip, rebuffing all thoughts of rebellion. *"Remove the cross, Jacqueline."*

Senses reeling, Jacqueline writhed against the ropes. "Yes!" she cried, but then, "No, I can't… Can't…"

Can't let Mircalla have me. Can't submit to these mists clouding my thoughts, arousing desires I don't truly feel. Can't be a victim again!

Mr. Smith would summon Claque. Vordenburg would make his way up the ladder too. If only she could stall for time.

"I can't," she whined. "Can't reach it. Help me."

Mists engulfed her, heady with jasmine, banishing every thought but Mircalla—her demands, her desires. Ravenous lust consumed her as Mircalla entered her mind.

"Remove the cross, Jacqueline."

"I can't, I can't. Help me!" Jacqueline screamed. "Help!" She slammed her chest against the capstan, vainly trying to catch the cross. She rasped, a trapped thing, spittle foaming in the corners of her mouth. "You have to help me!" she shrieked.

Angélique shot from the companionway from belowdecks. She leapt atop the capstan, snarling, finding nothing to attack.

Jacqueline snarled back, furious. "Get away from me, you animal!"

She butted Angélique with her head. When the wolf recoiled, she laughed and butted her again. With a warning growl, Angélique batted her, then swatted her face with claws.

Jacqueline matched her sister's snarl. "You bitch!"

Instantly, Mircalla appeared behind Angélique. Jacqueline cooed in wicked delight as the vampire seized Angélique by the scruff and hurled her across the deck. But the wolf regained her feet and sprang at Mircalla, catching the vampire's arm in her jaws and dragging her to the deck.

Jacqueline shrieked as Mircalla vanished, but her anger turned to wonder when a monstrous panther appeared, larger than the wolf, with eyes that gleamed red.

"Yes! Kill her!"

Angélique edged back, crouching to attack, but the panther pounced, digging claws into her shoulders and biting down on her snout. With a yelp, Angélique kicked the panther's head to free herself, her ear tearing as they separated. Angélique leapt atop the beast, raking open her belly. Then Angélique lunged, sinking her fangs into the panther's throat and thrashing her.

The panther vanished, leaving Angélique slewing on blood, her eyes wild as she sought her quarry.

Jacqueline laughed and mimicked a howl. "Wo-wo-wo-ooh! You lo-o-o-se!"

As Angélique floundered, Mircalla reappeared. Jacqueline cackled in delight. "Kill her! Kill the wolf bitch!"

Mircalla picked Angélique up by her forelegs and wrenched them from their sockets, then hurled her across the deck to strike the wall beside the companion door, where she lay stunned.

"Yes! Yes!"

Seizing her by the scruff, Mircalla punched Angélique's snout. Yelping, Angélique scrabbled vainly as Mircalla hoisted her and hurtled her at Monsieur Claque, who had gained the top step of the ladder. The two fell back together with a thundering crash accompanied by her interfering sister's agonized cries.

Mircalla turned slowly. Jacqueline's heart raced. Panting, she yanked vainly at her bonds.

"Remove the cross, Jacqueline," Mircalla demanded. "Get rid of it."

Jacqueline wedged her silver cross against the lip of the capstan and shoved. The cross flipped onto the deck, and the wounds on her breast burst open. She crowed triumphantly.

"Mircalla! I'm yours!"

A spray of water shot up from belowdecks, striking Mircalla full in the back. She yowled, writhing in agony. A second stream joined the attack. Billows of steam rose from the vampire until flames erupted. Mircalla vanished with a ghastly wail.

Jacqueline sagged against the capstan, unconscious.

12.

JACQUELINE AWOKE, HER HEAD HANGING OFF A BENCH ABOVE A PUDDLE of water dripping from her clothing. She shivered in the night breeze. With a groan she moved to push herself up, but found her hands secured behind her. A rope held her neck down.

"What happened?" she called out, hoping someone was near. "Angélique? Vordenburg? Anyone?"

Footsteps. A gentle hand soothing her back. "I'm here, madame," said Mr. Smith. "I'm glad you're conscious at last. Are you all right?"

She groaned. "She took me, didn't she? Putain! She didn't bite me though, did she? Hah!" She struggled again. "May I get up? I assume I'm drenched in holy water."

"Your foresight saved you," he told her, "but your—that is, the Duchess of Singlebury is wounded quite severely."

As the memory of the battle returned, she struggled against her bonds. "Angélique! Where is she? Zut! Get these ropes off me!"

"Indeed, we will." He began working on her wrists. "The Duchess will not allow anyone near her, but she seems to be in great pain."

"I need to see her. Her wolf blood will heal her, but—"

Her hands released, she found her shoulders too stiff to effectively move. The rope slipped off her neck and then from her body. Still, she couldn't push herself from the bench. As Mr. Smith lifted her up to sit, she swayed and slumped against the wall, fighting the lethargy that followed Mircalla's attacks. She untucked her bloodied chemise and stared ruefully at the ceinture of raw, open flesh. She scanned the deck and found Monsieur Claque stolidly at the helm. A few feet away from her, Vordenburg poised to spray her again, if needed. She waved him down.

"She escaped?" she asked. When he nodded, she cursed again.

"I believe I did grave damage to her, though." He patted the nozzle. "But she disappeared before complete immolation. I thought perhaps she still possessed you, tried to draw power from your strength."

Jacqueline put a hand to her throbbing head, finding an alarming lump. "What hit me?"

Vordenburg told her, "You struck your head when I dispelled the creature."

Jacqueline heaved a frustrated sigh. "I'm my own worst enemy. Take me to Angélique."

Mr. Smith cleared his throat. "Ah. Before that, would you take a look ahead?"

He helped her stand and walked her to the fo'c'sle. Rouen sparkled in the distance. Off the starboard bow, a glowing flame illuminated a thermal balloon floating less than a few kilometers away.

"Zut. At least we prepared for this too." Her hands balled to fists. "Let's hope we're more successful with this enemy. Below with you, Mister Smith. There are a few bottles of Bellesfées in Marthe's basket. Make use of one while I figure out what to do next."

"Madame Duval—"

"No arguments, Majesty. De Guise entrusted you to me. Let's go."

The two descended the ladder together.

Angélique lay on her side at the bottom step. She lifted her head and whined quietly. Jacqueline hurried to her but halted short of seizing her in her arms for fear of hurting her further, unsure of how much healing had taken place since the attack.

"Mon Ange, I'm so sorry!"

Angélique gruffed, then whined in pain and laid her head down again to let Jacqueline examine her. Though her fur was matted with blood, the wounds had already closed, and her eyes were clear. Jacqueline stroked the wolf's side and murmured in her ear.

"It wasn't me, it was her inside me. I could hear myself say those things, and I hated myself. My dearest, dearest, I am so sorry."

Angélique snorted, then sighed.

Rising, Jacqueline said, "So another enemy approaches. I can't afford another vampire attack as I deal with them, Mister Smith."

Angélique gave a short whoof and nudged Jacqueline's legs. Jacqueline stooped down again.

"Are you saying she's gone?"

Another whoof.

Jacqueline chewed her cheek. "Well, if a snarl meant she was here, I suppose a whoof means she's gone now." She hugged her sister's ruff tenderly. "Heal, mon Ange. Mister Smith will be here for you." She stood.

Smith caught her arm. "I have experience with weaponry, madame. I'd be interested in learning more about this gun of yours."

His eyes, usually so mischievous, were sharp and clear. This was a man who had faced down eleven attempts on his life, with scars where bullets grazed him, and now a small hole in his back. The thought of hiding himself away while others fought on his behalf was probably more than distasteful to him; it would be insulting to someone who had distinguished himself so brilliantly in the military. He had stoically endured the tragic death of his son only a year ago, though the loss had aged him. Who was Jacqueline to deny the King any favor, when she herself would soon need his?

"De Guise would argue, Mister Smith. You know he would."

"De Guise is not here."

Her anger flared. "You needn't remind me."

"He lies wounded defending me," Smith replied, equally piqued. "I would avenge his honor."

Jacqueline pressed her hand to her head. "Mister Smith, I understand your desire. I admire your courage. But I have defied de Guise too many times already, and he trusts me to fight to the last to defend you, just as he would do. You've already been wounded once while in my care. De Guise would never forgive himself if you should be hurt any further. You will stay belowdecks and enjoy my wine and my protection."

She held out her bloodied hand for her spyglass. She didn't stay to hear any argument.

The Montgolfier drifted into firing range of the revolving gun. In a few minutes, *Esprit* would be within a shot of a good rifle, but her envelope was so vast, a single ball wouldn't do much damage. Vordenburg had already maneuvered the gun turret and brought it to bear. Jacqueline jumped up to the fo'c'sle to peer ahead with the spyglass.

To her surprise, an old woman and a young man occupied the Montgolfier's gondola, dimly lit by the flame of the burner. Jacqueline spied no weapons. Those in the gondola scanned the skies, presumably for signs of *Esprit*. They appeared to be arguing. Suddenly, the young man laid hands on the woman's shoulders. Spinning her about, he pointed directly at Jacqueline. They didn't move. Didn't reach for any gun. Didn't make any attempt to divert their path.

Esprit could easily skirt the Montgolfier. However, Jacqueline itched to know why these two had insisted on tracking Jacqueline's movements. If they had sussed her ruse and come to complete their task, why were there no weapons at the ready?

Jacqueline snapped the spyglass closed but remained at the bow.

"Madame?" Vordenburg called.

"Steady, Baron. Claque, to me."

Once Monsieur Claque clomped up the ladder to join her on the fo'c'sle, she handed him a grappling hook and they waited. The balloon teetered and dipped in the night air. Jacqueline watched as the young man fought with the lines to keep their path on track to intercept *Esprit*. Slowly, the two ships closed.

"Now, Claque."

The autonomaton tossed the grappling hook and caught the gondola. Wind shoved the balloon well away from *Esprit*, but the rope tautened and held. The two passengers gave no reaction other than frowns. Jacqueline debated her next line of action as she hastened to the aft deck, Monsieur Claque at her side. The three stared at one another. Finally, Jacqueline decided on diplomacy.

"You pursue my airship," she called across the night. "That is not wise. What do you hope to gain?"

To her surprise, the woman answered. "We want the body of Général Égalité."

Jacqueline puzzled out the request. Égalité was the byname of the King's father, Louis Philippe II of the Bourbon line. The King himself had probably been a general in the Army of the North, so it made sense that as the Duc d'Orléans, he would use his father's byname during the Austrian Netherlands campaigns. All before Jacqueline's time, and she had never bothered to study history. She wondered, however, why the woman referred to him by that outdated name.

"We return Louis-Philippe to his family," she told the two.

"Then you must surrender him to me," the young man shouted. "That traitor to both France and Austria is my *grandfather*."

The woman placed her hand on his shoulder, but he shrugged her off. The shadows of his face deepened in the light of the burner.

Jacqueline leaned to the rail and hung her head wearily. *Esprit* now dragged the balloon and the wind worked against her. The ship veered to starboard, the engines straining to hold the course. Jacqueline glared across at the pair.

"You murdered the King of the French in cold blood with a cowardly shot in the back for a child of war?" she cried. She signaled to Vordenburg. He ignited the gas-fueled botefeux, poised to fire the revolving guns.

"Cowardly?" The old woman laughed bitterly. "That man led French troops against the Austrians, then betrayed them to join the Austrian army. He then proved himself to be no man of honor in Austria, though we welcomed him. My family took him in, trusted in him. *I* trusted him. And again, he turned coat and ran away."

Jacqueline measured the woman's words, weighing them against her cold frown and the young man's anger. The young man's pear-shaped face bore witness to his grandmother's accusations.

"Are you both mad?" Jacqueline said. "That was half a century ago! Where are the rest of your craven cabal hiding?"

"The ones who shot him have probably slunk back to their holes," the young man called. "Their reasons were political. Your cowardly king kissing the derrière of the queen of England. Neither my grand-mother nor I care a kroner for politics. That man stole her honor. She was outcast from the family estate, left to face the shame of bearing his child alone. I was happy to see him fall. I rejoice that he's dead. And now I would look upon his face and spit on him."

Jacqueline quaked. De Guise lay wounded at the hands of political revolutionists, and she faced a far different aftermath from what she had envisioned. She studied the grandmother. Despite the old woman's frosty, proud mien, tears slipped down her aged cheeks, sparkling poignantly in the light of the Montgolfier's flame.

So, the man who thought intimate encounters between the same gender were sinful and disgusting had abandoned his own pregnant lover, daughter of an aristocratic house. A wave of revulsion shook Jacqueline. Yet another assault on a woman. A bullet in the back wasn't unwarranted.

Or was there more to the woman's quest than simple vengeance? Fifty years. A child. She obviously hadn't suffered great hardship if she had also raised a grandson with such intelligence and skills to manage a thermal airship at night. The young man with the fire in his eyes—

she knew so many of his ilk in the cafés and taverns of the Boul'Mich. They called themselves Republicans, Orléanists, Socialists, Legitimists, but in the end, they were just plain malcontents, yapping to hear themselves yap, fighting to win a battle of their own making.

The old woman, however…

Jacqueline met her eyes. "Did you love him?"

The woman broke. Head bowed, shoulders sagging, she shuddered in silent sobs.

"The man I love, your assassins also gunned down," Jacqueline said.

The young man leaned to the rim of the basket, rocking the gondola dangerously. "What do we care if another filthy Frosch dies?" he shouted.

Jacqueline ignored him. She kept her eyes on the woman. Her grandson embraced her, glaring at Jacqueline, but the woman had nothing more to say.

Esprit's engines churned and chunked. Jacqueline was out of patience. Taking the rope from Monsieur Claque, she tossed it over the rail. The balloon lurched away. The two in the gondola cried out in dismay, but *Esprit* surged forward, leaving them to the west wind. Jacqueline patted Monsieur Claque's arm and they headed to the ladder. Vordenburg waited at the bottom, highly agitated.

As they descended to the main deck, a sharp ping from Monsieur Claque's torso shocked Jacqueline.

Boom!

Esprit's revolving gun fired. Jacqueline whirled.

Boom!

The woman shrieked. The young man bellowed. Something struck Jacqueline's shoulder, slicing through her coat, burning hot. With wild eyes she ran to the aft rail. By the light of the gas flame, she saw the young man bent half out of the gondola, aiming a rifle at her.

Boom! Boom! Boom!

The revolving guns shredded the gondola and its passengers, their limbs flailing, bodies jerking as they dropped through the air. The balloon shot upward. Flames caught the silk of the envelope and the Montgolfier slipped to earth as a ball of fire.

Jacqueline watched, agonized. Belowdecks, Angélique keened. Vordenburg hurried to the aft deck. Jacqueline spun on him and beat him back.

"What have you done!"

He grabbed her arms to halt her. "Not I, madame."

Jacqueline looked across the main deck. Louis-Philippe stood beside the turret of the revolving gun, arms folded, a look of grim satisfaction defying her. Vordenburg stopped her from leaping over the rail to attack the King. The Baron showed her fresh blood on his hand. Her blood, she realized. A ball had grazed her shoulder. It seared into her, but not as grievously as the immolation she had just witnessed. She shoved Vordenburg off.

"Go tell Angélique what happened. I'll make sure we maintain our course."

Jacqueline swung over the rail to the main deck as Mr. Smith turned to meet her wrath without remorse. Jacqueline trembled with constraint, wanting to punch the smug frown from his pudgy pear face, wishing she had Monsieur Claque's steam ports to vent her fury.

"She loved you," she said, her voice quavering.

He acknowledged the weight of her accusation. "Once. I suppose I once loved her." He set his hand to the gun. "Against my will, I was pushed onto this throne. I agreed to serve the people of France, Madame Duval, and I will give my life for that cause. I could not allow that young man to take your life and endanger all of France."

"Your own grandson."

He lifted his chin. "No one I knew." He indicated the blood seeping into her coat sleeve. "You should have that washed and bound."

"And you should have stayed below," she cried. She pointed. "Go. Now."

He tipped his head and headed for the ladder door.

Jacqueline stalked aft. "Vordenburg," she barked, "is belowdecks fully christened?"

Vordenburg paused at the companion. When he nodded, Jacqueline sighed with her whole body. "Make sure *everyone* stays down there, and stand guard with that canister."

He vanished down the ladder behind Mr. Smith.

Jacqueline pounded on the capstan and kicked it a few times. "Foute! Foute! Foute!" She threw her head back with a roar of rage. Monsieur Claque tilted his head, watching her. She bent double, then rested her aching head on the capstan. With another deep sigh, she was ready to fight again.

"Here's how it will be, Claque."

The autonomaton straightened.

"We've just passed Rouen. I'm setting the heading for north and east." She smacked a few gauges. "I need to cut back the engine slightly because we spent fuel dragging that—"

She swallowed and closed her eyes, then opened them quickly as the vision of the two riddled bodies flashed before her.

Damn the King and his open codpiece!

"We'll soon see the English Channel. Water. Now, listen carefully. I'd like to think we're rid of the two greatest obstacles on this journey, but I'm not sure I have any hope left. If Mircalla appears, I'll be incapacitated until you send a stake through her heart or use that canister on your left arm to spray her down with enough holy water to set her afire."

The Montgolfier fireball haunted her. She rubbed her eyes, fighting to erase it.

"If those who tried to murder the King were watching that balloon, they may surmise—Oh, I don't know." She waved her arm vaguely, then winced at the pain from the gunshot. "Just stand ready to take the King on a short flight. We'll be in view of Château d'Eu shortly. You and I. We get the King to Eu."

She headed to the directional capstans. "Then I don't care what happens."

Angélique gruffed from the ladder doorway. She glared at Jacqueline, then limped over to sniff her. She growled.

Her sister's common sense brought her down from her reckless fury. Jacqueline squatted and embraced her, burying her face in Angélique's bloodied ruff. She wanted to weep, but she knew she couldn't afford that release. Not yet.

"All right, all right." She brushed fur back from Angélique's face and scritched her ears. "Are you healed now? You'll know if Mircalla returns?"

Angélique lay down maw to paws. Jacqueline stroked her until the black mood dissipated. She stretched out on the deck beside her sister and set her head on Angélique, listening to her heartbeat.

"I've missed you so much, mon Ange. It was always just the two of us. Me following you, chasing you, rescuing you, hugging you. Everything's changed. I don't know what I'm doing anymore. I don't know who I'm supposed to be."

Angélique lifted her head and licked Jacqueline's chin. Jacqueline chuckled. "All right, I've finished. No more self-pity."

Jacqueline returned to setting the wings and the speed, then took her place at the ship's wheel. Once the course was set, she slid her coat off and examined her shoulder. The ball had left a gouge just above the bandage over the patch of skin Monsieur Claque had burned. The muscle, however, remained whole. She ripped her sleeve away and handed it to Monsieur Claque. He wrapped the gash and tied a neat bow.

"What's one more scar?" she grumbled.

A sudden sea breeze wafted over the ship, cold and moist and smelling of brine. *Esprit* tossed with it, but Jacqueline brought her back, then fought with the wind for the next twenty minutes. Every so often, she glanced at Angélique, whose wide-mouthed panting seemed to mock her every time she cursed. In the end, though, Jacqueline found release in bitter mockery herself. This was the longest flight she'd ever attempted on *Esprit* and—but for the vampire attack, the murderous pair in the Montgolfier, the gash in her arm, her disgust and anger at Mr. Smith for the man he had been fifty years earlier, and the horror brought about by a weapon she had designed for just that purpose— why, it was a fine night for a star cruise.

She cut the engine and lowered the hydrogen levels, keeping the envelope partially inflated. On her way from the aft deck, she rang the ship's bell to summon the King as well as alert the men-at-arms on the ground. Château d'Eu had a huge courtyard; Jacqueline made for it, bringing the hull just above the college church spire. *Esprit* settled and Jacqueline dropped anchor.

Alarms sounded throughout the château. Guards with torches, lanterns, and muskets stormed out to surround the massive airship. Jacqueline stood at the gangway, her feet spread wide, arms akimbo, hair wild in the sea wind. At the sight of her, the troops hesitated.

"Ohé gens d'armes," she hailed them, waving her good arm. "Would you be so kind as to secure the cables and prepare to receive His Majesty, the King of the French."

She unbattened the gangplank. Monsieur Claque hoisted it and locked it into place while on the ground, four soldiers laid hands on it and held it fast. They gazed up, astounded.

Jacqueline savored the confusion on their faces.

Mr. Smith at last emerged from the ladder unsteadily. He had evidently taken her advice and helped himself to the wine. When he came to her side, he set down his bag, faced her with a wide grin, and gripped her upper arms as if to knight her. She yelped in pain. She then gave him a vicious smile and clapped him on the back, enjoying the shock on his face.

"Your *Majesty.*" She emphasized the word, ice in her eyes. "I hope de Guise and I have discharged our duties to your satisfaction." She made a deep, formal curtsy. "It has been our honor to serve. Think kindly of us, and pray for him."

He took her hands in his. An unspoken apology darkened his eyes. She would make no apology for her anger, even if he had saved her life. He nodded and disembarked.

Troops swiftly fell in and snapped to shoulder arms as he strode down the gangplank, across the courtyard, and into the château. The four soldiers who stood on the gangplank gasped and tumbled off as Monsieur Claque yanked it out from under them. Jacqueline signaled the men holding the cables to release them.

"Anchors aweigh," she called, and followed through with the warning.

Monsieur Claque opened the hydrogen valves wide. *Esprit* soared toward the Channel, yawing and tipping in the wind, before settling into steady onshore breezes to carry it east. As they rose swiftly well beyond the range of any gun, Jacqueline set course for Bellesfées. Angélique came to her side and sat, panting contentedly, while Vordenburg rested on the bench beside the ladder door, his trusty canister next to him, jotting notes into his little book.

Jacqueline lifted her head to enjoy the sea breeze. The ordeal done, she patted the ship's wheel and stroked the wood handles.

"Good girl," she whispered. "Good girl."

Jacqueline waited until they were past Rouen to break out the basket of food Marthe packed. As Vordenburg carefully unwrapped cold meats and cheeses, Jacqueline uncapped two bottles of wine and handed him one. Vordenburg raised a brow.

"For just the two of us?"

She clinked her bottle to his. While he looked for glasses in the basket, she gulped from the bottle.

"Pfui!" Vordenburg held up a meaty bone with two fingers, appalled.

Jacqueline took it and tossed it to a grateful Angélique, then sandwiched some cheese between two slices of meat and munched.

"Listen, Vordenburg," she said between bites, "in an hour or so, we'll be at Chartres, where you repelled Mircalla. I know we didn't destroy her, and Angélique assures me she's no longer aboard. But is there a chance she'd linger about and return?"

Vordenburg patted the canister pump. "I saw smoke and flame arise from her body, and heard her scream. I have seen what damage a simple aspergillum can do, sprinkling only a few drops at a time. I know she is gravely weakened. She will need to return to her tomb to heal. Given that journey is more than sixty kilometers from Chartres, I don't know how she will make it there."

Jacqueline swigged wine again and dabbed her mouth on her sleeve. "She would need to feed, n'est-ce pas? And we have no idea where she would strike between here and home."

"Where is your cross?"

Jacqueline cast about without success. "Zut. I don't know. Did I—?" She recalled then she had snapped it off. It could have gone overboard. With a snort of exasperation, she took another swig of wine.

"Here's my fear, monsieur. Will she reach out to me again? Force me to abandon *Esprit* and find her? Feed her?" She grinned wryly. "I tell you, monsieur, I don't know when I've been more frightened."

His eyes widened. He too drank. He tucked the bottle back into the basket and reached into his pocket for his notebook. Jacqueline's wine was half gone before he spoke. "What is our altitude?"

"Nine hundred meters. Euh, make that twelve hundred," she said, checking the gauges again.

He tugged on his lower lip. "Two kilometers is the furthest reported summoning, but that was an ancient vampire in his full strength, and across the ground, not the air."

"Well, we can't go that high anyway."

He pondered a few more entries in his notebook, flipped back to earlier pages, then pored over a particular set of notes. Jacqueline, meanwhile, finished her bottle of wine and opened a second, noting with a smirk that the King had made off with an extra bottle. She stroked Angélique's side and enjoyed a bit more charcuterie. When she finished eating, she went back to check their course. The way was clear and cloudless. The night sky glittered with stars, and *Esprit*'s envelope reflected and magnified them spectacularly. It was probably the wine, but for the first time in many days she felt relaxed.

Relaxed, but not happy. There was nothing she could do if Mircalla summoned her. She would have to surrender, trusting to Vordenburg, Monsieur Claque, and Angélique. There was nothing she could do to effect or hasten de Guise's recovery. She would have to wait, trusting to the skill of the surgeon.

Jacqueline was never happy doing nothing. She swayed, swinging back and forth between the handles of the ship's wheel, wishing she were dancing with de Guise, the only one whose lips she desired on her breast.

Vordenburg shook his head, frustrated. "Abraham has nothing. Captain Hall made some notes, but nothing specific. Le Fanu's accounts are sheer romanticized fiction, and the man worships me for some reason. I think he's planning to make a novel of his notes. And of course, Coleridge's records are unfinished. We simply do not know enough about vampires to make any firm prediction. I am afraid I have no answer for you, madame."

Jacqueline grinned, her eyes flashing. "In that case, monsieur, I charge you with keeping me alive long enough to land *Esprit*."

Vordenburg closed the food basket and took his canister pump into his arms with a determined frown. With Monsieur Claque beside her and Angélique at her feet, Jacqueline hoisted her wine and defied the universe to cross her again that night.

13.

Jacqueline rang the ship's bell to alert Luc and Jean-Paul of their arrival, but she needn't have done; they were already at the airship's landing site. The sky, a pale periwinkle, resounded with the dawn chorus rising from the forest, lending a cheery welcome home. Once *Esprit* was anchored, moored, and battened down, its three passengers tramped wearily down the gangplank into the dewy grass. Angélique raced ahead.

"Is everyone safe, Luc?" Jacqueline asked.

"Quite safe."

"De Guise?"

"No change."

His response left her anxious to see her lover, but Jacqueline proceeded apace with Vordenburg, whose leg was overly taxed from carrying the heavy canister. Idly, she considered how to add wheels.

Once inside, Jacqueline trudged up the winding staircase, feeling as worn as the two-hundred-year-old marble steps. Cautiously, she opened the door to de Guise's room, part of her afraid she would find him suffering beyond her care, part of her ashamed of the tale she had to tell.

The darkened room, silent but for his even breathing, allayed both fears. Once her eyes adjusted to the twilight of pre-dawn at the windows, she hurried to make use of the water closet in the corner turret so as not to upset him by the blood on her clothes. Dropping all but her chemise on the floor, she filled a basin to gingerly wash her face, neck, hands, and arms, then pressed a cold cloth to the swelling on her brow. Although she couldn't see all the damage, she felt scratches on her face from Angélique's attack. The gouge on her arm stung, but it did not require stitches.

Battle scars, she told herself. Badges of honor, she told herself.

Muffled laughter spoke of Llewellyn and Angélique's reunion in the rooms down the hallway. Jacqueline longed for the same release. She dried herself, then crawled under the bedclothes to press against de Guise's body, her hand on his breast, her head cuddled in the curve of his neck. She slept.

Jacqueline awoke to de Guise tossing his head and moaning softly. Drenched in sweat, he radiated heat. Daylight filled the window and the sun hung high. Llewellyn sat beside de Guise, bathing his brow when he could reach him.

"Good afternoon," Llewellyn whispered.

She sat up. "What's wrong with him?" She tried without success to help Llewellyn hold the cool rag to his head.

"Infection," Llewellyn told her. "It's not uncommon."

"Gryffin, he's on fire!" she cried. "Can't we set him in cool water? A bath?"

"Not with an infected wound, no."

"Just his head, then. A shaving bowl. I'm sure he uses one. My father has one if he does not."

De Guise flailed, striking her cheek.

She recoiled in shock as Llewellyn pulled de Guise's arms away and held him down.

"Jacqueline, we're doing all we can do."

"How can you be so calm?"

"Because I must," he said sharply. "And so must you if you're to be of any help to him. If you can't, then go to your room."

Stricken, she glared at Llewellyn, but he ignored her, continuing his gentle ministrations. Her heart pounded in her ears. She couldn't think. Tossing the bedclothes aside, she stormed from the room.

In her own chambers, she halted as she passed her vanity and caught sight of her reflection. Sinking down in the chair, she stared in dismay. Blood stained her ragged chemise and her hair was a matted mess, sticky with Angélique's blood as well as her own. Her face torn, her eyes like a defeated bare-knuckler's... Defeated — that was the word. She had once again fallen to Mircalla's assault.

"No, damn you." She set her jaw defiantly. "I may have fallen, but you fell further, you bitch of hell."

Anne appeared behind her in the mirror, her worried eyes trained on Jacqueline's face. "Does that hurt? Shall I get a balm?"

Jacqueline turned around in surprise. Anne wore one of Angelique's old day dresses, taken in and hemmed to fit her slender young body, under a clean white pinafore. A chatelaine hung from her belt along with a ring of three keys Jacqueline recognized as those to her own wardrobe and rooms. Her hair was clean, combed, and neatly knotted into a chignon adorned with a simple strip of lace ribbon. She waited anxiously for Jacqueline's approval, plucking at her pinafore.

Jacqueline blinked away tears. Amid all the chaos and violence and death and despair, Anne had chosen a future at Bellesfées.

"Well." Jacqueline took the girl's hands in hers. "You truly look like a lady's maid. I hope you're ready."

"I am."

"Well, then. What is your family name?"

Anne tilted her head in curiosity. "Gaudin."

Jacqueline squeezed her hands. "A lady's maid is always called by her family name. From now on, you are Gaudin. Marthe has given you orders?"

Gaudin shook her head, then said, "I mean, no, madame. I'm supposed to say 'madame,' not 'mademoiselle.' Even though you're not married. Is that right?"

"It is," Jacqueline said. "An independent woman is called 'madame.' Except by Luc, in this house," she added with a chuckle. "Very well. First, I'll need you to bring out a fresh day dress from that wardrobe." She pointed. "A green one, please. I don't usually bother with a bustle or corset, but I will need a fresh chemise, split drawers, hose and garters, and a crinoline. I'm going to bathe, and when I'm through, you will dry my hair, brush it out, and put it up the same way yours is done. Can you do that, Gaudin?"

"Yes, madame." She grabbed the ring of keys on her belt and held them up. "Which key is the wardrobe?" When Jacqueline raised a brow, she said. "Oh. I can figure that out quick enough." She went to the wardrobe to try.

Jacqueline's bathtub in the adjoining room, still full from her previous bath, smelled faintly of burnt wood. She tipped a bit of rose water in to sweeten it, then dumped the rest of the bottle in. She ached too much to scrub herself, but the cold soak soothed her. The wounds on her arm, a fierce red, still wept. The water cooled them, so she dared to sink beneath the surface and gently wipe her face. The scratches there weren't as deep as she first feared. They might not scar at all. Angélique had been careful to spare her the wolf's full fury, hoping only to defend herself and to swat some sense into Jacqueline. Black-butter eyes could only become so black and no more.

Staying low in the tub, she combed knots from her hair so it floated around her like an aura. She then rubbed her skin with callused fingertips until she was pink all over. When she finally climbed out of the tub and wrapped herself in her dressing robe, her fear had left her, her panic had galvanized into energy, and her common sense had returned.

She emerged to find her clothing neatly laid out on her bed and her new lady's maid waiting, brush in hand. A cordial glass of sherry sat on the corner of her vanity.

"Did Marthe tell you to do that?"

"Yes, madame." Gaudin smothered a giggle. "And she called me 'madame,' too, and told me I must call her by her Christian name. Is that proper?"

"In this house it is. Usually, she would be called 'Madame Benet,' but your aunt was adamant she would not be called anything but Marthe."

"Hmm. Adamant. Does that mean stubborn? Tatie is stubborn."

Jacqueline rolled her eyes. "That, she is."

She sat at the vanity and motioned the girl to her. Gaudin began by rolling sections of her hair at a time into a towel, squeezing and wringing what she could. Once she finished, she set to brushing, lightly at first, then with more confidence. Finally, she added the cleansing pomatum. She was as serious and as gleeful as a tot with her poppets. Jacqueline had to admit, the girl did a better job than Jacqueline ever had done herself. When Gaudin stood back to assess her work, she frowned.

"Did that cat attack you, too?"

Jacqueline touched the marks on her collar and breast guiltily.

"Should I find some powder to cover up your scratches and your black-butter eyes? I can make you look really pretty."

Jacqueline smirked. "I don't think that's possible, Gaudin. Not that I doubt your skills. Besides, Monsieur de Guise would not know me in powder and rouge. I am who I am."

Angélique entered with coffee and brioches. "What's this? Someone has taken my place?" She set the tray down on the vanity. "Don't worry, child, I won't bite. That is, I won't bite *you*."

She hugged Jacqueline's neck and gazed back at her sister in the mirror. "Bof, you look a mess. I apologize for the scratches, but you deserved them." She kissed Jacqueline's cheek. Then she looked past Jacqueline to the new servant. "You did very well. What do we call you?"

"Gaudin," the girl replied with a curtsy. "And I call you 'Your Grace.'"

"Every girl's fairytale come true. Well, Gaudin, let me show you how to prepare madame's coffee and just how much preserves to put on her brioche."

Jacqueline snorted. "I'm not a helpless imbecile, mon Ange."

"No, but now that you have a lady's maid, it's time you learned to live up to one."

In the next half-hour, Gaudin also learned how to use Bellesfées' plumbing system, how to draw and drain a bath, how to make up the bed and turn it down at night, how to sort clothes to be washed or mended, Jacqueline's morning and evening clothing preferences — "on a normal day" — and more secrets of Château Bellesfées than she was ready to hear. In the end, she stared in awe at Angélique and met her amber wolf-eyes.

"And what is said in these chambers remains in these chambers, Gaudin," Jacqueline finished sternly. "You speak to no one about what passes between us, not even to Marthe. On that, *I* will be adamant. And in return for all this responsibility and work, you receive your own room, which you must keep clean yourself and do all your own chores, and a louis d'or each week."

"Ho ho! That's more than I ever got," Angélique said. But she winked at Jacqueline, knowing very well how much her sister had sacrificed over the past five years to pay for Angélique's dissolute habits. She reached over and pushed Gaudin's gaping mouth closed. "You must also learn to keep a look on your face that says nothing surprises you." She grinned at the girl. "In this house, that is most important."

Jacqueline sighed. "Alas, that is the sad truth."

Gaudin looked from one sister to the other hesitantly. "But, Your Grace, who dresses you?"

With a glint in her eye, Angélique said, "The same one who undresses me."

She pushed Gaudin's mouth closed again.

Jacqueline returned to de Guise's room. "I believe I'm sane now. How can I help?"

Llewelyn was in the process of cleansing the wound. Though De Guise was calmer, he moaned quietly each time Llewellyn daubed him. His entire left side blazed with inflammation, but there were no telltale black streaks of blood infection.

"Try to get him to drink some more water," Llewelyn told her. "He's able to swallow now."

She climbed up on the bed, lifted de Guise's head, and set a glass to his lips. She had to spill it into his mouth before he responded. He swallowed and groaned.

Llewellyn wrung out the cloth and set the basin aside. Beginning the task of bandaging, he passed the coiled linen under de Guise's body rather than rolling him back and forth. "He's been calling for you."

Jacqueline leaned to de Guise's ear. "I'm home, my love. You can lie still now. I won't leave you." She asked Llewellyn, "Do you need a rest? I can manage here."

He nodded. "I'll finish the wrap first. Angélique tells me your journey was waylaid, with more than pains for good Mister Smith's welfare. You seem to be wearing all of them."

"She doesn't know half of what happened." Jacqueline forced a bit more water on de Guise. "But I believe we've seen the last of the assassins, and the King will be able to keep his rendezvous with Queen Victoria next week."

"Vordenburg is still asleep."

"Unaccustomed to French wines." She chuckled quietly. "No, he saved us all. I'm very glad he was with us."

"And tomorrow, he and I will do our best to find Mircalla and put an end to her." Tying off the bandages and tugging the bedclothes up, Llewellyn yawned widely. "With your permission, I think I'll sleep now. Angélique will guard the house." He came around to carefully kiss her cheek. "I think he'll improve steadily now you're here."

She smiled. "I know I will."

He lifted her arm to examine the open wounds there. Clucking, he took up the bandages and balm to tend to her. "Angélique hasn't told me how this came about."

"No, but you must excuse her. She was belowdecks at the time."

He wrapped her upper arm generously then tied a decorative bow in the linens. As the two of them laughed, the melody of Angélique at the Pleyel piano came through the open windows.

"Now," Jacqueline said with a sigh. "Now I'm home."

In the evening, just after Jacqueline lit the argands on the mantel in de Guise's room, he opened his eyes. Seeing her, he gave a weak smile, but when he reached for her, he halted with a grunt. He licked his fever-chapped lips with difficulty.

"How long?"

"Not twenty-four hours since I kissed you last," she told him as she came back to the bed and kissed him again. His lips burned beneath hers, but from fever not passion. She made him drink some water. "But the King is safely at Eu."

"Ah, my brilliant love." He tried to lift his hand but failed. "Your face. What happened?"

"Oh, I'm quite battered. Gives me character, don't you think?" She shushed him when he protested. "We fought Mircalla. Or rather, Vordenburg and Angélique fought her after I failed to resist her call. They drove her off for now, somewhere over Chartres. Those who pulled the trigger here on the grounds have slipped away, but we encountered the menacing Montgolfier and —" She faltered. "Dispatched it."

"You're angry."

She kissed his brow. "Not with you, Alain."

A light tap at the door interrupted her. Vordenburg poked his head in, smiling to see de Guise awake and lucid.

"You are looking better, monsieur." Despite his jovial tone, his brow was knit, his face taut. "Madame, if you will?"

De Guise sighed. "Go, chérie. I'll be fine now."

She stroked his head gently. Clammy and still warm. She pressed her lips together. "I'll send someone up with broth."

He nodded, but he fell immediately asleep.

Jacqueline met Vordenburg in the hallway. "What is it? What's wrong?"

"I'm not certain if anything is wrong, but I will say it is unusual. Your housekeeper wanted to know where the food basket was, and I had to confess I'd left it on the airship."

Jacqueline groaned. "I'm sure she wasn't happy about that. I do apologize—"

"No, that is not my concern, but you see, she sent the little one, Anne, to retrieve it. When the girl did not return, Marthe went herself. Neither has come back."

Blood drained from her face. "Get Llewellyn."

"Hurry, madame. The sun is almost gone."

She shouted for Angélique as she hopped down the staircase, while Vordenburg tapped on Llewelyn's door. Angélique didn't answer. Jacqueline hoped it was because she had already sensed the danger and was changing to wolf.

"Claque!" she bellowed as she rushed out of the château. "Luc! Jean-Paul!"

On meeting the two groundskeepers at the edge of the vineyard, she sent Jean-Paul to de Guise's room, instructing the young man to keep him cool and give him water each time he awakened. When he left, she told Luc what happened. Monsieur Claque stomped up as she sent Luc to assist Vordenburg.

"To the ship first, Claque," she urged. "That's where Vordenburg sent them."

Together they ran across the field to where *Esprit* was moored. Jacqueline halted at the top of the hill above the ship when she caught sight of both Marthe and Gaudin at the aft rail. She called them. They didn't move. In the failing light of dusk, she counted at least another dozen pale figures along the rail of the main deck. All girls or young women. All silent, eyes closed, heads bowed as if they slept.

"What have you done now, you monster?"

Jacqueline ran down the hill to embark, only to find the gangplank gone. Angélique appeared at her side, but though her sister snarled, ramped, and circled, there was nothing either of them could do. Jacqueline waited impatiently for Llewellyn and Vordenburg.

"Who are these girls? Where could they have come from and how did they get aboard?" she fumed. "Luc! Hurry! The sun is almost gone!"

As she called out, a lurid mist gathered above the main deck, coalescing into a child. A girl. A dead girl. Or rather, recently dead. She still wore her funeral shift, caked in the dirt of the grave she had crawled from. Floating several feet above the deck, she gazed down hungrily at Jacqueline. Teeth bared, Angélique barked, furious but impotent.

Jacqueline's skin crawled. "Who are you? What are you doing here?"

The dead girl's eyes glowed red. Jacqueline quaked as the apparition drifted slowly to one of the older girls at the rail, then snatched her up by her hair. The unconscious girl never awakened. Before Jacqueline could react, the young vampire threw the girl to the ground where she lay in a bent heap, unmoving, her head twisted around.

Furious, Jacqueline lunged forward to beat at the hull. "Stop! What do you want?"

The vampire grinned and gripped another girl's collar. She soared straight up, then released her. Llewellyn, as wolf, streaked out of the dark and put himself beneath the falling girl. He yelped as she struck him, but the two rolled together safely.

The vampire giggled and chose another, this time tearing at the young woman's face and arms with her talon-like claws until her victim was a bloodied mass.

"Claque, take me up there. And stop her!"

Monsieur Claque lifted Jacqueline, ignited his engine, and jetted to the main deck. Setting her down, he turned to aim his wrist weapons. The vampire laughed until Monsieur Claque fired a thin stream of water that grazed her arm. She yowled as her arm smoked. More agile than the lumbering automaton, she darted away as he fired a stake. Coming around from behind, she kicked him. He crashed to the deck.

Jacqueline roared. "What is it you want from me?"

The vampire's voice simpered, a childlike treble, vicious as only a child could be. "I want you to watch."

Rather than give the demented beast what she wanted, Jacqueline cast about, searching for the missing gangplank, but even so half her attention remained on the unfolding events.

Vordenburg finally arrived, pumping the canister of holy water as he approached the ship. The vampire cocked her head curiously, then laughed again.

"My mistress tells me you're weak," she said. "Are you a weak little man?"

Monsieur Claque got to his feet. He snatched the vampire's hem and threw her to the deck. Unharmed, she flew out from beneath him and vanished, suddenly reappearing behind him. She kicked him again, this time into the companionway boards with such force the wood splintered.

She continued to giggle. "Silly machine."

It took every effort, but Jacqueline resisted responding. To do so would only feed the unnatural creature's desire.

As Vordenburg stood poised, waiting for an opportunity, Jacqueline found the gangplank. Wrestling it into place, she affixed it hurriedly so the men could climb. On the deck, she could not help but search the faces of the entranced girls. Both guilt and relief warred within her. None of them was from Forge-à-Bellesfées. They must have been Mircalla's many victims from across the Loire valley, her "larder."

"Why?" she called again, spinning to face Mircalla's minion. "Tell me what she wants me to do!"

"Nothing." The little vampire stayed just beyond Monsieur Claque's reach, flitting merrily between his failed attacks. "We want you to do nothing. My mistress called me here to feed. She wants me to be strong. She wants you to see what you can be. What you can have. She wants you to be *hers*. Like me!"

The vampire flew to the fo'c'sle, far out of the reach of Vordenburg's pump. Jacqueline lurched forward, though she had no hope of intervening. She watched in horror as the vampire seized another small girl in her arms and soared, sinking her fangs into the girl's throat. No delicate puncture, but the ravaging bite and bloodthirsty gulps of a monster.

Monsieur Claque lumbered up the ladder to the fo'c'sle. He aimed another stake. The vampire put her victim between them, still feeding. Seemingly weighing his options, Monsieur Claque raised his other arm and shot a full spray of holy water. At the same time, he launched himself at her. The vampire screeched and howled, her body writhing. Vordenburg gained the fo'c'sle at last and aimed a more powerful stream. Bursting into flames, the vampire dropped her victim to the deck, clawing the air with blackened hands. With careful aim, Monsieur Claque fired a wooden stake, piercing her heart.

The cursed child fell dead once more.

Jacqueline heaved an agonized cry, looking around in despair. None of the girls moved. "Mircalla still commands them," she called. "We need to wake them. We need to release them. Vordenburg, help me!"

Hurrying forward, she took Marthe by the shoulder. Still in a daze, the housekeeper spun around and slammed a meaty fist into her nose.

With a stunned cry, Jacqueline dropped, stunned and blinded. Before she could rise, Gaudin growled and jumped on top of her, shrieking as she swung her little clenched hands at Jacqueline's head. The explosion of pain set a dull buzz filling her head.

A harsh, cold rain fell.

14.

MERCIFULLY, THE BATTERING STOPPED. AS JACQUELINE ROLLED OVER TO her hands and knees, blood poured from her broken nose, mingling with the holy water that dripped from her hair and clothes. Through a cottony haze she heard weeping and moans, cries of terror, childish shrieks. Vordenburg and his holy rain had released the captives. Though the words sounded muffled, he kept repeating, "You are safe now. You are safe. Come, come. You are safe."

"Safe." Jacqueline spat bitterly, adding to the scarlet pool on the deck beneath her. When she tried to push herself upright, her hands slipped in the blood. She collapsed back to the deck, slicing her lip. In wolf form, Angélique and Llewellyn came to flank her, but wisely kept back until she regained her senses. Angélique whined and both wolves licked their lips worriedly as she pushed herself to her knees again.

"I'b all right," Jacqueline assured them.

Putting her arm around Angélique's ruff, she leaned on her to stand. For a moment, she just stood there, watching as Vordenburg and Luc shepherded the weeping young women, terrified from the moment of their awakening in a baptism of holy water. Monsieur Claque carefully cradled the flayed victim as he marched down the gangplank. Marthe and Gaudin were last to leave. Gaudin looked back and, seeing Jacqueline on her feet, ran to her.

"Madame! Madame! What happened to you? Are you hurt?" She took Jacqueline's arm and put it around her shoulder. "I'm here now. Let me help you."

It took an effort for Jacqueline not to recoil. But the girl scarcely noticed. She had no memory of what she had done. Jacqueline wasted no time assigning guilt; this was all Mircalla's doing.

"Help Monsieur Claque," Jacqueline told her. "See to that poor girl. And get the others to the banquet hall, quickly. Bring up the fires so everyone can get dry."

Every blunted word shot like a bullet through her broken nose.

"Yes, madame." Gaudin hurried off, delivering her mistress's garbled orders with an air of authority.

Unable to help herself, Jacqueline climbed up to survey the shambles on the fo'c'sle. At the sight of the slaughtered girl, she fell to her knees with a keen. The girl's throat gaped in a mass of gnawed flesh. Little blood remained in her body to stain the deck. Likely she was dead before Monsieur Claque had even sprayed the vampire. Tears first trickled down Jacqueline's face, then cascaded. Embracing the girl, she dragged her into her lap, cradling her, grieving as for a daughter.

What was the purpose of it all? A terrible display of power. A despicable show of force. The young vampire's mocking laughter as she reveled in her monstrous manifestation echoed in Jacqueline's head. She strained through her tears to find the downed vampire on the deck, a few feet away. She screamed in rage at the blackened thing. With low, anxious whines, Angélique and Llewellyn came to her side. They nuzzled her and each other in shared grief and fury. Together they mourned their loss, their failures. The keening of all three filled the night.

Slowly, she became aware of arms wrapping around her. Hands, prying her hands from the slaughtered girl, gently drawing her away.

"Come, mademoiselle," Luc coaxed.

Sobs wracked Jacqueline's body as Luc lifted her to her feet and took her into a paternal embrace. He rubbed her back and held her head and let her wail until she exhausted her rage, empty, drained even of pain. From a place of numbness, she heard Monsieur Claque retrieve the corpses and carry them from the ship. She hardly had the energy to care.

Whining, Angélique licked Jacqueline's legs and hands, pawing gently.

"The living need you," Luc whispered. "They need la Belle Dame de Bellesfées."

Recovered to her usual efficiency, Marthe managed to calm the young women and begin to get them settled, corralling some of the older ones to help her prepare food for them all. As Jacqueline entered the château, Marthe stopped her, handing her a bag of ice and ordering her to her room to wash.

"Don't know how you get into such trouble, ma fille," she grumbled.

"Be deither," Jacqueline replied thickly.

Gaudin had drained the tub earlier, so Jacqueline plunged her face into the wash basin in the water closet. Her eyes ached; she couldn't remember a time she had cried so much. When she lifted her face to the mirror and beheld the damage, she could only sigh and apply the ice bag to the swelling.

When Angélique came in, they hugged one another on the edge of collapse.

"I'm so sorry," Angélique murmured. "What can I do?"

"I don't know. We need to speak to them, but I don't know what to say." Jacqueline indicated her disfigurement. "I think you should be the one to explain. Terrible news should come from a prettier face. I'd only scare the devil out of them."

"If only that devil *could* be scared out of them." Angélique brushed a lock of Jacqueline's hair back from her wounds. "But we need a plan to address tonight and tomorrow. They should all stay here, where we can keep an eye on them. Vordenburg emptied his magic canister pump on them, so we'll need to send for the curé again before we set out to destroy Mircalla's tomb. Do we have any more of your little charms to give the girls?"

Jacqueline groaned. "It doesn't matter; they've all been bitten. Mircalla can control them now. Crosses may keep her from biting them unawares, but they won't stop Mircalla from summoning them again. I was wearing my cross aboard *Esprit* last night, and she made me take it off. Both Gaudin and Marthe were wearing theirs tonight."

She gently pressed her fingers to her nose; talking hurt. "Mon Dieu, where did they all come from? De Guise said nothing about two dozen afflicted girls." Then she gasped. "De Guise! I should—"

"Gryffin is with him."

Angélique sat Jacqueline down at the vanity and worked to make her a little more presentable. "We'll go downstairs together and tell the women exactly what happened to them. We'll learn where they come from and when they were first attacked. We'll turn their fear into anger and strength. And when we finish—"

Stepping back, Angélique appraised her work, her wolf-eyes narrowing in fierce satisfaction. "They will not be merely women, nor victims. They will be an army."

Angélique swept into the banquet hall with the flourish of a stage performer and the grace befitting the Duchess of Singlebury, Glamorgan. Llewellyn, Luc, and Vordenburg followed her. The girls seated at the great table fell silent at their entrance, although a few of the youngest continued to sob quietly, comforted by older ones. Jacqueline slipped in the back door and observed from a darkened corner of the hall.

Angélique began by praising them for their courage and reassuring them they would be safe within the walls of Bellesfées. Then she told them, "You were abducted by a horrible monster. She had no right to make you walk all the way here. Where are you from?"

As each responded, Jacqueline noted the older ones named locations that mapped a route from Meslay-le-Vidame, just south of Chartres, to Lailly-en-Val, recruited the previous night after Mircalla had been expelled from *Esprit*. The vampire must have seized on them immediately after her fall to restore herself, catching them in the fields or asleep in barns. Then she dragged them behind her on a relentless journey of nearly one hundred kilometers to her tomb, feeding and regaining her strength along the way. Other, younger women and girls were from nearby, some of them barefoot and in nightclothes — Mircalla's larder.

As the discussion continued, Jacqueline learned the nearby villagers had been bitten weeks, even months earlier, some several times. Not one of them remembered anything of their journey to Bellesfées, only the dream of the large jungle cat and the sweet fragrance of jasmine.

"Why did that man get us all wet?" one little girl demanded, her finger accusing Vordenburg.

"I sanctified you with blessed water," Vordenburg told them. "Blessed water repels the demon who brought you here."

They seemed relieved, and some of them thanked him. Another young woman wanted to know what the metal man was, and the girls were intrigued by the explanation of "clockwork automaton."

An older teen stood and straightened her drenched skirt shyly. "Madame, messieurs, I believe we owe our lives to you, and we are grateful... But I must ask, are we safe now? Can we return to our homes?"

Angélique looked back at Jacqueline in the corner. All heads turned to her. There were gasps and mutters as she stepped into the light, with her swollen eye, her bloody lip, and enormous nose, her face a battered mess. One of the little ones asked, "Is that the horrible monster?" setting off a chorus of frightened shrieks.

Angélique stilled the uproar with a sharp rebuke. "*She* is the woman who saved you all. She is the brilliant creator of Monsieur Claque. She provided him with wonderful weapons to destroy vampires. She invented the pump that sprayed you with holy water, saving your lives. Mesdemoiselles, you behold a true hero. Jacqueline Duval."

Jacqueline chafed at the hyperbole, but this was Angélique's performance, and she could but play along. She tried to look braver than she felt; her anger helped in her endeavor.

"Jacqueline Duval fought the vampire," Angélique continued her dramatic introduction. "You see the scars of her struggle against the demon. She fought for you, and she will fight to save you all until that demon is destroyed."

Jacqueline folded her arms "heroically" and gave a nod to the men. The four left Angélique to continue to weave her charms and bring the girls to a place where they would accept their internment at Bellesfées a few days more. Jacqueline had ordered enough food for a week's worth of guests for Angélique's wedding celebration, so there was plenty for a mere two dozen girls. They would sleep two or three to a room for protection, but she doubted they would mind. In fact, she doubted they would sleep at all—village girls in a great house, magical machines, delectable food, and the thrill of an adventure.

Provided Mircalla did not interfere before Jacqueline could defeat her.

Jacqueline sent Luc to Marthe, first reminding him that Marthe had no knowledge of what she'd done. He wasn't to let on his wife had broken Jacqueline's nose. "Don't tell Gaudin what she did, either," she added as he left.

The rest of them headed to the salon, where Marthe had laid a board for them. Gaudin waited in a chair at the table with a decanter of brandy, and she hurried to pour glasses. She carried one to Jacqueline.

"Gaudin, you're an angel. And the young woman whose face was attacked. How is she?"

Gaudin saddened. "It's terrible, madame. Marthe washed and cleaned the cuts, but—it's much worse even than your face."

Jacqueline splurted her first sip while the men chuckled quietly, but the circumstance was not one for humor.

"Gaudin, I want you to stay to hear our discussion. Afterward, you may go help the girl. After that, you may retire as you wish. I'll spend the night in Monsieur de Guise's room. Have my work clothes laid out for the morning."

Jacqueline's frown intimated the gravity of the discussion. Gaudin looked as though she was about to ask something, but she nodded and took her seat again.

When Vordenburg downed his brandy and poured a second, Jacqueline sniggered. "For someone who can't handle French wine, monsieur..." she noted wryly.

The vampire hunter winced and dropped into a chair, still shaking. "I decapitated the young vampire and her victim. Luc and I placed their bodies and the body of the girl whose neck was broken in the chapel for now, and I have soaked the remains with what water was left in Claque's reserve. Luc said he will bury them himself in the morning. Her Grace had me place the mauled young woman in her own chambers. She gave her a draught to make her sleep. I don't know how she'll survive with so much torn away. So much pain." He bowed his head to his hand. "How do we tell their parents? The creature... Her victims..."

"The creature was already buried," Llewellyn reminded them. "Her parents have already mourned her. We need not bring them any more pain by revealing her unnatural fate. As for the others, we don't even know who their parents are. The invalid will remain with us. Once she's healed enough, she can return home with an account of an animal attack." As he spoke, Llewellyn brought Jacqueline a plate before filling his own. "Perhaps, young Gaudin, you might assist Her Grace with the girl's convalescence?"

Gaudin dipped her head, although Jacqueline doubted she had any idea what Llewellyn had asked her to do.

"I have never seen such a display of force, not from any vampire," Vordenburg said. "This is not the pattern of the cursed. To continue to fight when faced with such opposition. Always, always, when confronted, they move on. If their chosen prey is shielded, they find someone who is not. This defies all history, all *Mircalla's* history. Why does she persist?"

Llewellyn sat with a grunt of surprise. "You don't know?" He indicated Jacqueline. "Mircalla's in love."

Vordenburg regarded him with a condescending smile. "Love? This is a demon. The vampire is an ever-hungry predator, an animal. You cannot think she truly loves another."

"Oh, you believe animals can't love? Still?" Llewellyn drew himself up. "It's time to expand your perceptions of the otherworld, Herr Vordenburg. Mircalla's desires run toward women, and she has fallen in love with Jacqueline."

Jacqueline scratched at her cuticles, frustrated. "It doesn't feel like love. It's ugly. Besides, what could she possibly find in me to love? Oh, I don't condemn her for her desires, any more than I condemn Custine for loving another man. Back in school, a few men made advances to me thinking I was another man, and some women flirted with me because they knew I was a woman. One loves whom one loves. I just fail to see any reason for this beautiful, powerful, immortal being to fall in love with *me*, a plain, brawny — and now, quite brutalized — polytech. I've no interest in her, and I've no desire to be like her. How could she be in love with me?"

Llewellyn's lips quirked. "Why does de Guise love you?"

The question startled her, especially because she had asked herself the same so frequently the past few days. She had to admit, "I honestly don't know."

Vordenburg gave a quiet chuckle. When she didn't show amusement, he looked from her to Llewellyn and back in wonder. "You cannot be serious. The fire between the two of you. The concern. The laughter. The light in his eyes when he looks at you. The way you melt when you look at him — you, the lady of brass and iron and steel. How can you not know?"

"I know I'm loved, monsieur," she answered sharply. Then she softened. "The *why* eludes me." She dismissed the topic with a wave. "So you believe she'll haunt me until one of us is dead? Splendid. And the night has just begun."

Vordenburg pursed his lips. "She has surpassed my understanding of her nature. She is old, but she is not an ancient vampire. I would not have believed her powerful enough to control so many of her victims at once from the tomb. And hold them there. After burning! She must be exhausted, but... Perhaps because they are so young? Or because her passion for you is so strong? To answer your question, I do not know."

"Why not come to me herself? Why send that young—" Jacqueline squeezed her eyes shut. The memory of the scorched corpse still sickened her. "She would have slaughtered them all. For amusement. I cannot understand."

"Nor will I pretend to," Vordenburg said. "But what was it she said? Mircalla wanted you to see the power you could have if you joined her. If you submitted to her."

"If I became like her; a vampire, you mean."

"A mate," Llewellyn concluded. "We all want a mate who completes us." He tapped his tinted glasses.

Jacqueline took his meaning. "I never needed anyone to complete me. Then I met de Guise, and I knew what it meant to be *more* than complete."

Llewellyn grinned. "Then you *do* know why he loves you."

A rumble of many feet, excited squeals, and peals of laughter signaled the gathering in the banquet hall had ended and the girls were being shown to their rooms. Angélique would see them settled and secure, then lock their doors so no one could be called away. Later, she would do the same for Jacqueline, locking her into de Guise's room. Luc would lock Marthe in. Everyone locked. Everyone safe. As safe as Jacqueline could make them, at least.

Jacqueline reached for Llewellyn's hand. He responded, reassuring her. "I didn't know I needed you too, Gryffin," she admitted. "And you, Monsieur Vordenburg. I need you all. Yes, you too, Gaudin."

Gaudin simply nodded and Jacqueline wondered if the girl understood any of the subtleties in their conversation.

When Angélique finally joined them, she drew her chair next to her twin's. Gaudin jumped up to pour another brandy.

Wrapping her arms around Jacqueline, Angélique laid her head on her shoulder. "I believe the girls will be content to spend a few days with us, but for myself, I had hoped for a less calamitous honeymoon and a little more time before a house full of children."

"Oh, I had such plans!" Jacqueline lamented. "Concerts and star cruises and recitals of poetry and music and so much more!"

"I know, m'amie." Angélique kissed her cheek. "And I bless you for your love. But what's our plan beyond tonight? Find and raid the tomb tomorrow?"

"Aye," said Vordenburg.

"Aye," echoed Llewellyn.

"And amen," Jacqueline finished. "I can accompany you, yes?"

Vordenburg agreed. "But first, a stop at the village church."

"And what does this raid entail?" Angélique prodded.

Vordenburg said, "We must dig down to expose the tomb to daylight, to weaken her. Then I will soak the tomb with blessed water so she cannot escape. Once she is trapped, we will dig it up, open it, and slay her. A stake to the heart and a beheading. It sounds simple, I know, but she will know we are coming because of her connection to Madame Duval. She will fight us."

"We'll rise at dawn then." Jacqueline tipped her head to Angélique's. "All of us." She stood and put Angélique's hand in Llewellyn's. "Come, Gaudin. Time for me to retire. You will help the Duchess with the injured girl, and then she will lock you into your room, so take some food with you to nibble on in case you get hungry tonight."

"But," Gaudin protested, "how will I lay out madame's work clothes?"

Jacqueline put her arm around her and ushered her from the salon. "Did you not hear me say we rise at dawn? That means you, too. I'll unlock your door and head to my water closet. You'll lay out my work clothes. I'll dress, and I'll show you how to put my hair up for a work day."

"Yes, madame."

"Questions?"

Gaudin shook her head, but her eyes held doubt.

"What is it?" Jacqueline paused and waited patiently for the girl to find her voice.

She gulped. "What is Luc not supposed to tell me? What did I do wrong?"

Jacqueline wanted to take her in her arms and hug the guilt away. She couldn't bear the fear in Gaudin's eyes. But this was not her child; this was her maid, her personal attendant. At Bellesfées, that meant Gaudin would never completely be a child again. She smiled and placed her hands on Gaudin's shoulders.

"You did everything you were asked to do, and more. I am very proud of you. And I'm very glad you agreed to be my lady's maid."

Gaudin dipped her head and said, "Yes, madame. Thank you, madame."

But she didn't seem relieved.

15.

Jacqueline gathered her chemise à la reine and peignoir, then paused at the vanity. The swelling in her eye had receded, though her vision remained blurred. Llewellyn had re-set her nose—a pain she hoped never to experience again—so at least it was straight, though huge for now. Her upper lip sported a red bulb around the cut. Her whole face was a mask of scarlet, violet, cobalt, and indigo, a fact that neither Angélique nor Llewellyn could truly appreciate although they did acknowledge the extent of the damage.

She grinned at the irony. After all her complaining about the face in the mirror, she wondered if she'd ever see that face again.

Helping her undress, Angélique brushed out Jacqueline's hair, mindful of wounds, and braided it. Llewellyn, meanwhile, went across the hall to dismiss Jean-Paul and change de Guise's bandages.

Llewellyn was laughing when Jacqueline entered. Her heart raced when she saw de Guise awake and propped up, and she fought the urge to throw herself into his arms. His eyes were clear though heavy with exhaustion. A weary smile lit his whole stubbled face, faltering as he took in the measure of her suffering. She hesitated, but then his smile returned with a hint of mischief.

He said, "They called you a horrible monster?"

Jacqueline spluttered. As she climbed up on the bed de Guise moved his right arm to embrace her.

"Can you blame them? Look at me." She pouted. "My nose looks like a potato."

"I am looking at you, chérie." He pulled her closer to kiss her gently, mindful of her injuries. "I am looking at the bravest, strongest, most brilliant woman I know. Every day I give thanks I have you by my side."

She stroked his brow. It was still hot to her touch; infection had abated, but he still fought the fever. "I'm more frustrated than brave or strong lately," she said. "All my life, the most vicious enemy I faced was molten steel. Burns and bruises I'm used to. I'm not accustomed to feeling weak and afraid. But I can do nothing to stop these attacks, and I'm afraid the time will come I'll fail to save anyone."

De Guise kissed her stricken arm above the wounds there. "Fear has nothing to do with courage, nor failure with strength, unless you allow them to rule you." He laid his head on her breast. "Angélique was right. You are a hero. You saved those girls."

Guilt rose up again. "Not all of them."

He kissed the wound where Mircalla had left her mark. "Learn to measure your worth by the greatness of your heart, chérie."

Llewellyn came around to Jacqueline. "Before you two get 'lovey-dovey,' I need to dress this arm. I just wrapped it this afternoon, didn't I?"

She gave a wry chuckle. "I've been busy being a hero."

"But not tonight," he told her. "Tonight, Angélique and I will be your sentinels and safeguards."

Jacqueline smiled gratefully. "I can think of no one I trust more."

When Llewellyn finished, he tucked Jacqueline into bed beside de Guise. "Remember what I said. The two of you need rest, and I do mean utter and complete rest."

De Guise grinned. "You mean, no 'lovey-dovey'?"

Alone with de Guise, Jacqueline told him the full tale of the flight to Eu and the horror of the savagery aboard *Esprit*. She kept her voice even so he would not know the depth of her alarm and sorrow. Though he gently stroked her back, she could not release the tension in her body.

"I close my eyes, but I still see them," she confessed. "All of them. The two in the gondola, the slaughtered young women, that *creature*, Marthe so brutal, Gaudin with that bloodthirsty look on her face." Her voice broke and she nestled closer. "Does that sound like a hero to you?"

"My love, that is exactly what heroes sound like. Only a monster can slash and slay and cry 'triumph' but walk away unmoved. As you saw tonight." He kissed the top of her head. "Enough talk of heroes, or fear, or worry. Tell me you missed me, as I have longed for you, chérie."

"De Guise—"

"*Alain.*"

"My love." She kissed his bare breast and breathed in his scent. A calming peace finally eased through her. "How is it you love me?"

His heart thumped beneath her lips, eliciting a grunt of pain. He cleared his throat and said, "I would show you how, but I'm afraid we have strict orders for complete rest."

Jacqueline snickered, then exploded in laughter. His mischievous grin made her laugh even harder. Sitting up, she gasped for air, bursting again into giggles. Though tears streamed her face they did not hurt.

Outside the chamber door, Llewellyn growled a reminder of his instructions, driving her to howls of even more laughter.

Jacqueline slept so deeply Llewellyn had to wake her in the morning. De Guise stirred but remained asleep. Slipping from his arms, she went to her room to fetch the key to Gaudin's chambers. To her surprise, the girl was already there setting out her work clothes.

"Madame Llewellyn came for me," she explained. "She told me to make two long braids to wind around your head."

Jacqueline smiled at the girl's confidence. She bent to wash her face, humming happily at her reflection. The swelling had receded from both her eyes and her lip. She felt whole and human again.

Gaudin was unusually quiet as she coiffed her. Jacqueline tried to make conversation, but the girl simply nodded or shook her head.

"You'll help keep the girls inside the château? Maybe some of them can help Marthe in the kitchen. And assist Angélique with her charge — what's her name?"

Gaudin shrugged.

"She'll be frightened and in a lot of pain. Maybe you could play checkers. Like Mister Smith did when you were sick."

Frustrated by the girl's lack of response, Jacqueline turned from the vanity. "Tell me what troubles you, Gaudin. I can't leave you behind today if you're in distress. I must focus all my attention on the work I have to do. So, talk to me now, and as I promised, nothing said in these chambers will go any farther."

Gaudin lowered her gaze. "I'm not in distress."

Jacqueline tapped her foot. "Gaudin, I place my trust in you. That's what it means to have a lady's maid. You never need tell me anything you don't wish to tell me, but I do ask you to be honest."

Gaudin raised her chin, a little defiantly. "Did you mean what you said about love?"

It was not the question Jacqueline had anticipated. She stifled the urge to laugh; the girl's somber frown deserved respect. "I usually mean exactly what I say, although it may shock or disappoint people. Have I disappointed you?"

Gaudin shifted and scratched her nose.

Jacqueline coaxed her. "Tell me what I said. Then ask me your question."

"You said 'one loves whom one loves.' Maman — that is — my mother tells me I should marry soon, now that I'm — you know."

"A young woman. You've had your monthly règles." Again Jacqueline patted her hand. "You don't have to marry if you don't wish to marry. Here at Bellesfées, you're your own woman. You can marry whenever you find the right man. You may even stay here as my maid once you're married, if you wish."

"But I don't want to marry."

Jacqueline smiled. "Not yet, you mean. You want to marry for love."

"No. I mean ever. Because —"

Jacqueline met the haunted look in the girl's eyes. Gaudin looked down again, her cheeks ablaze. Jacqueline took her hands and squeezed.

"Just like the demon." Gaudin's lip quivered.

Jacqueline hugged her. "You're not a demon, Gaudin."

"But the curé said it's a sin."

"Perhaps it is." Jacqueline stood to dress. "I don't know. I'm certain the curé would also say it's a sin for me to spend my nights in Monsieur de Guise's bed, or he in mine."

"Isn't it?" The girl's voice strained with the weight of guilt.

Jacqueline sighed, frustrated and annoyed, but not by Gaudin. She yanked on hose and her work pants and peeled away her night chemise.

"I can't tell you what sin is for you, Gaudin. If the curé says it's a sin, I'm sure he will be happy to hear your confession. At the least, you'll do penance. At the worst, you'll be looked down upon by everyone except those who truly love you. If I could, I'd send you away to school to learn Greek and Hebrew properly. Then you could read the Holy Scripture for yourself, study it, and wrestle with God as Jacob did, and as I have done, to learn what God wants from you. Confess yourself to God. I've found God to be far more forgiving than the church."

Jacqueline slipped her chemise over her head, tucked it, and tugged on her vest.

"Vampires aren't even mentioned in Scripture, but I'm very sure what Mircalla is doing is more than a sin, and I don't believe my desire to destroy her is a sin. Not because she's in love with me, as His Grace surmises, but because she's forced herself violently on me, and on others without their consent. She has stolen something from them they didn't offer, and she has murdered defenseless people for her own gain. Those things I know are wrong, and Scripture agrees."

Jacqueline tossed her coat around her shoulders and inspected the mended bullet tear. "You did a fine job with my coat, Gaudin. Thank you. Would you be good enough to bring Her Grace and the unfortunate girl some breakfast after you've had yours? After that, you are to assist the Duchess."

Gaudin did not look any happier. Jacqueline feared she had left the girl with more questions than answers. Better now than later, she told herself. A young woman like Gaudin would have enough to worry about later.

Jacqueline went first to the chapel where Luc had just finished laying the corpses of the vampire and her victims on a porter. Together they went to the forest and followed a path to the backwater of the Loire where Monsieur Claque had prepared a single grave for the three lost girls. One by one, Luc lowered the bodies in, nestling them close, as if for comfort. When he stepped away, Jacqueline moved forward and, with a sorrowful smile, laid silver crosses on them in benediction. After a solemn moment, Monsieur Claque interred them.

She wished she knew what to say over them. The little vampire, a child who should be gathering summer flowers. The young girls, almost women, who should be flirting and learning to dance. Jacqueline had no wisdom to impart, and inferred no deeper meaning from their deaths. They stood in silence as dark turned to day, cloudy and glum.

They returned to the château without a word. As Luc headed to the barn, Jacqueline caught his sleeve. He clapped her shoulder and gave her an encouraging shake.

Jacqueline met Llewellyn in the dining room for breakfast. "Where's Vordenburg?"

"Gone to the village already."

"Good. I refueled Claque's air jets and reloaded his stake gun. He's ready."

"Are you?"

She rubbed the ache in the back of her head. "No. Not at all."

Llewellyn slid the pot of coffee and the bowl of boiled cream her way. "You could stay here. Your presence would encourage the girls. Show them the panharmonium. Angélique can play for them. Pass a lovely summer day doing whatever it is girls do."

"Hah!" Jacqueline snorted. "As if I know what girls do."

Llewellyn tut-tutted. "I have heard the stories of the wild twins of Bellesfées. Angélique filled many hours reminiscing about the two of you tearing up the vineyards, dancing on the lawn, chasing the barking frogs."

"None of which we can do until Mircalla is gone," she observed. "I want them all inside. Honestly, Gryffin, I would rather stay back, but I'm a liability to them. With you, I can be bait."

"Bait." He chuckled. "Angélique said the same thing. Vordenburg assures me vampires burn in sunlight."

"Yes, but they can move about by day if they stay out of the sun, and clearly Mircalla can summon from the tomb. I know she brought some of them with her as she returned after her fall from *Esprit*, feeding and gaining strength as she made her way back to her tomb. But these others, from the nearby villages. How else could all these girls have appeared from so far afield, except that she commands them, as she commands me."

Jacqueline gulped coffee. "That terrifies me more than anything. What she might convince them or me to do. You believe she's in love with me. What if she asks me to slay her rival? What if the girls murder de Guise while we are away on this quest? Vordenburg says she can't reach their minds here within the warded château, but I don't trust that to be true, now that we know her powers exceed Vordenburg's knowledge of her. That's really why Claque is staying behind—to protect de Guise. You saw what happened last night. Gaudin and Marthe had no idea they were attacking me. I might just as eagerly slit de Guise's throat completely unaware of what I was doing. And the girls..." She recalled the vampire's childish gloating. "Girls are vicious."

EF DEAL † 169

Llewellyn chewed thoughtfully. "Jacky, would you want de Guise to be with you, spend the rest of his life with you—"

"Absolutely."

"—if he didn't love you?"

Jacqueline stared at him.

"Mircalla wants you, that is plain. And she wants you because of who and what you are. But she doesn't want to possess you. I think she wants you to want her, for who and what she is." He removed his sun-glasses. "When I met Angélique—perhaps she told you—she forced herself on me."

Jacqueline protested. "She wasn't herself, Gryffin, not really. Not since—"

"I know that now." He grinned at the memory. "I knew at the time what she had done was out of fear. She hoped to seduce me and know my mind, force me to feel love for her in the midst of the danger she was in. She didn't realize I had already committed myself to her the moment she defended me against Count Draganov's men. My loyalty became affection, affection became tenderness. But when I learned who she was—Angélique Laforge, a woman I already admired, who had already enchanted me, a woman I *wanted* to love—I dared hope she could love me as well. We cared for one another through peril and death, and in the end, we realized our true love.

"My point, Jacky, is this: if Mircalla loves you, truly loves you as I believe she does, she will dedicate herself to making you love her. She first professed her tenderness toward you. She then forced herself on you, and you resisted. So she tried to convince you with promises of power. I think her goal is to woo you and win you. She'll visit you again, and again, and again until you surrender yourself to her. She'll try to build an understanding, as delicate and as strong as your brass musicians, thread by thread."

"Hmm. I may need your sword to snap those threads."

He laughed. "My mameluke will serve you better. I'll make sure you have it."

Yet, his words kindled a spark of an idea for a new design. At the same time, a low distant rumbling outside raised a fresh fear. "Llewellyn, a storm," she said. "No sunlight today."

The two rose hastily.

"You find Vordenburg," Jacqueline said. "Make sure he returns safely. Let's hope Mircalla is still too drained from her display last night to have left her tomb."

"What about you?" Llewellyn called after her as she hurried from the dining room.

"I have work to do."

Jacqueline ran upstairs to her room and riffled through her wardrobe until she found the gowns she needed. She then went to Angélique's chambers. As she swept through the door, Gaudin jumped up from the chair where she napped beside the bed. Jacqueline hushed her and bid her go back to sleep. Glancing at the unconscious young woman in the bed, she shuddered at the extreme of her torture. Such could not happen again. With a grunt of determination, Jacqueline entered Angélique's dressing room and opened the wardrobe. Her sister's profligate tastes of the years past finally had a worthwhile purpose. Sorting through the colorful frocks, she snatched down three that met her needs as Angélique entered.

"I won't complain," she commented. "After all, you did pay for them. But—"

"They're silk," Jacqueline explained on her way out. "We've seen what my work can do against a bullet. Let us see what it can do against a vampire's bite."

A roll of thunder accompanied her words.

Jacqueline stopped to visit de Guise before getting to work. He was awake, unshaven but groomed, and reading. He looked up in delight.

"You haven't left yet? The storm?"

She bent over to kiss him. "I have a new plan, a new design. I may be at work the whole day, but I wanted to see you once more before I vanished."

He caressed her face, his brown eyes warm. "Go be brilliant." He tugged her down for one more kiss before releasing her. "Come home to me, chérie."

Jacqueline smiled. "Always."

She headed to the music conservatory, pausing at the servants wing to call Monsieur Claque to her as she loaded the dresses and her gown on the porter and sent it up on the lift. Checking to make sure all her tools and supplies were in her kit, she headed to the concert hall with Monsieur Claque, meeting the porter and leading it to the clarinetist.

"Eh bien, monsieur," she said, gauging its form and size, "I believe you will do nicely."

She yanked her welding cap over her braided chignon, pulled her gogglers into place, and ignited the blow lamp. In a few minutes, she had removed the musician's head.

Heavy rain fell steadily. The leaden skies indicated there would be no sun the rest of the day. Gaudin brought Jacqueline's luncheon along with a dessert of peach ice cream, but Jacqueline was so preoccupied with her work she never noticed the tray until the dessert was peach soup. Once the soldering was finished, she began wrapping and sewing down six-ply silk over a webbing of silver and brass.

And on she worked, until galloping feet up the stairs broke her focus. She blinked about in surprise as the girls poured into the concert hall, with Angélique a shepherdess surrounded by her flock.

"Take seats, mesdames, mesdemoiselles. You must all be seated," Angélique told them. She grinned at Jacqueline, then feigned shock. "Where's my clarinetist?"

Jacqueline spread her hands in apology. "He was just my size."

"It's Jacqueline Duval!" cried a little girl.

"It's the hero!" came a chorus in response.

Immediately, they crowded forward, but Angélique signaled them back. Two dozen voices called out a hundred questions at once and Jacqueline didn't know how to answer any of them.

Angélique clapped her hands for attention. "Jacqueline Duval is working on a new creation. We cannot disturb her. Come see what she has already built, though. Take seats."

They "Aww"ed in disappointment until Jacqueline started up the panharmonium. She led the older ones to the front row seats and showed them the pedals, gave instructions, and left Angélique to amuse them for the next few hours. She bent back to her design and was lost to the music and voices surrounding her until she finished, testing the joints and making final adjustments to close any gaps in the silk.

Finally, Jacqueline became aware of hushed murmurs. She turned to see the crowd of girls around her again. With a flourish, she smiled and displayed the completed suit of silk armor. The younger ones giggled.

"Is that worn under a gown?" an older one asked.

"Under my clothing."

The young woman pursed her lips doubtfully. "It looks uncomfortable."

"About as uncomfortable as a bustle or stays," Jacqueline assured her.

"How do you put it on?"

Jacqueline winked at Angélique. "With help. You can do anything difficult with help. And aren't you all supposed to be helping Marthe with dinner? She can't feed you by herself, you know."

As they filed out, Angélique whispered, "Gryffin and Vordenburg have news for you. Is your suit of armor complete?"

"Not quite," Jacqueline said. "One more adjustment."

She picked up the stake gun she had removed from Monsieur Claque and reignited the blow lamp.

16.

JACQUELINE WAS SURPRISED TO FIND THE MEN GATHERED IN DE GUISE'S room. They greeted her, and she took her place on the bed beside de Guise. She rubbed his blond-stubbled chin with a teasing grin, relieved to find his skin was not so fevered beneath her touch.

"Our assassins have returned to the village," Llewellyn said without prelude. "I caught their scent near the inn. We've been contemplating the best way to deal with them."

"Alas, I am not a soldier," Vordenburg lamented. "Not in this kind of war."

"And I'm not fit for battle," de Guise grumbled. "And before you say it, Llewellyn, you can't take on all of them yourself."

Llewellyn huffed. "I beg the honor of argument. My first commission was in Her Majesty's Royal Navy fighting Caribbean pirates, long before you and I met in Prague. Musket, sword, and saber, sir, I'm quite adept. Add to those skills my lupine agility and heightened senses, and I assure you, I am a formidable opponent."

De Guise saluted with a flourish and a grin. "What would you suggest then, sir?"

"I would suggest that first, I enjoy a good supper, so I'm not tempted to eat anyone."

De Guise gave a short, hearty laugh, but quickly suppressed it, gripping his side.

"More seriously," Llewellyn continued, "I want to know why they returned. Jacqueline said they believed they'd accomplished their goal."

"Perhaps with lack of news of the King's death, they wish to know why we had a surgeon here, or a funeral procession. They were watching your departure to Eu, Jacqueline. Llewellyn confirmed that after you'd left."

De Guise reached for water, but Jacqueline quickly got it for him and helped him drink.

"That does make sense," she agreed. "Word of an assassination would have spread. They've returned to finish their task. But I have faith in Llewellyn," she said. "I know his strength first hand, and he's every bit as capable as you, de Guise."

"Is that so?" De Guise feigned suspicion. "I trust you speak only of his martial skills."

It was her turn to tweak his nose.

"It's settled then," Llewellyn said as he rose. "I'll go."

"And do what?" Jacqueline stopped him. "Will you simply kill them? And how do we explain that to the prefecture? Why can't we report these men shot at our château and nearly killed a man and have them arrested?"

The men exchanged dark looks. "Because no one can know de Guise has been removed from the field of the King's defense," Llewellyn told her.

"We can say I was shot, then. I mean, I was *shot*, and I certainly look the victim, don't I?" She indicated her arm. "You and I, we capture these men, we drag them to the gendarmerie, make our accusations and show the wound. You bear witness you saw them fleeing through the woods of Bellesfées. It will be enough to hold them, perhaps send them on to the Orléans prison to await trial. Besides, they're foreigners. The local prefecture will not deal with them kindly, especially if I convince them of my utter dismay and horror, and offer a considerable reward for the capture of these—what is the word you use? 'Blackguards'?"

Llewellyn weighed her plan. "If we go, we go now, so we can return before dark."

"It's already dark. It's been dark all day," she observed.

As if to punctuate her meaning, thunder returned in the distance. De Guise sighed unhappily. She kissed his brow.

"You know I'm right," she said.

He didn't answer.

The château hallways were busier than they had ever been, so many girls darting about from room to kitchen, from kitchen to a different room, with Marthe the queen bee giving orders above the hum. Jacqueline found Gaudin still guarding the injured girl, who was kept in a stupor with Angélique's supply of narcotics to ease her pain.

"You must find time to rest as well, Gaudin. I'll have need of you tonight, I think."

"Yes, madame. Her Grace has sent other girls to help me. I'll be fine."

"Well done. I'm going to the village with Monsieur Llewellyn. Do you have a message for your mother and father?"

"If you see them—" Gaudin hesitated, then said, "tell them I'm a lady's maid at the château, and I'll send them a portion of my pay as soon as I can."

Jacqueline regarded her with astonishment. Then she smiled in approval.

Jacqueline changed into a day gown for greater effect in the village, albeit without the full undergirding a lady should have worn. She was just too sore to bear stays or bustles. Llewellyn met her at the entryway and the two set out.

Bellesfées's macadamized drive traversed over three kilometers of wooded lane, sheltered from the heaviest of the storm. The center of the village lay another two kilometers beyond. Llewelyn carried an ornate carved-handled umbrella that covered them both, although it didn't keep their clothing dry. They soon squelched through mud. Once they reached the village, they slowed approaching the inn. Llewellyn confirmed the scent of the assassins, and as they entered the courtyard, he verified no one else hung about.

Following Llewellyn's instructions, Jacqueline stepped inside and turned her back to the gathered group as Llewellyn closed the umbrella. They removed their wet overcoats and hung them on hooks. Jacqueline sported an ostentatious bandage on her wounded arm.

"Back corner," Llewellyn murmured close to her ear. He offered his arm and led her into the common room.

Jacqueline's eyes narrowed on the offenders. She pointed and cried, "You!"

The handful of village men in the room rose to glare at the strangers seated there, while other travelers lowered their glasses or utensils and kept their heads tucked down.

"See what they've done to me!" Jacqueline pleaded to the room, letting her voice break with anger and shock. "They shot me! On my own lands, in my own home! I am Jacqueline Duval de la Forge-à-Bellesfées, and those men tried to kill me. Look!"

Blinking back crocodile tears, Jacqueline untied the large bow to reveal the gash and burn on her arm. Satisfied with the angry mutters she evinced, she then indicated her damaged face.

"I fainted from the pain and the sight of my own blood, and thus struck my face upon the mantel. Those Autriche-*chiens* did this. An attack on Bellesfées! An attack upon my person!"

The four men in the corner had nowhere to retreat. The villagers moved in on them, calling out threats.

Llewellyn whisked a sword from the handle of his umbrella and tossed the umbrella aside. "Messieurs! Take them to the prefecture! A louis d'or for each of you for defending la Belle Dame de Bellesfées."

Confronted by the tavern crowd, the cornered men drew long knives from their belts and took aggressive stances. The villagers fell back. Being simple workmen, they weren't prepared for a fight.

Llewellyn was.

Llewellyn surged forward and kicked the men's table into their legs, trapping them. He grabbed a chair with his left hand and swung it at the first man's head as he and the man beside him raised their arms to defend themselves. At the same time, Llewellyn's sword flashed so swiftly Jacqueline couldn't see what he had done. Two knives clattered to the floor as the two men who had wielded them grabbed their wrists. Blood streamed between their clenched fingers. A third man raised his arm to throw his blade. Llewellyn lunged, striking upward into the heart, and withdrew.

Llewellyn nodded to Jacqueline. "Always withdraw," he told her, "so they bleed."

Crimson spread across the man's chest. He clutched at the wound and fell forward gasping. The fourth man dropped his knife and surrendered.

"Murderers!" Jacqueline cried. "Seize them!"

With the brigands disarmed, the men of Forge-à-Bellesfées had the courage of their beers. They laid hands on the three left standing and piled on blow after blow until the assassins lay unconscious. They then dragged all four down the muddied road to the prefecture after receiving the promised reward from the Duke of Singlebury.

Llewellyn flipped another louis d'or to the patron behind the bar and took the rag from the man's shoulder to wipe down his blade. "I wish to inspect their rooms," he said. "We'll take their effects to the jail."

"Of course, monsieur."

"Your Grace," Jacqueline corrected him.

The man's eyes widened, and he bowed. "Your Grace!"

He led Llewellyn and Jacqueline to an upstairs room with three beds, a wardrobe and oil lamp, and a trunk, where they found two breechloaders along with ammunition.

"These aren't Austrian," Llewellyn said, examining the guns. "Dreyse needle-guns. No wonder they could fire from the woods and still hit something."

Jacqueline secured their papers from the nightstand. "Austrian. But I don't recognize these registrations. They don't appear to represent any authority." She crumpled the papers into her pocket, exasperated. "Malcontents. No one."

"They always are," Llewellyn said. "Zealots. Fieschis or Fawkeses. Let's get these papers to the prefect and be gone." He went ahead of her and took her arm once more at the foot of the steps. "Would you like to carry the rifles or the umbrella?" he asked with a smirk.

"The rifles will go inside my coat," she answered in kind. "It is not fitting for la Belle Dame de Bellesfées to carry her own umbrella when there is a gentleman about."

Llewellyn laughed. He wrapped her coat around her, mindful of her now-exposed wounds. She then slid the rifles into the long pocket inside her coat and tightened her belt, stowing the ammunition in the various outside pockets. She beamed up at him.

"This was quite amusing, Your Grace."

"Indeed, it was, Madame Duval."

"And educational. 'Always withdraw so they bleed.' I shall remember that."

After depositing their evidence and more louis d'ors with the prefect and making certain three were locked away safely and the fourth was dead, Jacqueline and Llewellyn walked back to Bellesfées. They stopped first chez Gaudin, where the girl's parents wept with gratitude not only at the news of their daughter's recovery but also of her new station and promised income.

"You've done a good thing," Llewellyn said as they left.

"It's only what is right."

"Noblesse oblige?"

"It's a social contract of mutual benefit." Jacqueline sighed. "I have to rebuild my workshop. I'll need all of them to accomplish that. The workers of France are treated oppressively enough by the government, by the wealthy, by the bankers and industrialists. I don't think Mister Smith will enjoy more than a few more years on the throne, given his flippancy toward these very serious economic matters."

Llewellyn chuckled. "Why, Jacky, you're a socialist after all."

As promised, they returned to Bellesfées before sunset, even if the sun wasn't present. Vordenburg welcomed them with relief and helped with their coats.

"Where are the girls?" Jacqueline wondered at the emptiness of the halls. "Banquet hall?"

"The music conservatory," he answered. "The duchess is leading them in song."

Llewellyn excused himself to join Angélique, while Jacqueline went upstairs to de Guise's room. He was asleep, guarded by Monsieur Claque, but he roused at her light kiss on his brow and gave her a tired grin.

"Our assassins?"

"Will trouble us no further. Llewellyn was quite dashing. One is dead, three imprisoned in our prefecture."

De Guise frowned. "I thought there were six? Isn't that what Llewellyn said?"

"Yes, the two others—" She swallowed. "Fell. Remember? From the gondola. The Montgolfier."

De Guise wasn't convinced. "Did the woman in the gondola appear to be the kind who would skulk in the woods to fire off shots in the dark?"

Jacqueline straightened, her pulse quickening. "What are you saying? There's one more man out there?"

He rubbed his head, his brow knit with both pain and worry. "Find Llewellyn again. We'll talk."

Jacqueline went down the back staircase, closer to the conservatory. She halted at the empty kitchen, where laden dinner platters lined the preparation table. No Marthe. No helpers. Jacqueline walked along the servants' wing, but all was silent.

With twenty-four girls in the house.

Supposedly singing while Angélique played piano.

Jacqueline's dread increased when she found Llewellyn's and her wet coats on the floor of the entryway along with Llewellyn's umbrella.

Jacqueline silently unsheathed the blade from the umbrella handle and crept upstairs, pausing to make certain there was no one else in the hallway. She went to Angélique's room first. Gaudin sat by the sleeping girl. Jacqueline laid a finger to her lips. Closing the door, she locked it. She then went down the hallway and locked de Guise's door. As she did, she heard him call quietly, "Careful, chérie."

Jacqueline pulled off her muddy boots and hose and slipped out of her wet gown, leaving them outside her chambers. Like a ghost, she glided down the back staircase in her chemise and drawers. Step by cautious step, blade poised, she made her way from the kitchens. When she got to the conservatory wing, she halted beneath the concert hall stairway to listen. The hall doors were closed. She caught the muffled scrape of chairs. Then a rough murmur followed again by silence.

Jacqueline opened the panel beneath the staircase to access the controls for the gas lighting in the conservatory wing. By small increments, she lowered the lighting in the stairwell to inky blackness, hoping no one would notice the glass panes in the hall doors going dark. She then tiptoed up the stairs and flattened herself beside the door, listening, her mouth agape so her heart didn't pound so loudly in her ears, slowing her breathing to still the trembling in her arms. She didn't know whether she was more frightened or angry. It didn't matter. Two dozen young girls, Marthe, and probably Vordenburg, Llewellyn, Luc, and Jean-Paul needed her to be neither.

A harsh voice hollered, "If you don't stop your blubbing, I will blow your head off, you noisy Fotz."

The sixth Austrian. His words were followed by a small girl's wail.

He sounded close. He likely faced the gathered group with his back to the entrance, but Jacqueline couldn't know for certain; he might be standing off to the side. She wanted to hazard a glance through the glass. If she stood far enough back, she might not be seen in the dark.

By now, Angélique and Llewellyn would have her scent and know she was very near. This was one of those times having the ability to communicate with the wolves would be convenient. She would tell them to find a way to—

"She's frightened!" Angélique cried. "She's just a little girl. Don't you know she's frightened for her life?"

"Shut your mouth!"

"You come in here with a musketoon and think we won't be frightened of you? We're all seated. Our men are on the floor. We've done everything you asked."

Jacqueline sighed with relief. *Bless you, mon Ange!*

Plenty of distraction for Jacqueline to poke her head around to locate the assassin, about two meters to the right and three meters forward, clutching a small girl by her hair. And clever Angélique, revealing he brandished a musketoon, which she couldn't see from the door. A single shot, no reloading before she could strike him down, presuming he missed her. The girls sat frozen in fear. Vordenburg slumped unconscious by the wall. The other men lay face down with their hands behind their heads. How had Llewellyn been caught by surprise?

"Dame, I will put a ball through your open mouth if you do not shut it."

"Don't you dare point that gun at me."

That was Jacqueline's cue. She ploughed through the doors and dove to the floor, rolling over her sword. The man shoved the little girl away and pivoted from Angélique to fire in a panic at Jacqueline. The ball shattered the glass panel of the door. Girls screamed and the men leapt up. Jacqueline flexed to her knees and thrust Llewellyn's blade up into the man's groin. She withdrew, giving a quick nod to Llewellyn. He grinned and winked.

The brigand dropped the gun. He gasped and fell forward as Llewellyn and Luc seized his arms. His wide eyes glazed over and he looked down. Blood soaked his trousers and pooled on the marble.

Jacqueline stood and pricked the man's jugular vein, but the wound to his femoral artery was fatal. He would live just long enough to see the fury in her eyes before his closed.

17.

LUC AND JEAN-PAUL TOOK AWAY THE AUSTRIAN'S BODY.

"That one is for the boars to feed on," Angélique snarled after them.

Llewellyn revived Vordenburg, and Marthe comforted the girls. Jacqueline clung to Angélique, her quaking body so charged with electricity she felt she would collapse, now that the crisis had passed. Angélique held her tightly.

"You were wonderful, m'amie. Where did you get that sword? And when did you learn to use it?" Angélique squeezed her. "You truly are a hero. Don't ever doubt it."

As Angélique released her, a swarm of girls engulfed them calling for "Jacqueline Duval! The hero!"

Jacqueline answered their cries with a solemn frown. When they quieted, she told them, "You were *all* heroes. You were very wise and very brave. It is not easy to be either of those when someone treats you brutally. You didn't run away. You kept very quiet."

"Except Lisette," muttered someone, who was shushed.

"I'm proud of you," Jacqueline said. "All of you. You saved one another by not being foolish. You saved one another, and you saved Bellesfées. I thank each and every one of you."

She bowed to the girls, and they gazed back in astonishment. The older ones acknowledged the solemnity of the occasion and took the younger ones under their arms.

"I would ask one more duty of each of you," Jacqueline said, and her voice softened. "Would you help Marthe put dinner on the table in the banquet hall?"

Marthe wiped tears from her ruddy cheeks and blew her nose into a towel. She nodded wearily and gave a half-hearted smile to the group surrounding her. She kissed Jacqueline's cheek—"You're a good girl.

Both, good girls." — before herding the others from the concert hall, barking orders.

Llewellyn clapped Jacqueline on the back, startling her. "You did well. I'm sorry it came to this. It's all my fault. I didn't expect another man. When I caught the scent, I thought it was the smell of the clothing from the inn."

"As did I," Angélique added. "And Vordenburg always smells frightened, so when that man barreled through the doors holding a gun on him—"

Jacqueline shushed them both. "It was no one's fault. It was his unfortunate choice to lay siege to Bellesfées." She shuddered. "Another corpse to my tally. I have to wonder what is the difference between a hero and a monster."

Llewellyn lifted Jacqueline's right arm and pried her fingers from the hilt of the blade. Jacqueline stretched and flexed her hand, staring at it. It hardly seemed her own, yet she could no more disown it than she could deny the memory of what it had just wrought. Passing the blade to Angélique, Llewellyn put his arm around Jacqueline's waist and accompanied her all the way to de Guise's room.

De Guise had wrestled himself up to sit in his agitation. He gave a cry of relief when they entered. Llewellyn helped Jacqueline onto the bed and she folded herself against de Guise, still trembling.

"She's one extraordinary woman, de Guise," he said. He came around to make sure de Guise hadn't opened his side with his restless movements, then tucked him in. "I would say she is the most extraordinary woman I've ever known, but then, I did marry Angélique."

Llewellyn picked up clean linens and sat down beside Jacqueline to bandage her arm. She had forgotten about her gash and the burns, about all of her wounds. She had forgotten everything from the entire day beyond two words: *Always withdraw.*

Jacqueline set her hand on de Guise's chest, and he curled his hand around hers. She sighed, releasing the anger and fear that had driven her, letting the serenity of de Guise's presence replace them.

Deep in the night, Jacqueline awoke frozen in terror with the echo of a velvety voice calling her name. Tranquil silence eased her fears, but she waited, listening.

De Guise's even breathing lulled her. His light blond hair caught the glow of the argand. Jacqueline traced his face with her fingers. In profile, his bow lips formed a lovely arch she wanted to kiss. Such a perfect nose, too, something she would no longer have. She watched his chest rise and fall, and laid her hand on his breast to feel his heartbeat. Her hand came alive with a jolt of electricity that sent a wave of heat through her, arousing a moist warmth between her legs. Her fingers caught in curls and she followed their lines down his body, her own heart racing. She longed to straddle him and press her breasts to him. To slide her thighs along his and lower herself onto him and feel the whole of him filling her as she took him in. To gaze into his eyes, triumphant, as he gazed up in wonder at her power over him.

Jacqueline snatched back her hand. She tumbled out of the bed and ran to the bathtub to climb in. She turned on the cold water and thrust her head under the flow. As the tub filled, the rest of her cooled as well. The ache of her wounds eased. The ache deeper within that had so frightened her abated. Worse than arousal, a rapacious need to claim a victory she hadn't earned. She hugged her knees and rocked until her thoughts settled into just one question:

Did de Guise ever feel the same selfish hunger when he looked at her?

Jacqueline was not willing to accept it. She had saved the King; she had defended Bellesfées. She was a force to be savored, not tamed or taken.

No, this was not the fire that lit his eyes when he looked at her. Gentleness, tenderness, giving more than taking—the difference between lust and love. For the first time, she felt worthy of his love. For the first time, she felt equal to it.

But the realization brought another question: Was this what Mircalla felt for her?

"Yes. Yes, Jacqueline, my beautiful Jacqueline. Now you know what I feel, how I feel."

She jerked upright, sloshing water on the floor. Mircalla's voice— silky, alluring, but not as a dream, not in some hypnotic trance. No mists. No jasmine. No clouds in her mind.

"Mircalla," she whispered. "Your thoughts, not mine." She clenched her jaw. "Monster."

Mircalla's laughter cut through Jacqueline's soul. *"And what are you?"*

Jacqueline bowed her head to her knees. "Leave me."

"*How can I leave you, my beloved? Day by day I have watched you work. Such a facile mind, such physical strength and elegant grace, such wonders you create. The scent of your body, the tenderness of your caress day by day. I love you, Jacqueline. How can I leave you?*"

With a shudder of horror, Jacqueline realized she had harbored Mircalla all along: the black cat from the workshop. Now she understood how Mircalla had first been able to attack her, why the wards had not been effective. Jacqueline had let the cat in long ago, petted it, accepted it.

"*Why will you not let me caress you as you have caressed me? Touch you, as you long to be touched? Give you all I long to give you?*"

"No."

"*Why? Because the thought of my love sickens you? Or are you afraid of your own desires?*"

Jacqueline pressed her hands to her ears. "Your love doesn't sicken me, Mircalla, it's your hunger and savagery I reject. You don't love me; you desire me, that's all. In life, you might have declared your desire, and I would not revile you, but neither would I requite your affection. I will never love you. That's who I am. I love whom I love, whom I *choose* to love. I do not choose you."

"*You will. My Jacqueline, my beautiful Jacqueline.*"

"I am not yours. I am my own!" she roared to the ceiling.

After a long silence, Mircalla replied, "*I will have you, Jacqueline. You are mine. You and I are one forever.*"

Jacqueline stepped out of the tub and stripped off her chemise and drawers. She stood naked and defiant. "This is *my* body. Scarred and battered and broken and burned. It's not beautiful, but it's *mine*. You have the power to do what you will, to take what I can't give you; but *I* decide who may possess my heart. I will never be yours, and I will forever despise you for what you did to me."

She stormed out of the water closet and halted when she saw De Guise watched her from the bed. His eyes glistened with tears. She clasped her hands over her mouth.

"Not you, de Guise. I did not rail at you."

"Didn't you?" His voice broke. "I know I've taken you from all that you were, and I can't offer any promise of tomorrow. I wouldn't—"

Dripping wet, Jacqueline climbed onto the bed and knelt, aching to embrace him, afraid to hurt him. "Oh, Alain, Alain, my love, my dearest, only love, you didn't take me. I gave myself to you. I give you all I am, gladly, freely, lovingly."

"Stop." De Guise winced, then groaned. "Chérie."

He heaved himself over and seized her in his arms, although he cried out in pain. "I'm sorry." He gasped. "I can't—I can't protect you. I can't—"

Silencing him with a kiss, she gently pushed him back onto the pillows. Her fingertip traced the bow of his lip as she lifted his hand to her heart, eliciting a quiet moan. She leaned over to press her breasts to him, then slid down to nestle into the curve of his shoulder, leading his hand to caress her as she swirled the silvery blond curls on his chest.

"I don't need protection, my love," she whispered. "I need gentleness. I need you beside me, with me. I need you to let me love you."

They held one another until their breathing calmed, their bodies relaxed.

"I can't lose you," he murmured. "Jacqueline, chérie."

"I promise you will never lose me. I'm yours."

She drew the coverlet up over their heads, a fortress against the rest of the world. "It's my turn to protect you. I'll fight her. I will defeat her. I only need you to be here when I do."

De Guise closed his eyes. "Where else can I go? You are my home."

They passed the remainder of the night awake, silent, and content. Mircalla did not intrude again. The sky paled to lilac, then pink-tinged mother-of-pearl as the sun rose. The dawn chorus was swiftly drowned out by the bustle of the château. Still they didn't stir. Quiet murmurs in the hallway outside the chambers alerted them that Llewellyn and Angélique would soon be in to attend them. Only then did Jacqueline remember her chemise lay in a soaking heap on the water-closet floor. She tucked the bedclothes around her just as Llewellyn entered.

"Whoop!" He disappeared.

A moment later, Angélique came in with Jacqueline's dressing gown. "All that shouting last night. He's supposed to be healing," she scolded good-naturedly. She slipped the gown around Jacqueline.

De Guise grinned. "This was more healing than you know."

"Jean-Paul has fetched the curé once again, and he's not happy with us dragging him up here every day." Angelique laughed. "Ah, if only he knew what else he'd find."

Jacqueline bent over to kiss de Guise. "I'll come to you before we leave. One way or another, this ends today."

"They will sing of our glory in the legends to come," Angélique declared, blowing de Guise a kiss on their way out.

The thick silk armor was more difficult to don than Jacqueline had anticipated, but Angélique and Gaudin fitted her into it and fastened it closed. It encased her from her neck to her calves in six layers of silk and brass mesh.

"At least it's fairly light, and more flexible for breathing than a corset," Jacqueline said.

They checked for gaps in the silk, making certain her throat was well protected. Gaudin helped her put her work clothes on, including the new silk chemise Gaudin had prepared at Jacqueline's request: the sleeves slit between the wrist and elbow to allow for the weapon on each arm.

Angélique stepped back to admire the results. "A regular corsair. I think there's a musketoon lying about, if you wish."

"Zut, that reminds me." Jacqueline sighed. "I need to commission a glazier."

"Vitrier, très vite!" Angélique quipped. "I can take care of that later, Jacky. Have you finished dressing? What coiffure goes with those guns? Gaudin, can you make tresses?"

"Yes, madame. Along the sides, or as a crown?"

"Neither," Jacqueline said. She went to her vanity, but to her dismay she found she couldn't bend enough to sit. She gave specific instructions, and stood while Gaudin and Angélique worked together to plait her hair away from her face, then roll the rest into a secure chignon close to her brow instead of at her nape.

Angélique applauded. "With a battered face, broken nose, black-butter eyes, and a head like a bald monkey, you look truly terrifying, dear sister. Let's go scare the hell out of that vampire."

She hooked arms with Jacqueline and they went down to the break-fast room. They were surprised to discover a handful of young women awaiting them, for the women's breakfast was being served in the ban-quet room.

"What's this?" Jacqueline asked.

The slender blonde with large blue eyes said, "We heard you plan to hunt down the vampire today. My name is Adèle Frontenac, and I wish to accompany you. On my father's estate, I hunted deer and boar. I would dearly love to blow that demon's head off."

Her imperious tone took Jacqueline off guard. The young woman hardly looked the type to hunt monsters. Her bedraggled, tiered-balloon skirt, just brushing the tops of worn low boots, and torn lace-trimmed sleeves revealed her to be from a bourgeois family. Her father was probably frantic at her disappearance.

Before Jacqueline could answer, a second stepped forward, stout and dark-eyed, dressed in a plain day dress, tunic, and boots, all showing the wear of her travels. "I'm Giselle Boulot. My family has a butcher shop, so I'm very strong and skilled with the knife. Please let me come too."

A third, Renée Guichet, and a fourth, Patrice Yves, gave similar credentials. The fifth—the oldest of them, boyish and sturdily built, wearing the formless culottes and overshirt of a field worker—simply said, "Têtue. No family. You said you can accomplish anything difficult with help, right? You saved my life twice. I figure that means it's yours, so take me with you, Jacqueline Duval."

Jacqueline searched their faces. They did not look as though they hungered for her blood. Each young woman returned her gaze evenly. Their arms bore witness to their physical ability. They leaned forward intently, itching for her assent. Têtue wore the typical Parisian defiant sneer, daring Jacqueline to test her.

Planting her hands on her hips, Jacqueline said to the first four. "Frontenac, Boulot, Guichet, Yves, you'll accompany my wolves. If you can shoot, you'll be given guns. And shovels so we can dig that much faster. Têtue." She nodded at the brawny girl with a grin. "Something tells me you'd be good with a wooden stake in your hand."

Têtue folded her muscular arms. "I have very strong hands, Jacqueline Duval."

Angélique nudged Jacqueline and whispered. "I like this girl. Can we keep her?"

Jacqueline hushed her sister, then turned to the young women. "Call me 'Duval.' If you've had your breakfast, go find my maid Gaudin to fetch you all trousers."

The women in skirts made noises of protest, but Jacqueline cut them off. "We are heading into the rough woods, and your skirts will only catch and rip and hinder you. If you object to trousers, you may stay behind. Otherwise, once you're suitably clothed, go to the salon and explain to Baron Vordenburg my instructions."

As the women left, Têtue paused to say, "Thank you, Duval."

Vordenburg fumed outside the salon. "What do you mean bringing all these girls?" he said when Jacqueline finally appeared after bidding de Guise goodbye. "You realize—"

"I realize," she replied, "you and I have been fighting this thing on our own, and we haven't succeeded. We're not the only ones aggrieved by Countess Karnstein. These *women* deserve the right to avenge the wrongs done to them as much as I do."

"But how do we trust them? Mircalla has bitten them. Mircalla could make them turn on you at any moment."

"They won't," she said, although she did not tell him about her midnight conversation with Mircalla. "Baron, I believe I have a solution to Mircalla's call."

As Luc joined them with weapons and shovels, she motioned them inside.

Llewellyn and Angélique had met the four women assigned to them in lupine form. The women fawned over them in delight, unaware they cuddled the Duke and Duchess of Singlebury. Llewellyn particularly enjoyed the scratching behind his ears. Têtue watched from the mantel, an amused smirk on her face. She straightened to attention when Jacqueline came in. Jacqueline handed each young woman a large empty wineskin shorn of its spout and threaded with leather cord to cinch it.

"Today, ladies, we learn a new coiffure. Each of you—" She stopped at Têtue, with her ragged, cropped black curls. "Each of you with long hair, that is. Bend over as far as you can, grab your hair at the base as far forward as you can, and begin twisting until you have a knot you can tuck at your forehead."

She assisted them as needed, pinning the knot close to their brow instead of at the back. They tittered at their silly appearance.

"You think you look funny now? Wait for the bonnets."

Jacqueline demonstrated, pulling the wineskin over her head and cinching it tight against her brow. It flopped behind like a baggy cap.

The women burst into laughter, but they followed suit, and soon they were all in giggles except Têtue, who caught on immediately.

"The holy water."

"The holy water," Jacqueline confirmed. "When we were sprayed with holy water, Mircalla lost her hold on our minds. I believe Mircalla will not be able to touch your minds at all if your heads are kept soaked in holy water. Baron Vordenburg will fill these caps, and they'll hold the holy water close to your heads."

No longer glowering, Vordenburg plucked his notebook out and wrote furiously. "Abraham will enjoy hearing this one," he said with a chuckle. He clapped the notebook shut, tucked it away, and took up his walking stick.

Jacqueline opened a cabinet and brought out a tray of glasses and a decanter of sherry. She poured for the women, Vordenburg, and herself. Four of the young women again giggled. Not Têtue. When Jacqueline raised her glass for a toast, Têtue said, "What about your wolves?"

The wolves chuffed in laughter. Jacqueline answered, "They prefer vermouth."

"To our league of extraordinary women," Vordenburg said. "Knights of the Order of Van Helsing."

"Huh. The Order of Duval, I think," said Têtue.

18.

THEY RODE SOUTH ALONG THE LOIRE TOWARD BEAUGENCY, WHERE THEY crossed the river and headed southeast toward Jouy-le-Poitier. In her cage of wire and silk, Jacqueline was forced to lie uncomfortably against the buckboard of the wagon. To pass the time along the way, Vordenburg educated the young women on what he had learned of Mircalla's strengths and powers.

"Remember not only can she fly, but she can vanish and reappear behind you almost immediately, so walk side by side and be ready to turn back-to-back. Her hands are talons, like an eagle's claws. You saw what happened to that poor girl who now lies in the Duchess's chambers. Do not let a vampire get too close to you."

"She's already been too close to us, monsieur," Boulot replied. She patted her rifle. "She won't make that mistake again."

"Do not be overconfident. She has bitten you all," Vordenburg reminded them. "We hope the holy water that soaks your heads will prevent her from overpowering your minds, but we cannot be altogether sure. I do not know how many times she has bitten any of you, but she may have invited you to drink her blood. A vampire's blood heals the most mortal of wounds and lends strengths and powers beyond the limits of human abilities. You might think that is good, yes? But if that has happened, then after a third bite from the vampire, you soon begin to thirst for human blood, leaving behind your human appetite for food and becoming a vampire yourself. Then nothing can save you—*unless* the vampire is destroyed before you drink another's blood."

The young women made no retort, their swagger diminished. Jacqueline chewed the inside of her cheek. Some of them had first been bitten the night Mircalla fell near Chartres; she didn't know about the others. However, none of them had burst into flames when their caps were filled with holy water, so she had to trust they would be able to hold their own against Mircalla's call.

They secured their wagon at an inn at Lailly-en-Val before eleven o'clock, and from there they plunged into heavy woods where the spicy scents of oak, plane, pine, beech, and birch soothed their raw nerves. Warblers and woodlarks filled the air with their songs, weaving a surreal tapestry of serenity, and the women added quiet chatter to the undercurrent set by woodpeckers and frogs.

After a little more than a kilometer, Vordenburg indicated a vague path due east. "According to the villagers nearby, far back here, about four kilometers, we will find a very old and long-abandoned burial ground. I believe her tomb is there."

"Isn't a cemetery sanctified?" Frontenac asked.

"Not this one," Vordenburg said. "It's early Roman. Pagan." He surveyed his distaff troops with a worried frown. "I do wish we had Monsieur Claque with us."

"He was very little help against Mircalla aboard *Esprit*," Jacqueline reminded him. "He's clumsy and slow to react. Someone had to guard de Guise. You'll have to make do with me."

"Us," Têtue corrected her. She answered Jacqueline's surprise with a shrug. "You've got us."

Jacqueline couldn't argue.

They moved cautiously, allowing the wolves to take the lead, Frontenac and Yves with Llewellyn, Guichet and Boulot with Angélique. Vordenburg already leaned heavily on his walking stick, and his red face betrayed the debilitating effect of his concussion from the Austrian's attack as well as the weight of the canister on his back. Jacqueline and Têtue made the rear guard. Jacqueline carried Llewellyn's mameluke, a sabre-like cavalry sword very much like the kilij she had wielded in the Catacombs. Unlike the elegant umbrella blade, the mameluke would easily take a head.

Though merry birdsong continued, the women fell quiet as the forest around them grew denser. Swarms of gnats circled their heads and dove at their eyes and noses as the odor of sweat rose from their bodies. Jacqueline's stiff armor made every step ache, the drenched silk chafing her skin. She gave thanks for the shade of the forest and the holy water soaking her head.

Suddenly the wolves balked, halting the procession. The women's fear was palpable. Whining, Angélique came to Jacqueline and pawed her leg.

"Wait here," Jacqueline told the others, and followed Angélique back along the path to a secluded clearing. Angélique changed form.

"Girls from the chateau," she whispered. "They've followed us."

"What! We must go back."

Angélique disagreed. "We've come too far."

Jacqueline fretted. How had they escaped Marthe's watchful eye or Monsieur Claque's patrol? "Either Mircalla has summoned them to overpower us, or they foolishly believe they can join us in the battle. I can't let them."

Têtue stepped into the clearing, startling them both. "Why not?" she said. "Why can't they fight too?"

Jacqueline frowned at the intrusion. "I told you to wait."

"Guarding your back, like Vordenburg said." Têtue's eyes narrowed on Angélique, and she grinned. "Clever trick. I was wondering about those sun-glasses. Can you teach me to do that?"

Jacqueline rubbed her brow. "It's not safe for the others. Some of them are only six or seven years old. They can't possibly be of any help."

Têtue shook her head. "The little ones couldn't have followed us so fast. I'll bet what you smell is the older ones, like us. There were two cabriolets and a coach left in the mews, but only two horses in the stable. So, at most it's only six, assuming two of them know how to drive. That's not likely. They'd have to get past Luc, hitch the horses, and track us down. Little ones couldn't get away with that, and there were only two other women old enough to brave it."

Angélique regarded her with an appreciative grin. "I really like this girl, Jacqueline. Can't we keep her?"

Jacqueline flexed and unflexed her grip on the sword. "They won't be protected. They aren't armed. I don't have more weapons tucked away in my pockets, or wineskin bonnets."

"Futter the weapons." Têtue pointed to the sword. "I can sharpen sticks while we walk." She folded her arms, not so much defiant as patient. "You know I'm right, Duval."

Angélique was still chuckling as she melted into the wolf.

Têtue's eyes glinted jealously. "Please tell me you'll teach me that."

The news of more girls dismayed Vordenburg, but Jacqueline had committed to the change in circumstances. She felt it was safer to backtrack and meet up with the newcomers than to wait for them to catch up.

"There's still plenty of daylight," she observed.

Angélique and Llewellyn conferred. Llewellyn loped further up the trail while Angélique herded the wolf brigade after Vordenburg and Jacqueline. They got back to the clearing and sat on the ground except for Jacqueline, who paced restlessly. Vordenburg checked the caps to make sure the women were still well protected, adding water where needed. Têtue began gathering solid sticks longer than the half-meter stakes she stocked. The young women asked for more vampire lore, and Vordenburg recounted the legend of Varnae, a vampire so old and powerful he could walk abroad in direct sunlight.

"Or so say the legends. But his legend is only found in pennybloods, those dreadful serial publications in London that usually spin nonsense, perpetuating tales for the purpose of drawing more sales. No one in the Order of Van Helsing has ever verified the story, or even given it any credit."

"And what is this Order of Van Helsing?" Boulot asked.

Vordenburg placed his hand over his vest pocket and the notebook there. "A secret group of men and women who research information about vampires; who hunt them, destroy them."

"Like us?" Boulot looked around. "Probably not like us. We don't read or write."

"I do," Frontenac said.

"We could learn," Yves suggested. "Better that than staying a wife to an old goat."

Jacqueline clenched her jaw. "You're married?"

"I'm sixteen. I've been married for more than a year. To an old man my father owed money." Yves curled her lip in disgust. "He can't even give me kids."

Têtue gave her characteristic shrug as she whittled stakes. "I was a widow at thirteen, married a second time at fourteen. That man was a brute." She blew away sawdust and tested the point, frowning. "I left."

Angélique gruffed. Jacqueline knew she was saying again, "I like this girl."

Têtue wrapped her arm under Angélique's neck and scratched behind her ear. Angélique sprawled in delight. Then she sat up and whined. Jacqueline stiffened at the warning.

As Têtue had calculated, two more young women strode up the path. When they spotted Jacqueline and the others, they ran to join them. They drew up short at Jacqueline's angry glare and Angélique's snarl. Neither was older than fourteen. They lowered their heads, not daring to meet Jacqueline's eyes.

One of them nudged the other. They held up bladders threaded with ribbons. "Jean-Paul said—"

Jacqueline threw her hands in the air with a cry of frustration. "You think this is some grand adventure, a stroll across the meadow? Do you understand what we're walking into? I can't make you any safer than I have done, except to send you back, and I can't ensure any of us will live through this encounter. Some of you have family to return to, perhaps even loving husbands or children. They're already worried for you, I have no doubt."

"We're following you," Geneviève said. "We follow Duval."

The others repeated, "We follow Duval."

Têtue folded her arms. "We are the Order of Duval. We're *your* army."

Jacqueline argued no further.

When they finally caught up to Llewellyn, they found him pacing anxiously, and he sprang forward to greet Angélique, biting her ruff. Snarling, she returned the play bites.

"What's happening?" Yves asked, alarmed. "Why are they fighting?"

"They're talking," Jacqueline explained. "If I had to guess, he's found Mircalla's scent and they're discussing how to approach."

"Danger," Frontenac called. "Everyone, side by side."

Jacqueline suppressed a smile at the young woman's sense of leadership. "Not just yet. These wolves can scent things almost two kilometers away, so we may be about thirty minutes from our quarry."

Angélique returned to Jacqueline's side and nudged her forward up the trail. The others followed, the wolves setting a slightly faster pace now that they had the scent of their prey. In less than half an hour, they spotted a row of lichen-covered nubs that formed the remains of a wall and pale stone humps listing beyond—an ancient burial ground overgrown with trees, thorn bushes, and underbrush. They could not measure the extent of its reach into the forest.

The wolves sat, ears forward, hackles raised. Setting their shovels aside, the wolf brigade readied their guns and formed a ring at the opening in the wall behind the wolves. Jacqueline ordered the young women to stay outside the burial ground but stand ready for their call. Then she approached the edge of the cemetery, for a moment hesitant to step forward. Drawing a deep breath, she straightened her shoulders as Vordenburg moved up next to her, priming his canister. With a grim set to her jaw, Jacqueline nodded to her sister. Angélique and Llewellyn moved ahead, snuffling the ground. Jacqueline kept pace, using the sword to slash her way through the rough brush, with Vordenburg following her.

Mircalla's voice rasped, no longer honey sweet. "*Jacqueline, why are you doing this?*"

Jacqueline shuddered. "She's awake!"

Pausing to prime and ignite her specialized weapons, she glanced back but couldn't see the others clearly through the brush. Vordenburg pushed ahead to keep up with the wolves.

"*I will kill them. I will kill them all.*"

Jacqueline called, "She wants you all dead."

"We can hear her," Têtue replied. "She's telling us to kill each other." She laughed.

The wolves pressed farther into the forest.

"*Do not doubt me, Jacqueline.*" Mircalla's voice struck like a stone in Jacqueline's mind. "*I will kill them. I will kill everyone, and you will have no one but me to love you.*"

Jacqueline quaked. Mircalla meant the ones at Bellesfées. De Guise.

"*You cannot fight me. Will you not surrender? Will you watch them all die for your stubbornness? Come, Jacqueline. I can complete you so much more than anyone else ever could.*"

The wolves yipped and snarled, circling one of the stone markers and a mound of fresh, loose dirt. They had found the tomb. Vordenburg stuck his walking stick into the earth. The wolves pawed at the dirt and began to dig. Vordenburg called for the others to bring shovels.

"*I'll let you watch each one die. I will let you watch de Guise die.*"

"And I'll despise you all the more," Jacqueline replied through her teeth. "I've seen your power. You have not yet seen mine!"

Têtue called again, closer now. "Duval, she wants us to kill the Baron."

"Keep back," Jacqueline warned.

Têtue's voice strained. "I can't. She doesn't have my head, but she's got my body. All of us. We can't help it."

"What!"

To Jacqueline's dismay, the women stumbled toward her and Vordenburg, fighting each step Mircalla forced them to take. Clothing caught on thorns and bracken, thwarting them. Still, they faltered on with leaden steps. They tumbled over roots, cursing when Mircalla made them drag themselves to their feet. Like a band of mindless revenants, they shambled forward wielding the stakes, shovels, or guns.

"I can't drop my rifle," Boulot called shrilly, "and I'm getting ready to fire. I don't want to."

Before Jacqueline could answer, Llewellyn and Angélique charged the women, teeth bared. Boulot fired wide as Llewellyn knocked her to the ground. When he seized the rifle in his maw and threw it, Boulot tried to crawl after it. Llewellyn bit her leg as a ball sailed past his ear. He whirled and brought Guichet down before she could fire again. As she tried to rise, Llewellyn thrashed her ankle until she screamed.

Frontenac and Émilie, brandishing the shovels, rushed forward to attack Angélique, all the while crying, "Look out! Run! I'm sorry!" Frontenac's blow landed on the side of Angélique's head. With a snarl, she retaliated, nipping them both until they fell to the ground shrieking, "Thank you! I'm sorry!"

"Stop us, Duval," Têtue hollered. "Cut us down."

Jacqueline stood ready to defend Vordenburg with the sword. Têtue and Geneviève still advanced step by constrained step, wielding stakes. The two wolves launched themselves at their backs, pitching the women to the ground. When Geneviève tried to rise, Llewellyn swatted her head. She dropped again, and he lay on top of her to pin her down.

Têtue didn't move. Angélique yelped and nosed her. Frantic, she circled and pawed at her until she turned Têtue on her back.

Têtue gripped a stake impaled under her breast. She gazed dully up at Jacqueline, gulping for air. She sneered. "Futter that bitch, yeh?"

Jacqueline's heart shattered. She wanted to scream. Instead, she forced herself to match Têtue's bravado. "Indeed, you did. Well done, Têtue."

Jacqueline could not even bend over enough to reach Têtue's brow with her fingertips. Her mind raced as she stared at the stake and the trace of blood around it. "*Don't withdraw. Don't withdraw!*" Her soul ached with the weight of the girl's sacrifice. Jacqueline looked desperately into Angélique's eyes.

The amber eyes narrowed. Angélique growled and gruffed. Llewellyn whined a response.

"Têtue," Jacqueline whispered. "Want to learn a really clever trick?"

Têtue's eyes flickered open. She tried to nod.

Angélique bit deep into her left forepaw. Taking the stake in her maw, she pulled it from Têtue's chest. Blood gushed out a two-centimeter hole under Têtue's sternum. Angélique placed her bleeding paw into the wound, mingling her lupine blood with Têtue's blood.

Jacqueline worried the grip of the sword. Her pulse beat in her ears. Twenty seconds. Thirty. "Come on, come on!"

"It's—all right." Têtue closed her eyes again, still smirking. "Worth it."

Then Têtue gasped as her body jolted. Angélique pulled her paw away, but Têtue seized her around the neck. She clung to the wolf, wide-eyed. "What—what—I—" She fell back, her arms spread wide. She began to laugh. "Some—trick!"

Jacqueline blew out a sigh of relief as the blood ceased to flow from the hole. She wiped her tears on her sleeve. "Damn you, Mircalla," she muttered, then shouted, "Damn you, Mircalla!"

Geneviève groaned where she lay beneath Llewellyn's weight. "I think she's gone," she said.

Llewellyn let her rise and went over to lick Angélique's paw.

"I'm free," Guichet called. "But I can't stand up. Can someone help?"

One by one, the women struggled to their feet and limped to sit on the grave markers. They cursed Mircalla and cursed their own weakness. Mircalla had released them, but the wolves had left necessary wounds that now rendered them useless.

"Why did she let us go now?" Frontenac asked. "Because we couldn't do what she wanted?"

"Maybe using up all that power to get to us tired her out," said Boulet. "We resisted. That had to have cost her something."

"It is possible," Vordenburg said. "She summoned all of you to the castle, but she did not appear herself. Now, she tries to command you, and again, she does not appear. I don't think she has left the tomb since she buried herself, so she has not fed in two days. I cannot believe her strength will last much longer." He shifted the canister on his back. "I am not sure mine will last either."

Jacqueline debated her choices, but she came back to the fact that bringing the young women along had accomplished more loss than gain. In the end, it was Vordenburg, Llewellyn, and Jacqueline left to continue the work.

Vordenburg took up a shovel and dug into the loose mound over the tomb. Jacqueline helped. Together they managed a wide hole a half meter deep. By then, the Baron could barely stand. Jacqueline let him lean on her as he activated the pump and sprayed holy water into the grave.

"If this reaches her tomb before sundown, she will be helpless tonight," he insisted. "We can dig her up tomorrow. And this time we *will* bring Monsieur Claque."

Jacqueline watched his progress. They had no idea how deeply entombed Mircalla lay, no idea how long it would take for the holy water to seep down. Shaking her head, she clapped Vordenburg's shoulder.

An explosion of sound and pain rammed her into the grave.

"Yves!" someone shrieked.

Women bellowed in anger. Angélique and Llewellyn barked and yelped, circling Jacqueline wildly, their clamor worse than the screaming in her head. She gasped. An agonizing spear of pain shot through her left side. She couldn't open her eyes, couldn't find air to speak. She dug her hands into the mud to keep from falling into the blackness that swallowed her. Shouts echoed.

"Duval! Duval!"

"Yves shot Duval!"

"Madame, are you alive?"

Wolves howled and alarm-barked.

"Madame Duval! Can you hear me?"

A voice like a rusted weathervane in the wind pierced her thoughts. *"Jacqueline! My love! What has she done! That stupid little fool!"*

Mircalla's wrath struck Jacqueline like a brick wall. She felt her skull crushing her brain as Mircalla filled her mind with raging hatred.

Women screamed. "Yves!"

They screamed again. "The wolves!"

A soft hand tugged away Jacqueline's chemise. "I'm here, m'amie," Angélique whispered in her ear. "I need you to lend me some clothes. We have to leave. My left hand is useless. Can you put your arm around me?"

No. She couldn't. She couldn't move. She gulped like a landed fish. How many ribs could one ball break?

"Your coat, Vordenburg, if you don't mind," Llewellyn said.

A moment later his strong arms hoisted her up and across his shoulder. Jacqueline wailed as pain ripped into her. She was grateful she couldn't fully bend.

"Yves is dead," Frontenac cried with a choked sob. "I took the gun from her, and she just collapsed. She's dead."

Vordenburg growled. "Mircalla."

"She was supposed to shoot *you*," Guichet cried angrily. "Why did she shoot Duval?"

Têtue answered, her breath still halting. "Yves knew — the armor. Fought — control. That's why — bitch killed her."

Quiet. Quiet. Why couldn't they be quiet? Jacqueline hissed, struggling for air. Where were they now? Where were they going? Why were they leaving? So close!

"*So close!*" Mircalla echoed. "*Come to me, Jacqueline. Come to me and live!*"

How close had Yves been? Ten meters? Closer? Jacqueline felt sticky wetness down her side. She was losing blood, so she knew the ball had struck deep, even if it hadn't pierced the silk.

If.

Had it?

She hoped not. The silk would stanch the wound. Llewellyn knew all about that.

Wonderful Llewellyn! How wonderful Angélique found someone wonderful to tame her. How wonderful we both found wonderful men who understand us and love us despite our quirks. What a wonderful adventure we enjoyed together. Angélique and Gryffin, me and de Guise. Alain. Beautiful beau Alain. Beau. With his beautiful brown eyes and beautiful bow lips and beautiful blond curls. So many b's.

"B — b — b —"

"Shhhh." Llewellyn shifted her from his shoulder to lay her out on the ground. She wailed again. "Broken rib," he said. "Just one, I think."

He pressed his palms around her side. "Frontenac, come here and press just—so."

A new level of agony shot through Jacqueline. Her eyes flew open and she gasped. She found she could take in air. She gaped around at the gathered faces.

Solemn. Worried. Angry. Fierce. Defiant.

Not a single tear.

"Well done." Jacqueline closed her eyes. "Well done."

Too weak to stand any longer, Vordenburg sat and pumped the canister while Frontenac poured the last of the holy water. The women bore their wounds stoically, insisting they felt strong enough to fetch the wagon and cabriolet in Lailly-en-Val, but Vordenburg objected to their going without protection.

"It's only a few kilometers," Frontenac argued. "Let those of us who can help do this much."

Vordenburg heaved a frustrated sigh. "I cannot guarantee your safety. Mircalla has expended tremendous power. I cannot believe she could have accomplished all she has done and still have any remaining strength." He pulled at his chin. "But it tells me something that she had to release all of you to control just one. Maybe."

"Duval?" Frontenac waited for Jacqueline's assent, her wide blue eyes searching Jacqueline's face.

Jacqueline squeezed Angélique's hand. *Yes, yes, get them away, get them home. Get me home. Let me die at home. Let me die and cheat that bitch.*

Angélique sent the others on. Têtue and Guichet, too wounded to walk, stayed back. Llewellyn returned to the cemetery to retrieve Yves's lifeless body. Then he took Têtue away from the others and rested her against a mossy tree, where he sat beside her and spoke so quietly no one else could overhear.

"Wonderful Gryffin," Jacqueline murmured.

Angélique caressed her sister's face. "Thank you. Such courage deserved reward. She did ask."

"Beau Alain."

"Indeed he is, m'amie."

Jacqueline closed her eyes. Her tongue cleaved to the roof of her mouth. Everything ached with a searing heat, yet she shivered. Every cut, scratch, scorch, bruise, gash, and gaping wound radiated agony throughout her body. If only Angélique would stop touching her.

"Vordenburg, is there anything left in that thing?" Angélique said. "Jacqueline needs water right away, blessed or not."

"Here. My cap," offered Guichet.

"*Come to me, Jacqueline,*" Mircalla urged. "*I can save you. I feel your pain. I can make it stop. You'll find peace. Drink from me. You will be loved. So loved.*"

"So loved," Jacqueline mumbled.

"Yes, Jacky, you're so loved." Angélique's voice broke.

Water seeped into Jacqueline's mouth, loosening her tongue, trickling down her throat. She coughed, sending another spear of agony through her. She tossed her head to get away from the hands that held her. Someone pinched her chin and again water poured. Again, she thrashed and moaned. As de Guise had thrashed in his fever, begging her to be careful for him. To live for him. To come home to him.

Jacqueline tried to struggle. "No. Can't. Mircalla—"

Mircalla would kill him. Mircalla would force Jacqueline to kill him.

But Mircalla could heal Jacqueline. Vordenburg had said so. Vampire's blood— Something about—Power…

Jacqueline knew what power could do. She had spent her life harnessing power of every sort. Electrical, chemical, mechanical, steam… Oh, yes. Jacqueline understood power.

Mircalla's voice was once again soothing and sultry. "*I am here, Jacqueline. I will heal you. I will come for you.*"

Jacqueline fell back into Angélique's arms. "Come, then."

19.

A HELLISH SCREECH AWAKENED JACQUELINE, A DEMONIC CRY RISING from infernal depths, filling her with terror. She screamed, then wailed as pain slammed her side.

Jacqueline lay trapped in her silk armor falling through the night sky. She gaped wide-eyed until she recognized the panoply of gold stars on the bleu-de-France field above her — the canopy of her bed.

Angélique's arm slipped beneath her head and raised her to sip water. Llewellyn tucked pillows beneath her so she could recline. He examined the linens that wrapped her so tightly she could barely breathe. Questions she couldn't voice dizzied her, spinning wildly through her head. She looked from one to the other. Then she glared.

"They're all safe," Llewellyn assured her. He held her hands and massaged them. "Bruised but proud. Bowed but not beaten. Ready for the next battle. We took Yves to the chapel, prepared her—"

He meant they decapitated her, Jacqueline realized with a groan.

"—and wrapped her. Angélique and I will find her family once this is over. Têtue will be up and about soon. She's anxious to discover her new-found form. Vordenburg is resting. Poor fellow had to be carried from the wagon, though the girls recovered quickly enough. It would appear your suspicions about them drinking vampire blood were correct, but as of now, that is all to their advantage. It's a few hours past dinner, but Marthe brought a plate. Gaudin loosed your hair and brushed it out while you slept. She's beside herself with worry, but she's been an angel tending to all of them." He smiled encouragingly. "Have I left anything out?"

Thunder shook the château.

"Ah, yes. We got home before the rain."

"I can hear you, Llewellyn," de Guise bellowed from across the hallway. "For pity's sake, tell me if she's awake."

Jacqueline blinked back tears and relaxed. De Guise still lived. Mircalla had not been able to reach this far.

If that shriek meant what Jacqueline believed it meant, Mircalla wouldn't be able to accomplish anything further that night. Holy water had seeped down through the soil and enveloped her tomb. She was locked in for now.

"Drink," Angélique insisted.

She pushed the glass away. "Girls." She winced. "Not. Safe."

"I'll take care of it," Llewellyn said. "I'll have Marthe and Gaudin take them all home tomorrow. Jean-Paul might enjoy going with them."

"I swear by all that's holy, Llewellyn—" de Guise called again.

"I'll swat you with a towel if you do," Llewellyn replied, mimicking Marthe. He winked at Jacqueline and went to calm de Guise.

"Are you hungry?" Angélique asked.

Jacqueline closed her eyes again. Angélique lowered her to the pillows.

"Impressive armor. So brilliant. It saved your life. Llewellyn won't let us remove it until the bleeding has completely stopped and we can stitch you closed. Jean-Paul is fetching the surgeon. Again. The man will think we're lunatics out here, shooting one another for bourgeois pleasures. I'll also have him look at little Lisette. The girl is wracked with coughing, poor thing. Don't worry. The news has spread, the château was attacked by assassins. We'll be able to explain it away, all of it."

Jacqueline finally convinced Angélique she wasn't listening. Angélique pressed a cheek to hers, then slipped belladonna into Jacqueline's mouth. "Sleep, m'amie," she whispered.

The light dimmed. The door clicked shut. Low voices across the hall assured Jacqueline that de Guise was satisfied with her health.

They were so cheerful. They had failed, and they could not wait to go back to fail again.

No. *She* had failed. She had failed *them*, failed them all. She had *never* failed before. Accidents, yes; stupidity, yes; but failure? Never. None of her tutors, none of her professors, none of her colleagues—ever. De Guise may have forgiven her, but how could she forgive herself? Young women dead. Her household invaded and possessed. The King shot. De Guise...

And she was not innocent. The two in the gondola—their blood was on the King, but had she not fashioned the weapon for just that purpose? The Austrian villain—she could have disarmed him, disabled him. What had she become, killing a man? Yves, Têtue—what sort of hero inspired others to die for her sake?

Outside the window, rain poured and thunder grumbled. Tears slid from the corner of her eyes, pooled in her ears, and dripped to the pillow. Mircalla was a problem she'd wished on no one, least of all on herself. She hadn't invited this monster onto her lands, into her village, into her life. Yet, no one but Jacqueline could resolve this. Vordenburg claimed the right and owned the knowledge, but he had neither the ability nor the strength to accomplish his goal. He too would end up dead if she allowed him to pursue Mircalla further.

Mircalla had bound herself to Jacqueline. The demon would not suffer de Guise to live nor cease her attacks on Bellesfées until Jacqueline was hers.

Jacqueline saw only one choice. She would make certain Mircalla didn't attack again.

In the morning, Llewellyn gave orders before the surgeon arrived. Marthe and Gaudin weren't happy to leave, but Jean-Paul declared he would seat himself between his mother and his cousin, musket at the ready, and the "ladies" would be delivered safely to their homes.

The Order of Duval, as they now called themselves, had already recovered from their wounds, a fact that disturbed Vordenburg. They demanded to remain until Duval healed. Jacqueline acquiesced, but to those five only, along with little Lisette and the minion's victim. The younger ones shouted her name over and over as the wagon trundled away. She was too weary to smile. If she failed again, what would become of them, Mircalla's "larder"?

Llewellyn set to work with wire cutters to gain access to the gunshot wound.

"Also cut around the hips and free my legs at least. My wrists, too," she said. "Easier to feel my pulse."

"Very wise. And the weapons?"

"Leave them." Jacqueline was thankful he didn't argue or ask her to explain further.

When the surgeon gently unpacked the wound, the shot rolled into his hand. He looked at her in amazement and dropped the ball into the surgical tray. "You are a very fortunate woman," he commented. "If the ball had not been slowed, you would be dead." He scrubbed his hands in a basin. "Are you ready?"

Jacqueline nodded to him. He placed a silken bag over her head. The air became sickly sweet. She recognized the scent of nitrous oxide as it took hold of her.

"Oh, dear. Am I so mutilated you have to cover my face with a bag?" she mused. She giggled. Amused. A musing mind with amusing mutilations. There should be music for amusing mutilation musings.

Darkness and sleep enveloped her.

In anesthesian dreams, Jacqueline danced with de Guise on the deck of *Esprit*. They spun beneath the stars even as the stars whirled. Fireworks blazed all around them, but the night breezes kept them cool. De Guise kissed her — warm and deep and soft.

But then it was not de Guise. A cold mouth — harsh, demanding, hungry.

Jacqueline sighed with longing.

Jacqueline's eyes fluttered open. Torturous pain throbbed through her, along her left side, into her left arm, and across her brow. Her whole face drew to a taut grimace. She couldn't suppress a cry, and immediately regretted it when pain shot into her ribs.

Llewellyn sat beside her head on the pillow. He gently stroked her brow. "How do you feel?"

The surgeon, scrubbing his hands in the water closet, called, "You should feel lucky. The ball struck the rib and cracked it, then grazed along it a couple centimeters, but nothing pierced the lung. The silk stopped the bleeding in very good time, and the tight mesh held the rib in place as well as the silk that stanched it. I thought it best to keep you in your defensive suit, given the circumstances. Not that I know what the circumstances are, and I won't ask, but it's tight enough to hold the bandages in place, give you support, and help you heal."

He came to her side, drying his hands. "Hot water at the ready? Madame, my hospital could use your plumbing designs. A water closet such as this on each ward? Perhaps we might come to an agreement, as it appears a hospital and surgeon on retainer could be to your benefit."

He wrapped his instruments and placed them into his black bag. "I also re-stitched your forehead. His Grace has given his word he'll keep you sedated for at least twenty-four hours. I'll return tomorrow to check on your progress, but I'll look in on Monsieur de Guise and the girls before I leave."

He studied her eyes and face, then touched her shoulder reassuringly. "Very lucky indeed."

As Llewellyn showed him out, Angélique hurried in. She curled up beside Jacqueline and stroked her hair. "The surgeon says you did very well and should be up in three days."

Jacqueline groaned. "We don't—have—three days."

Llewellyn said firmly, "It's no longer your concern, Jacky. We'll take care of it."

Angélique tenderly wrapped her arms around Jacqueline's neck. "Calm yourself. Vordenburg says we have a reprieve. He's gone to Tours today to beg the archbishop for some sanctified host wafers. He claims they can't be crossed by a vampire. He'll place a circle of—"

"We're beyond that." Jacqueline shook her head. "Vordenburg isn't strong enough for this. None of us is."

"But together—"

Jacqueline's temper flared. Her pulse hammered at her side. "Together, Yves was murdered," she said between clenched teeth. "Têtue would be dead, and so would I be."

She pushed Angélique away with her good arm. "Remember what she did to you on the ship? What her little minion did to Claque? We can't defeat her. She has power over too many of us."

"Not as much as she thinks," Llewellyn reminded her. "Those young ladies healed up in hours. They've got the power to resist her."

"But I don't. She has hold of me and she won't stop until I—" She clamped her mouth shut. She couldn't say it. "There's only one way to stave off these vicious attacks."

"There's never just one way," Angélique argued. "You taught me that. If a way doesn't exist, you make one. If that doesn't work, you make another one." She sat up with a worried frown. "Jacky, I've seen you design the most brilliant—"

"Stop using that word!" Jacqueline then wailed at the pain her outcry brought. She eased her breathing, but her anger remained. "I'm *not* brilliant. Yves is dead. Mircalla is not. I'm not a hero. Damn you for making anyone think I am. For making *me* believe it."

Tears welled in Angélique's eyes. "You're *my* hero."

Jacqueline turned away. Llewellyn lifted a glass to her lips and she drank. He then tipped a teaspoon of a thick, cloyingly sweet jelly flavored with oranges, cinnamon, cloves, and cardamom onto her tongue.

"You'll sleep now," he said. "Charles assured me this will numb any pain for a long, long while, and I gave you enough to last into the night. I'll be back to check on you." Llewellyn drew Angélique away. As the two left the room, he said, "Charles says she'll be sedated at least twelve hours. I think you and I should get some well-earned human sleep as well."

Angélique answered with a quiet sob.

Jacqueline damned Mircalla from the depths of her being. For the woman's supernatural beauty that made Jacqueline doubt herself and de Guise's love. For the vampire's vicious display of savagery that rendered Jacqueline powerless. For Mircalla's devious manipulation of the young women who had sworn to fight for Jacqueline Duval, the hero.

She was not a hero. But she was Jacqueline Duval. She never before had cause to be ashamed of who she was or doubt what she could do. And as Angélique had rightly observed, who she was could not prevent what happened to her, or to anyone else, but she was no less Jacqueline Duval. Surely that would count for something. It had to.

The sunlight that filled Jacqueline's chambers did little to ease her anger, but it wasn't long before the sunlight turned to the delicious aroma of baking bread and the taste of music. Pain left her, replaced by tingling roses and sultry flügelhorn through her entire body. She gazed up at the diamond-studded day sky overhead and hummed to the star-song they sang to her.

But how could diamonds sing? Surely, they were birds. Birds sang. Birds could fly. Surely, they called her to fly away with them. Surely, she could fly.

Her enormous, burly, muscular arms lifted her easily from the bed. Jacqueline grinned at them in amazement as they stretched themselves out to become elongated vines and drew back again as willowy limbs. How had she ever thought them hideous? So lithe, slender, feminine, flowery.

Her reflection in the standing mirror dazzled her. Curls like a glowing halo draped her face, crowned with a ruby tiara. A single red rose beneath her left breast adorned her white gown. Not one, but two corsages—one on each arm. By heaven, she was—

"*Beautiful. My beautiful Jacqueline. Come to me!*"

Jacqueline understood what beauty truly was. Beauty was power, and Jacqueline knew what power could do.

"I'm coming." She went to the window and opened it wide. "Where are you?"

"*Come to me!*"

Jacqueline coiled to leap off the balcony. The sweet bouquet of wine coursed along her left side. Then she caught the scent of the lush wall of lilies and orchids and wisteria covering the château wall where none had been before. She descended the floral stairway, as long ago she had descended the stairs for her début ball: a lovely gown, a tiara, bouquets of flowers. The day sky so blue wrapped around her and caught her in its folds like the ocean drawing a starfish back into the depths. She glided along its waves to stand on an Oriental shore of exotic jade and emerald.

To her delight, she now had two carmethene roses on her gown, and more were budding. She danced away to the melody of a memory. She twirled, her arms outstretched. As Da Vinci had predicted centuries before, her whirling arms lifted her. She sailed over the pond and up the hill. She was glorious.

From the top of the hill, Jacqueline launched herself into the wind and soared to the west, racing the sun. She waved to the cows she passed and said thank you, no, she was well, how are you? A green-blue ribbon adorned the landscape of sparkling châteaux, verdant fields, a spectrum of colorful trees and so many flowers, fragrant and alluring. All the pretty horses called to her and she said thank you, yes, she knew the way. She knew many things. She was very, very smart, you know.

Most wonderful of all, beyond the ribbon of river, a wall of juniper and pine marked her new world. A yellow road stretched into the distance, and she longed to dance on its golden stones. She alighted and pushed open the massive oak gates with her dainty arms. She was indeed powerful. She entered the sylvan halls of the dead.

The gloom of early evening enveloped her in a siren call. Her ruby tiara tightened, as did the glorious carmine band on her arm. Where had that come from? Garnet streams forked along her face, dripping from her chin and jaw. Too much dancing put a sharp pain in her side. When she gripped it, her hand came away full of alizarin roses. The roses melted, leaving her fingers slick with madder. Her carmine gown blew away as dust.

Gripping her side to hold in the pain, Jacqueline staggered forward through the dusky woods shot from above with sunbeams. She chased the ragged remnants of what power remained to her. Trees reached out. Branches grabbed her with gnarled fingers. They could not stop Jacqueline Duval. They could not defeat her single purposeful design.

She stumbled and fell headlong into mud.

Jacqueline lay face down in Mircalla's grave, now a miry wallow. She strained but couldn't raise herself. Exhausted, wracked, she fought to recall how she got there. She tried to swallow. Her mouth was dry, her throat parched. Bitterness coated her tongue. Mircalla's voice was thick with oranges, cinnamon, cloves, and cardamom.

"I will give you drink. Come."

Jacqueline closed her eyes. Too tired to respond. Too drained to fight. Tangy pine, sweet mildew, and earthy molds filled her nose. The woods were silent. She was alone but for Mircalla, and she had opened every wound in her body to bleed into Mircalla's tomb. Mircalla would feed on her blood and rise, and Jacqueline would save Bellesfées at last.

She was Jacqueline Duval. She alone had the power to free Bellesfées from the vampire's attacks on the ones she loved. She would anger De Guise one final time, but he would live.

Not beautiful. Not glorious. Smart, yes, but broken. Dying. Her only choice was surrender. She was happy to surrender if it meant the others were beyond Mircalla's reach.

How much blood had she lost? Enough to die before Mircalla could claim her prize? Enough left to soak through the holy water and free Mircalla before Jacqueline expired? How far down was the tomb?

A surprising radiance soothed Jacqueline's head and her aching body with a gentle heat. She opened her eyes and looked up. Shafts of late-afternoon sunlight broke through the forest roof like altar fires amid living pillars of a temple, bathing her in warmth.

Jacqueline dared to hope. She had found another way after all.

With grim determination, Jacqueline fumbled at her forearms and ignited the tanks attached to each arm. "Yes, Mircalla. I'm coming to you."

Jacqueline thrust her hands into the mud and shoveled. Every breath stabbed through her. She whimpered with each movement until her cries grew to sobs. Soon her enfeebled left arm hung almost useless, but she drove herself through the pain. More pain meant more blood flowing from her. More blood in the soil meant the closer she was to freeing Mircalla. She dug deeper, pulling and shoveling, oozing life.

A shadow eclipsed the sunlight. A wolf sniffed at her ear and licked her cheek, then growled menacingly.

"I can do this," she rasped. "Angélique—"

The wolf whined. Jacqueline looked up into the unfamiliar brown eyes of a silver and black wolf. Joy flooded her.

"Help me, Têtue," she begged. "Hurry."

Têtue curled her lips back over her fangs.

Jacqueline met her glare. "Help," she said again. "I can accomplish anything with help."

Têtue sniffed around Jacqueline's head. As Jacqueline shoved her hand into the mud once more, Têtue joined her. Soon the thick mud cleared away and they shoveled damp soil. The hole was now up to Jacqueline's shoulder. Têtue dug away at the sides to give Jacqueline more room to maneuver.

The sunbeam glided further and further away. Jacqueline's heart pounded against her rib with agonizing pain. She refused it. She had to dig. *Faster!* She had to reach Mircalla. She had to release her from the tomb before bleeding out, before the sun set. Jacqueline thrust her arm to scoop another handful of dirt.

A claw erupted from the soil, seizing Jacqueline's arm. Têtue yelped and recoiled. Talons stained with rot dug into Jacqueline's unshielded wrist, slicing open her flesh, slashing a vein. A venomous burning climbed Jacqueline's arm, matched by the ice of shock that gripped her body as her blood poured out into the dirt.

"You came for me!"

"I came for you," Jacqueline whispered.

Jacqueline met Têtue's gaze and jerked her head to the side. Têtue gruffed and inched back to hide behind a crumbling grave marker where she crouched, her eyes narrowed on Jacqueline. Jacqueline's vision dimmed. Consciousness drained from her. Her shallow breathing wasn't enough to hold in the outpouring of her life's blood.

A cold mouth closed on her wrist to drink the flow. *"Deeper, Jacqueline. Come deeper."*

Mircalla wrapped both talons around Jacqueline's arm and pulled her farther into the hole, sucking ravenously at Jacqueline's wrist. Jacqueline was too weak to cry out.

"I will take your pain, Jacqueline. My love will heal you. My blood will heal you. Bring me to you."

Jacqueline gulped for air. Her head swam. Pain blinded her. The hole began to fall in on her, closing her into the tomb with Mircalla. Têtue growled and whined, circling. The sun now lit the grave marker where Têtue waited. She alarm-barked for Jacqueline, then howled.

Jacqueline answered with a wail. Heaving her body up, she rolled over to free herself from the hole. Mircalla held tight. Têtue yelped.

Jacqueline bit into Mircalla's arm and ripped away flaking grey flesh.

Mircalla's blood gushed into Jacqueline's mouth—thick, tarry, sour as rancid meat. Jacqueline swallowed. She drank. Power surged in her. Relieved, grateful, she gulped with vicious purpose, hungry, furious, demanding. Strength returned to her. Strength overfilled her.

"My beloved! My Jacqueline!"

Jacqueline hauled Mircalla from the grave. Shriveled, gaunt as death, Mircalla slithered from the tomb and up through the mud. She lay twisted in the shade of the forest, coated in slime. She hissed, turning her face from the late-day sky above.

Têtue sprang at her. Mircalla caught her nimbly with one claw and hurled her away. The wolf fell stunned against a stone, whining, her eyes desperate as she struggled to rise.

Still, Jacqueline drank. Pain ebbed. The tightness of her wounds eased away. The piercing jabs in her brow vanished. Dark, ravenous energies coursed through her and filled every portion of her body.

Healed and whole, replete with savage wrath, Jacqueline released Mircalla and lay back with a grateful cry. She bellowed, alive and ready to slaughter. She looked at Mircalla in awe.

No longer the beautiful, exotic Countess Laroche, gaunt, putrescent Mircalla gazed back at Jacqueline with lidless, death-greyed eyes set in a shrunken face crowned with white wispy patches of hair plastered to her skull with mire. Mircalla's smile widened, revealing elongated fangs, yellow, limned with Jacqueline's blood.

Wrapping a skeletal arm around her, Mircalla drew Jacqueline closer. She caught the last drops trickling from the corner of Jacqueline's mouth on her gnarled, bony finger, then slid her finger across

Jacqueline's tongue. With a voice as ancient, unholy, and hollow as her tomb, Mircalla whispered with a sigh.

"My Jacqueline."

Her arms snaked around Jacqueline's waist. She pressed a kiss to Jacqueline's cheek. Withered lips grazed Jacqueline's lips.

Jacqueline pushed Mircalla to her back and crawled onto her. Her thighs squeezed the vampire's cadaverous hips. Mircalla leered up at her and laughed, a wheezing rasp of fetid exhalation. When Jacqueline cupped her hands over Mircalla's sunken breasts, the vampire moaned with hunger and reached for her, voice grating like iron on stone.

"My Jacqueline. Mine!"

Jacqueline fired.

Mircalla's eyes bulged, gaping in disbelief at the stake lodged in her heart. She threw Jacqueline from her with a hellish yowl. Jacqueline rolled aside and got to her feet, poised to fire the stake gun again.

Mircalla drew herself up, whipping the air like a serpent wriggling to free itself from its own skin. Her body spasmed. She writhed, screeching, spitting. Throwing her head back, she spewed pitch black, two centuries of death. Her arms flailed. Her talons raked a beam, the last of the day's sun. Fire flared along her arm. Keening, Mircalla fell into a blaze of saffron sunlight. Flames engulfed her. Her death shrieks filled the forest until she burned away to ash.

Jacqueline stepped into the vampire's dust and sprayed it with holy water, then scattered the mud with her bare feet.

RÉSOLUTION

JACQUELINE SLEPT PEACEFULLY THROUGH THE NIGHT, HER HEAD RESTING on Têtue's flank. They rose with the dawn chorus, birdsong like a hymn of rejoicing as they made their way to the inn at Lailly-en-Val by noon, famished and eager for a hearty meal. Remembering Jacqueline's previous generosity, the innkeeper made no comment about her bizarre mud-and-blood-stained habiliment nor the wolf at her side, despite the grumbles and sidelong looks they received from his other patrons. He set a beer and a full board in front of her and gave Têtue a skinned rabbit. Jacqueline savored the aromas of hearty roasted vegetables and heavy malt, but they couldn't cleanse the taste of Mircalla's blood from her mouth. She poked meat to the side, then fed it to Têtue.

They had just finished when Llewellyn and Angélique burst in. Têtue leapt up and cavorted around them, sneezing her excitement. Jacqueline stood more slowly, awaiting their judgment. Hysterical, Angélique threw herself at Jacqueline and clung to her, nearly bowling her into her chair.

Llewellyn cried, "Anyel, her stitches."

Angélique sprang back, but Jacqueline pulled her into an embrace and let her weep.

Llewellyn raged. "You could have killed yourself. How the devil did you get out of your room without our sensing it? People up and down the road have been babbling about the crazed, bloody Belle Dame de Bellesfées running around in her bloody nightgown. Walking all this way with a bullet hole. For what? For a beer? *You brew your own Pils!*" he shouted.

Jacqueline met his angry gaze and waited for facts to register. Llewellyn softened suddenly. He gripped Jacqueline's shoulder and examined her in doubtful confusion. "How—?"

"Don't. Don't touch me." Jacqueline pushed his hand away, tears starting. "I can't tell you. I can't say it. Not yet. A story for the fireside. Tonight." She sat again and finished the last of her beer, petting Têtue and hugging her close. "I'm sorry to ask, Gryffin, but I have no pockets. Would you mind?"

Llewellyn studied her, his anger fading. He paid their bill of fare without comment and bundled them into the cabriolet, while Têtue loped off with a joyous yip. Jacqueline remained silent, her head in Angélique's lap, while Angélique combed mud from Jacqueline's hair with her long fingers.

"He's not angry with you," Angélique said. "He's angry he wasn't able to help you."

Like de Guise.

Jacqueline wondered if being loved meant people would always be angry because of her, because of who and what she was.

Têtue had run overland; she was changed and dressed, though barefoot, when she met them at the drive.

"That was fantastic!" she crowed as the twins descended from the cabriolet. She threw her arms around Jacqueline and whirled with her. "*You* were fantastic! What a warrior. God, I love you! Mwah!" She pressed a kiss to Jacqueline's mouth. "Oh, you're absolutely fantastic. You should have seen her, Your Graces. Incredible! She—"

"No." Jacqueline placed a finger to Têtue's lips. "Tonight. Fireside." She held Têtue at arm's length and gazed into the young woman's new brown wolf-eyes. "I couldn't have succeeded without you, Têtue. A true knight of the Order of Van Helsing." She solemnly returned Têtue's kiss.

Têtue snorted. "Huh. It's the Order of Duval. Don't you forget that." Then she sobered. She took Angélique's hand and laid her cheek against it. "I can't thank you enough, Your Grace. My old life wasn't worth spit. Didn't mind throwing it away for Duval, but you gave me a new one, a better one. I can't repay that."

Angélique hugged Têtue. She said to Jacqueline, "Maybe I should take Gaudin with me, and you can teach Têtue a thing or two about how not to wear hair."

Jacqueline eyed Têtue. "Another wild daughter of Bellesfées. What do you say, Têtue? Would you like to stay on?"

Têtue looked from one sister to the other, half in gratitude, half in doubt. "I'm not good with hair," she said.

The twins laughed. Angélique draped her arm around Têtue's shoulder. "Well, then we could be family, at any rate. You certainly now own the blood."

Têtue's eyes glistened. "Family. I think I'd like that."

De Guise began bellowing as soon as he heard voices. Jacqueline sent the others on and went to his room. She entered hesitantly, dreading the next moments. His eyes widened at the sight of her. Joy, wonder, curiosity, amazement lit his face, followed by grim recognition of what she must have done to accomplish such a transformation. She waited, undefiant, unapologetic. De Guise was alive and would live; no price was too high to pay.

She answered the dark questions in his eyes. "I love you."

De Guise opened his arms, and she went to him. She kissed him gently, and she wept at last as if to wash away the obscenity of her deeds and the shame of her self-doubt. He held her as she told him as much as she could remember. The afternoon deepened into evening.

"You can blame Llewellyn this time," she said, "giving me so much dawamesc. I floated, absolutely numb, my mind twisted in a hyperaesthesia of colors and sensations. That's probably why the wolves couldn't sense any fear or pain—I had none. I'd already made up my mind this morning that I would meet Mircalla's demand."

His heart thumped beneath her ear. "Jacqueline—"

She kissed him quiet. "I was the only one who could get close enough to destroy her. And I wanted her dead. To save you, to save all of you. I would have summoned her to me, but the dawamesc provided other means. Judging by the wounds I suffered, I must have climbed down the ivy of the château and run all the way to the grave, utterly unaware of what I was doing."

Jacqueline tucked her head to his breast again. "But when I arrived, I knew I was dying. I feared my blood on the tomb would free her, and she would avenge herself on you if I died there, denying her the prize she longed to possess. I needed to save myself first. I needed the power of Mircalla's blood to save me. I counted on her desire, and I used her. I hoped to get well enough, and then near enough to drive a stake into her heart."

She pressed her eyes closed. "I fed on her, just as she had fed on me. It was a shameful ruse and an unspeakable obscenity."

De Guise tipped her chin up. "I begged you to consider your own safety for my sake. I don't blame you for your choice."

Jacqueline sighed, still uncertain. "I'm not proud, but I am satisfied. You're alive. We're all alive."

He traced her face, his eyes full of worry. "Do we know what vampire blood in you will do once the vampire is gone?"

"No." She bit her lip. "But I'm healed and whole. I can't ask for more than that."

De Guise squeezed her and kissed the top of her head. "So, with Mircalla gone, you won't be trying to feast on me?" he teased.

She grinned and kissed his breast, nuzzling the blond curls there. "Oh, I am determined to feast on you, my love, as soon as you are feast-able."

"Well, I can tell you that the surgeon has ordered me up and about as soon as tomorrow. Short strolls, accompanied, no stairs, and no exertion. But—" He smiled and combed his fingers through her hair. "Soon."

Llewellyn knocked and entered, followed by one of the clockwork porters. "I know the doctor said tomorrow, but we are soldiers, you and I." He clapped his hands sharply. "No more malingering like a cheap bourgeois, de Guise. Stand."

Jacqueline sat up. "Don't be ridiculous, Llewellyn. How will the porter get down the staircase?"

Llewellyn feigned hurt. "Are you the only genius in this household, Jacqueline Duval? I think not."

De Guise looked askance at his friend. "I'm neither groomed nor dressed, Llewellyn. I cannot be seen like this."

"You offered your life for the King," Llewellyn said. "You'll be seen for the worthy soldier you are, for tonight we feast."

Jacqueline snickered when de Guise said dryly, "We were just discussing feasts."

"Oh, good. A feast there shall be indeed," Llewellyn said, oblivious to their private joke. He lifted de Guise and helped him onto the clockwork cart designed for toting luggage and bags. De Guise groaned and leaned to the upright on one side, unable to straighten.

"Here," Llewellyn said, handing him a pillow. "Press this firmly against your wound."

Jacqueline fretted. "Are you sure?"

De Guise clutched the pillow as directed and stood. "Sacrebleu, Llewellyn, where do you learn these things?"

"I told you. Pirates." Llewellyn wrapped de Guise's dressing robe around him and belted it. "You'll need this, with all these young ladies running about."

Jacqueline stepped up beside de Guise and held onto the other upright. Llewellyn fixed an eye on her and shook his head. "Go to your room, Jacky. Take one look in the mirror. I'll say no more."

"I'll see him safely down the stairs first," she insisted as she stepped down.

"If that's how you wish to make your triumphal return," Llewellyn allowed with a grin.

Llewellyn led the automaton out the door and to the stairs. Jacqueline gaped in wonder. The entire contingent of the Order of Duval lined the spiral staircase. They had placed bolsters on each step and laid down sheets of scorched metal salvaged from the workshop. The porter slowly chugged to the edge of the stairs, and the women relayed it down the makeshift ramp.

"Now *that* is brilliant!" Jacqueline declared.

Frontenac saluted her thanks.

De Guise no sooner arrived at the bottom of the staircase when Jacqueline heard a wagon pull up to the entrance of Bellesfées through the open doors. She couldn't summon enough indignation to be angry as Marthe, Gaudin, and Jean-Paul trooped in, home from Chartres against her orders. She skated down the ramp in her bare feet.

Jean-Paul forestalled her scolding. "We got the last girl to Dammarie, and Maman said get home, and I couldn't disobey when she's sitting right next to me," he said with a shrug.

Jacqueline pinched his ear playfully. "Not even with the musket?"

Marthe made no excuse for herself, but she kissed Jacqueline's cheeks. "You're looking better, but you're a filthy mess, as usual," she said. "I won't ask how you managed it. You're a good girl. Both, good girls. How many for dinner now?"

"No need to fuss, Madame Benet," Frontenac spoke up. "We've prepared it already."

Marthe *hmmph*ed and headed to the kitchen.

Gaudin gaped at Jacqueline. "Oh, madame, you—you're—"

Jacqueline placed her hands on Gaudin's shoulders reassuringly. "I'm safe, Gaudin. I'm fine."

"You're—*disgusting!*" the girl cried. "I'll get you fixed up right away." Gaudin flew up the stairs, dislodging the women of the Order. Jacqueline followed, laughing.

As the bathtub filled, the fragrance of roses wreathed Jacqueline, cleansing her spirit of wraiths and demons. She peeled away her armor and all her bandages, now unnecessary, and stood naked in front of the mirror, examining her smooth flesh. Scars from every cut or burn she had endured throughout her life had vanished. Even her hands were now more elegant than the Marquis de Custine's. Everything was soft again, everything new. She would need to make new calluses on her rejuvenated fingertips.

No hint that she had given away her life to that monster and drawn life from it. No badge of honor. And still no reason she could see for anyone to call her beautiful. Wild hair, firm jaw, muscled arms and legs… The same face in the mirror.

It no longer mattered. Mircalla was right in this much: Jacqueline had an eternal beauty. She was more than loved; she knew who she was and what she could do. That was all the power she needed.

Vordenburg arrived from Tours just before eight o'clock. He halted in the dining hall doorway, horrified at the sight of Jacqueline.

"What have you done?" he cried. He raised his walking stick and advanced to strike her. "Mein Gott, no, madame!"

"Steady on, Vordenburg." Llewellyn set his hand on the Baron's shoulder. "Fireside. Tonight."

Jacqueline acknowledged the Baron's implicit accusation. She bid him sit to her left. He obeyed, though he trembled, eyeing her with trepidation, fingering the crucifix he wore. A divan was supplied for de Guise to lounge beside Jacqueline at the head of the table. The Duchess and Duke of Singlebury sat at her right in full English ducal regalia, awing the young women. Gaudin had supplied the six vampire hunters with day dresses from the twins' vast wardrobes. They wore their hair à la Order of Duval, in tresses and topknots above their brow, although adorned with ribbons or lace to appear less menacing. Têtue, seated beside the duke, wore the Llewellyn tartan in a clipped bow of crimson, black, and white. Jacqueline insisted Gaudin dine with them, and she summoned Marthe, Luc, and Jean-Paul as well. Marthe's displeasure colored her face.

"Not proper," Marthe muttered as she took a seat and glared at the smirking Jean-Paul.

Jacqueline gazed around the table. She struggled to quell the conflicting emotions that filled her. So much horror and death. So much risked and lost. But the women were free, and Bellesfées was safe. Jacqueline believed that was worth her macabre deeds, though she could not yet fully reckon the cost. Vordenburg had said a vampire's blood had no power over any of them once the vampire was destroyed. Yet, Jacqueline still felt the surge of energies, still sensed the change within her, within each cell of her body, in every thought that filled her head. Mircalla had given her the power to slay with cold, calculating intent. What other power did Jacqueline now hold?

Shaking off melancholy once again, she stood and quieted the gathering. Despite her admonition to Têtue, the young vampire hunters seemed to be aware of events. Perhaps they sensed the release of Mircalla's hold on them. Perhaps they had merely deduced the source of Têtue's celebration. Their eyes sparkled with anticipation and suppressed joy. Jacqueline confirmed their expectations.

"We're all safe," she announced. "Mircalla is dead."

Vordenburg jumped up so quickly his chair fell over, and he nearly did as well. He stammered, dumbfounded. Têtue attested to the truth of the news, and the young women applauded and cheered, further offending Marthe with their unseemly behavior at the table. Jacqueline held up her hand again for quiet as Vordenburg regained his seat.

"My first thoughts are for Yves." Her voice caught.

Faces sobered.

"Patrice Yves knew what Mircalla had commanded, but she refused to kill Vordenburg, and she gave her life to save you. She's the true hero of our war. Tomorrow I'll do my best to find her husband, her family, and return her to them in honor." Jacqueline raised her glass. "To Patrice Yves."

"To Yves," came the solemn response.

"My second thoughts are for all of you." She dipped her head. "My legion of vampire hunters. Warriors. You fought a battle I daresay no soldier in France has ever fought, not even the King himself. You think your efforts failed, but without your struggles against Mircalla, she would not have been so weakened. You are the only reason I could destroy her. You saved Bellesfées, and you will always be welcome here as daughters of Bellesfées. Whenever you wish."

"How about always?" said Têtue.

Some chuckled. Others did not. Jacqueline answered, "As long as you wish, if you wish."

Frontenac stood and raised her glass. "To the Order of Duval!"

Jacqueline wagged her head and laughed as they toasted. "Finally," she said, "to Baron Vordenburg, faithful officer in the Order of Van Helsing, without whom we could not have even begun our fight."

As the applause finished, Boulot leaned over to whisper in Vordenburg's ear. He blushed, but he nodded, and she grinned. Jacqueline guessed the young woman had found a calling in the vampire hunter's company.

"I wish I could tell you," Jacqueline continued, meeting each one's eyes, "how I overcame a gunshot wound, a broken rib, mental disarray, physical frailty." She blushed. "In truth, I don't understand how I could possibly have accomplished the journey to Mircalla's tomb. I don't even know how I managed to crawl out of my bed yesterday morning. But Têtue—"

Jacqueline raised her glass to Têtue, seated beside Llewellyn and sporting modified Ayscough sun-glasses like her lupine kindred. Jacqueline bowed to her. "Têtue sensed me. She followed and helped me dig up Mircalla's tomb. As witness to it all, tonight, after we dine, it will be Têtue's turn to tell the tale of the end of Mircalla, Countess Karnstein, the vampire."

Everyone's glasses were emptied and eagerly refilled. Platters of roasted chicken, vegetables, potatoes, and fruit passed along the table, and chatter continued lively throughout the meal. Frontenac conversed with a degree of authority with Guichet. Geneviève and Émilie tugged Jean-Paul's ear one way and the other, which the young man did not mind despite his mother's disapproving scowl. Vordenburg spoke animatedly with Boulot, while Têtue was deep in discussion with her new family. Jacqueline left her chair to lounge on the divan beside de Guise, savoring kisses between sips of wine and bites of dinner.

The room went suddenly silent. Jacqueline looked up and broke into a delighted smile. Her father, a tall, lean man with ash hair, stood in the doorway holding a small package. He gazed upon the bizarre gathering in shocked surprise.

"This is your idea of a wedding celebration?" he inquired.

Jacqueline and Angélique leapt up together and ran to him. "Papa!"

Michel Duval laughed heartily as his daughters embraced him. "My girls, my girls. Have pity on an old man."

Llewellyn hurried to receive him, and Vordenburg stood and bowed. De Guise, reclining in his dressing gown, tipped his head.

"De Guise?" Monsieur Duval raised a brow. "Are we comfortable?"

"As a matter of fact, Duval, we are not," de Guise replied with humor, "but with a little more wine I'll arrive there."

"What's this?" Monsieur Duval pushed his daughters back. "Tears? Do I want to know why?"

Jacqueline wiped her cheeks. "Love and joy, Papa. You're home."

He eyed them both suspiciously. He looked around the room again at the bevy of young women, then back to his daughters. "Something tells me I do *not* want to hear this tale." He held up the package he had brought. "I do have presents for you in my bag, and a special gift for the newlyweds," he said, "but when I arrived at the station in Orléans, the stationmaster gave me this for you, Jacky, and some dandy named Charles bid me tell you, Angélique, you owe him a salon reading."

Llewellyn groaned as Angélique laughed.

Jacqueline examined the box addressed in English to *The Mistress of the Forge at Bellesfées, Jacqueline Marie-Claire Duval.* "The Royal Seal," she noted. "*Bof!* A gift from Mister Smith?"

Her father asked, "Who is Mister Smith?"

De Guise's eyes gleamed. He grinned at her and winked. Jacqueline peeled away the wrapping to uncover an exquisite mahogany coffer. Inside was a note addressed to de Guise. Under that lay an ostentatious medallion: a red ribbon securing a silver filigree crown attached to a silver Maltese cross against a laurel wreath; on one side a cloisonné of crossed flags—the blue, white, and red of France—and on the obverse a gold engraving of Louis-Philippe, King of the French.

Jacqueline snapped the coffer shut with a *pfft* of disgust. "I hoped never to see that hypocritical, adulterous, pudgy pear-face again." She tossed the coffer onto the table

Her father patted her on the back, laughing. "That's my girl. À bas les aristos!"

Jacqueline kissed her father's cheek and handed the note to de Guise. "Just let him remember me fondly when Armand's suit comes to court."

Llewellyn opened the coffer curiously. His face lit up. "Jacqueline, that's a knighthood in the Legion of Honor. Dame Jacqueline, Chevalier de la Forge-à-Bellesfées. Well done!"

Jacqueline shrugged and looked up at her father. "I'm not the first of the family to get a trinket from the old pear."

Her father squeezed her again.

"But a knighthood comes with a pension," de Guise said as he read the missive from the King, "which is fortunate, as it appears I am without a position."

Jacqueline's heart leapt and she caught her breath. "He dismissed you? You're—free?"

"In a manner of speaking," he replied. He reached for her hand. "Let us say, rather, I'm home."

Their kiss was met with applause and felicitations. Vordenburg rapped his walking stick. Jean-Paul whooped, ducking when Marthe swatted him. Têtue thrust two fingers into her mouth and whistled shrilly. Within seconds, Monsieur Claque thundered into the dining room and halted. He answered the whistle with a *poot* of steam.

Amongst all the uproar, Monsieur Duval doffed his travel coat and poured himself a glass of wine as Luc hastened to set a chair at the foot of the table for him. His grey eyes twinkled as he surveyed the many faces around him.

"For twenty-one years this table seated only the three of us. I think I'm going to enjoy having a large family."

Angélique and Llewellyn exchanged sly smiles. Jacqueline caught their intimation and clapped her hand over her mouth, tears springing.

Monsieur Duval raised his glass. "Here's to coming home."

ACKNOWLEDGEMENTS

DANIELLE ACKLEY-MCPHAIL IS A GEM OF AN EDITOR. OR RATHER, SHE knows how to take rough stones and make the author polish them until the gem gleams. She's not only a wonderful editor and publisher, she is her authors' greatest cheerleader. I count myself blessed to be part of eSpec Books and to call her a friend.

Mike McPhail's insights into the characters that bring them alive on the cover fascinate me, but he is a wise conversationalist with whom I've had many enlightening discussions, and not just about cover art. He too is a blessing.

If you are reading this, take the opportunity to visit the eSpec website to see the wealth of their work. Better still, find them in a dealers' room at a con and meet them personally.

This book poured out of me so swiftly, it was a dizzying whirl when I finished it. I had so much research left over from my work on *Esprit de Corpse* that the story had already been fixed in my mind before I finished the first novel. To me, this book felt like the natural next chapter, and it flowed and was finished in four weeks. But it was truly a "rough" draft.

I was fortunate to have the Bucks County Writing Workshop members at the time who were willing to suffer through more than thirty pages at each critique session, helping me craft Jacqueline's magnificent aerostat and plot out the nature of the supernatural elements. Bobby Cohen and Jim Kempner were incredibly helpful in getting my engineering-fu on "track."

Thanks especially to LCW Allingham, Chris Bauer, William J. Donahue, and Natalie Dyen for their insights into the plot and pacing, and especially into the characters and their development. More importantly, thank you for your friendship which has been priceless, whether we're talking through the craft or yakking at a bar. You are the most significant writers in my writing life.

I'm grateful for Beverly Black, my beta reader from the BCWW, who helped me find the stupid and kept me on track with the story despite all the names, pushing me to find the core of the plot and leave the frills on the cutting-room floor.

Most of the information about the historical figures I gleaned from mindful Googling, finding fascinating details about Louis-Philippe that I could find nowhere else, including the accusation that he had more mistresses than children in his lifetime, and the wonderful quotation "When it comes to kings, it is always open season." Likewise, Dumas and his role in the Club des Hashischins, the Haight-Ashbury of their day, with links that took me down lovely rabbit-holes. All the details of weaponry and aerostats of the time period are also traceable online.

Given the constrictions of the COVID-19 quarantine, I'm very glad to have also found the following books:

Chopin in Paris by Tad Szulc
Carmilla by Sheridan Le Fanu
The Wolf-Leader by Alexandre Dumas, *père*
Les Misérables by Alexandre Dumas, *père*
The life of Marie Amélie last queen of the French, 1782-1866. With some account of the principal personages at the courts of Naples and France in her time by C. C. Dyson
Les Fleurs du Mal by Charles Baudelaire
An Englishman in Paris, by Albert D. (Albert Dresden) Vandam
Dumas' Paris by Francis Miltoun

My husband Jack is my rock, and I could not be a writer without his support, his thoughtfulness, and especially his love. Thank you for understanding what drives me to hours of isolation at the computer. Although it seems like I do this apart from you, I could not do this without you.

ABOUT THE AUTHOR

EF DEAL IS A NEW VOICE IN THE GENRE OF SPECULATIVE STEAMPUNK with her debut novel, *Esprit de Corpse*, but she is not new to publishing. Her short fiction has appeared in various magazines and ezines over the years. Her short story "Czesko," published in the March 2006 F&SF, was given honorable mention in Gardner Dozois' *Year's Best Science Fiction and Fantasy*, which gave both her and Gardner great delight. They laughed and laughed and sipped Scotch (not cognac, alas) over the last line.

Despite her preoccupation with old-school drum and bugle corps — playing, composing, arranging, and teaching — Ef Deal can usually be found at the keyboard of her computer rather than her piano. She is Assistant Fiction Editor at Abyss & Apex magazine and edits videos for the YouTube channel Strong Women — Strange Worlds Quick Reads.

Esprit de Corpse from eSpec Books is the first of a series featuring the brilliant 19th-century sisters, the Twins of Bellesfées Jacqueline and Angélique. Hard science blends with the paranormal as they challenge the supernatural invasion of France in 1843.

When she's not lost in her imagination, Ef Deal can be found in historic Haddonfield, NJ, in a once-haunted Victorian with her husband and two chows. She is an associate member of SFWA and an affiliate member of HWA.

THE ORDER OF DUVAL

Abigail Reilly
Alex Jay Berman
Andrew Kaplan
Andy Holman Hunter
Anthony R. Cardno
Aysha Rehm
Bailey A Buchanan
Barry Nove
Benjamin Adler
bill
Bill & Kelley & Kyle
Brendan Coffey
Brian D Lambert
Brian Klueter
Brooks Moses
Buddy Deal
Caitlin Rozakis
Candi O'Rourke
Carla Spence
Carol J. Guess
Carol Jones
Caroline Westra
Cheri Kannarr
Christine Lawrence
Christine Norris
Christopher Bennett
Christopher J. Burke
Coats Family
Colleen Feeney

Craig "Stevo" Stephenson
Crysella
Dale A Russell
Danielle Ackley-McPhail
Danny Chamberlin
Denise and Raphael Sutton
Doniki Boderick-Luckey
Donna Hogg
Duane Warnecke
E.M. Middel
Ef Deal
Ellen Montgomery
Emily Weed Baisch
Erin A.
"filkertom" Tom Smith
Frank Michaels
Gary Phillips
Gav I
GhostCat
GraceAnne Andreassi
   DeCandido
Greg Levick
Ian Harvey
J.E. Taylor
Jack Deal
Jakub Narębski
James Aquilone
Jamie René Peddicord
Jennifer Hindle

Jennifer L. Pierce
Jeremy Bottroff
Joe Gillis
John Keegan
John L. French
John Markley
Jonathan Haar
Judy McClain
Karen Palmer
KC Grifant
Kelly Pierce
Ken Seed
kirbsmilieu
krinsky
Lark Cunningham
LCW Allingham
Lee
Lee Thalblum
Lisa Kruse
Liz DeJesus and Amber Davis
Lorraine J Anderson
Louise Lowenspets
Lynn P.
Maria V Arnold
Marie Devey
Matthew Barr
Michael A. Burstein
Michael Barbour
Morgan Hazelwood
Mustela
Niki Curtis
Paul Ryan
pjk
Rachel A Brune
Raja Thiagarajan

Reckless Pantalones
Rich Gonzalez
Rich Walker
Richard Fine
Richard Novak
Richard O'Shea
Rigel Ailur
Robert Greenberger
Robert Ziegler
Ronald H. Miller
Ruth Ann Orlansky
Scott Schaper
Shawnee M
Shervyn
Sheryl R. Hayes
Sonia Koval
Sonya M.
Steph Parker
Stephen Ballentine
Stephen W. Buchanan
Steven Purcell
Subrata Sircar
Susan Simko
The Creative Fund by BackerKit
Thomas Bull
Thomas P. Tiernan
Tim Tucker
Tom B.
Tracy Popey
Tracy 'Rayhne' Fretwell
Will "scifantasy" Frank
'Will It Work' Dansicker
William C Tracy
wmaddie700